THE STREET OF THE CITY

Frannie was a working girl who lived on the poor side of town. Across the river glamorous people glittered in high society.

Wealthy Val Willoughby, impatient with their shallow world, was captivated by Frannie's sweet sincerity, and gladly crossed the river to court her.

But sophisticated Marietta Hollister considered Val her personal property and jealously resented his association with such a common girl.

Her spiteful vindictiveness threatened to poison both Val's reputation and Frannie's.

Bantam Books by Grace Livingston Hill
Ask your bookseller for the books you have missed

GRACE LIVINGSTON HILL

THE STREET OF THE CITY

*This low-priced Bantam Book
has been completely reset in a type face
designed for easy reading, and was printed
from new plates. It contains the complete
text of the original hard-cover edition.*
NOT ONE WORD HAS BEEN OMITTED.

THE STREET OF THE CITY
*A Bantam Book / published by arrangement with
J. B. Lippincott Company*

PRINTING HISTORY
Originally published 1942
Bantam edition / February 1977

*Bantam Books are published by Bantam Books, Inc. Its trade-
mark, consisting of the words "Bantam Books" and the por-
trayal of a bantam, is registered in the United States Patent
Office and in other countries. Marca Registrada, Bantam
Books, Inc., 666 Fifth Avenue, New York, New York 10019.*

Chapter 1

THE RIVER WOUND like a crystal ribbon at the foot of the hill below the house, a clear shining pathway of solid ice, blue as the sky above it, until it curved about the hemlock bluff where the tall feathery trees cut it sharply with dark delicate points against its shining surface. Then beyond, the gleaming pathway swept toward the town, and on to the dingy group of munitions plants, and farther to the open spaces banked by the buildings where airplanes were made.

The old lady was sitting in her sunny window with a bit of sewing, now and again glancing out the window, and following the bright course of the river. She had been watching the river for years, in all seasons, but she loved it best in this shining garb of winter, with its solid pavement of bright ice in its soft white setting of snow.

Lady Winthrop, as her friends called her, had come to the house as a bride. It was a pleasant house on the hillside with the river at its feet, and she had had long years to get acquainted with her river. She knew and loved every phase of it. How it had been with her in every change of her life. How she had communed with it during the early days of her young wifehood, shyly watching, learning slowly its quiet moods: singing with it when there were twinkling sparkles on its bosom; or gathering comfort from its steady peace when there was sorrow in the house, sadly, patiently waiting when gray skies spread gloom over its stolid surface; or, in times of storm and stress, watching its steady strength, hurrying on angrily, as if so much depended upon its haste.

And sometimes when her life had given quiet, and a space for thoughtfulness, she had seen in that river as it were a way into the Heavenly City. Especially was

1

this so in the winter evenings at sunset, when the sun, a great ball of fire, was going down in the break of the distant mountains and casting ruby light over the ice like flaming gold. Often taking a moment out of her busy life she would stand at her window watching it, and would repeat softly to herself: "And the street of the city was pure gold, as it were transparent glass."

Or later, when the sun was slipping over the rim of the world and its last brilliancy flared over the ice like a great conflagration, she would murmur: "And I saw as it were a sea of glass mingled with fire."

But today Lady Winthrop was not seeing fire in her river. It was early morning and she was watching for her day's parade of people, passing by on that pathway of ice. Groups of workmen walking by the river because it shortened their way, rather than going around by the bridge and the road. Bevies of laborers hurrying to their tasks, rough clad, striding along at the edge of the stream with grim, set faces, or bandying rough jokes with raucous laughter. Some wore the hard determined look of men who were in this warfight to make the most out of it; and others bore themselves as men who had sacrificially laid aside their work in their chosen field of labor to do what was to be done for right's sake and for loyalty to their country.

But there was one young man who had been going by for several days now, in fact ever since the fierce cold came that locked the river into a deep floor of crystal. He had appeared that first morning after word had gone out that the skating was fine, and he had come sailing smoothly into view with gleaming skates that almost seemed to be tipped with silvered magic, and had glided by with quick firm strokes, and such assurance and grace as only a natural gift can acquire.

He was young, yet not a boy, for his movements had that control that belongs to maturity.

Lady Winthrop had watched him every day, wondering who he was, where he came from, and what was his place in this new world that the war had brought suddenly into being?

Lady Winthrop liked to watch his tall straight form

moving with such easy precision down the bright ice.
She had been watching him morning after morning now,
since the ice had been so fine. She felt glad and comfortable in looking for him because the cold had been so
steady. The ice would not be gone, nor spoiled by rain,
or a heavy snowfall, not today, anyway. The sky was
clear. There would perhaps be several days yet when
he could go down this same way to wherever it was he
went in the morning, and he would probably return
the same way in the evening. Each day she studied him
from her post in the window, caught a glimpse now and
then of his vivid young face with the determination of
manhood in its lines, and liked it, wished she might
see it nearer by. She had even climbed to the attic and
searched in an old trunk till she found an old pair of
field glasses that she had not used since Judge Winthrop
died, a relic of their happy days together and the summer and winter trips they used to take.

She studied him one night as he came back from his
day's work, and after that keen look put down her
glasses, quite satisfied that he was worth her interest.

And so this morning she had settled down by her
window, field glasses on the table beside her, watching
for him. It was almost the time he usually came by,
and she wanted another good look at him to be sure he
wasn't someone she used to know a few years ago. She
was lonely and sad. Her own two boys were long since
grown up, and away at the war, one a naval commander
in the Far East, the other an officer in the army. She
had given them freely, and would not spend her days
in sighing for them, but she was trying to get all the
cheerful interest she could find in the things about her.

And now suddenly there came into view another
skater, a young girl, so tiny she almost seemed a child.
She had seen her two or three times before, skating almost uncertainly the first time, as if somehow her skates
were untried, or perhaps rusty and had been idle a
long time. But here she was again like a little bird, flying
along as if she had wings. The skates looked brighter
now, or did she imagine that? She had probably been
polishing them up. At any rate she seemed to make

swifter progress than the first times. And she was a fine
skater, very graceful, like a bird of swift wing. Lady
Winthrop might be old, and she no longer took frequent
trips by herself down the slope of the hill, but she
could remember the feel of her own skates long ago
when she too used to glide down that long smooth
stretch of ice, and she felt the swing of her body as if
she were out there skimming along. She felt the ex-
hilaration of the keen bright air, the cut of steel on ice,
and drew a deep breath of wistfulness. Oh for the days
when she could skate! How great it would be if even just
for one day she could have her young skill and strength
back, and go down that bright path toward the city herself!

And then suddenly she laughed aloud at herself, a
sweet old trill of a laugh. She was actually envying that
young girl!

Who was she? A student? Or perhaps a teacher in
one of the city schools. But she looked so young, and
why had she never seen her before? She might be a
worker in some defense plant, a stenographer or typist.
They gave good salaries in some of those places she had
heard. She hoped her salary was adequate for her needs.
It was not many times she had seen this girl go down
her Crystal Street as she called it, and yet here she was
thinking of the child as if she were a friend!

The girl wore such a look of steady purpose, the look
of a worker, not just a girl out for fun or exercise. Ah!
Here was another skater of whom she would like to
know more. She must find out who she was if possible. Perhaps she came from one of those new houses
across the river, the small ones built alike up around
the bend of the hill. She could see them from her kitch-
en windows; they were small frame houses, high on the
bluff. She must find out about her. Perhaps the servants
could discover who she was.

And that young man must be a stranger in the neighborhood, too. Did his people live up in that new sub-
urb farther up the river, the place they called Cliveden?

How well those two skaters would look together!

Did they know one another? Queer thoughts for the dear old lady to have about two young people who were utter strangers to her, two people she had only seen from a distance a few times!

She watched the girl go gliding down the river, till she disappeared at Hemlock Rocks, and a moment later reappeared beyond them again and skimmed away into the silvery distance. A mere little speck of a girl in simple garb, with a graceful motion. That was all she could see even with the glasses.

But she could not help thinking again how well those two skaters would look together. If they only knew each other. Both of them living up in the same direction, perhaps they did, and perhaps some day she would see them come down by her house together.

But where was the young man? It was almost five minutes past his usual time for going by. She hoped nothing would hinder him. It would seem as if the day held a big disappointment for her if he didn't come. It would be something left out from what she had come to expect of a day, not to see him. And that was silly of course, because it had been only four or five days that she had been seeing him at all. She couldn't expect it to go on forever. There would presently come a thaw and spoil the ice, or a snow storm and spoil the skating—unless a crowd came out and swept it clean, and that would hardly be likely, sweeping the whole way to town!

Then suddenly she heard footsteps crunching hastily through the crusty snow up the hillside. Young, hurried, frightened footsteps, a quick insistent pounding on the door beside her window, and a little girl's voice full of fright calling wildly:

"Oh, please, *please* won't you help me? Please won't you come quick and open your door? Something has happened to *my mamma!*"

Lady Winthrop hurried to open the door.

"Why, *my dear!*" she exclaimed. For there stood a little girl about five or six years old, a very tiny little girl, with no hat or coat on, and shivering, with her small, red, cold hands clasped tightly, and tears flowing down her cold round cheeks. Her large beautiful eyes were full of terror.

"What is the matter?" asked the old lady tenderly. "Come into the house and let me close the door. It is very cold!"

"Oh no, I can't come in," said the child excitedly. "I must go to my mamma! Won't you come with me *quick?*"

"Why, you poor child! You are trembling with cold. You poor little thing! Who are you, and what is the matter with your mother?"

"I'm Bonnie Fernley," wailed the child frantically, "and I don't know what is the matter. My mamma just dropped down on the floor with her eyes shut, and she didn't answer me when I called her. She was clearing off the table and all the dishes she was carrying are broken on the floor! Oh, *won't* you come *quick* and make my mamma wake up?"

"Oh, my dear! I'm lame and I can't come myself, but I'll send somebody! Where do you live?"

"Right across the river in that red brick house. Come out here and I'll show you."

"Wait, child! Who is your doctor? I'll telephone him." The child began to cry again.

"We haven't got any doctor. We just moved here! Oh, I must go quick! My mamma is all alone!"

"Wait!" said Lady Winthrop sharply. "You can't go that way! You have no coat on, and it is very cold!"

"No! *No!*" said the child jerking away. "I can't wait!"

The old lady reached to the couch and caught up a soft bright knitted afghan, wrapping it quickly around the little shaking shoulders. Then she swung the door wide and looked out on the white morning scene, and her shining glass pathway. And then straight into the scene at the upper bend of the road wheeled the tall skater coming at full speed.

The old lady did not pause to consider. She lifted her soft frail hands, hollowed them about her lips, and made a deep sound like a big boy calling to his mates, a sound that boomed out and became a far-reaching "Hal-loo! Hal*loo!*" and then turned sharply into another syllable, *"Help! help!"*

The skater looked up sharply as the word rang out with a carrying quality that an old lady would not have been supposed to be capable of sending out.

"H-ee-lp!" cried Lady Winthrop with all the power of her frail little body thrown into the cry.

And now she was standing out in the center of her porch, her little lavender shawl fluttering wildly, with bright strands of her lovely silver hair caught by the sharp morning breeze. She was waving her hands frantically as she cried.

The skater threw up his head attentively and faced her, whirling almost in a circle and coming about in front of the old house on the hill and the pretty old lady.

"Are you calling *me?*" he shouted, coming to a halt on his shining runners and looking up.

"Yes!" answered the old lady, nodding her white head excitedly.

"What's the matter?" called the young man.

"A woman in trouble!"

"Where? Up there?"

"No, over across the river. This child will show you."

She put the little girl before her, pointing to her, and the child started to plunge into the snow, and come to him.

"Wait!" shouted the young man, "I'll come up and carry you. There's a big drift there!" and he swung to the edge of the river deftly, and began breaking a way for himself up the crust of the snowy hillside.

Lady Winthrop took her handkerchief out of her pocket, softly, swiftly, wiped the little tear-wet face of the child, and tucked the afghan closer about her shoulders. Then she lifted her head and watched the strong firm steps that broke into the white crust of the hill. The young man was looking up now, taking the hill in great strides, studying the two on the porch.

"I'll carry that child," he announced as he arrived. "Sure, I can manage that all right. Are you coming, Madam?"

"No," said the old lady sadly, "I have a sprained knee, and I'm very unsteady on my feet. I'm afraid I couldn't make the grade. Both my servants are out on errands. I'm here alone."

"Well, can you tell me where I am going, and what I am to do when I get there?"

"This child's mother has been taken sick. She will tell you. They are strangers to me, have just moved into that red brick house across the river. She says her mother is lying on the floor. That she fell."

"She wouldn't answer me," said the baby catching her voice in a sob. "Her eyes were shut tight!"

A tender pitying look came over the young man's face.

"And what is their name?" he asked. "I imagine there ought to be a doctor at once."

"Yes," said Lady Winthrop, "I was just going in to telephone my doctor. His office hours will be over but I think I can catch him. The name is Fernley, isn't that right, dear?"

The child nodded.

"It's number ten Rosemary Lane," she added. "It's the old brick house. We just moved there last week. Our things haven't all come yet."

"I see," said the young man. "Well, let's get going. Lady Winthrop, you had better go inside. The wind is pretty sharp this morning. Better get warm at once, or there will be two sick ladies instead of one."

The old lady looked up surprised.

"You know me?" she asked.

"Sure," said the young man with a pleasant grin, "go in and get warm!" He plunged sharply down the crusty hill with the child held firmly in his arms. He landed in a smooth glide on the ice and flew away upstream.

The old lady watched for an instant to make sure the child would be all right with this engaging young stranger, and then turned swiftly in to her telephone, not even stopping to shiver, though it was a good many years since she had permitted herself to be as cold as she was now. There had always been that afghan to throw about her if anyone came to the door and she had to stand a moment talking to them. But she wasn't thinking about being cold now. She was thinking of that little child, and a poor mother lying unconscious on the floor. She must get the doctor before he started on his rounds!

She waited frantically for the number, wondering what to do if the doctor was gone. Was there some other doctor she would feel like sending in his place if her doctor was not available? Then she was relieved to hear the doctor's voice answering.

"Yes, Mrs. Winthrop? You're not ill, I trust? Yes, of course I recognized your voice. There isn't another voice like yours. You see I sent Miss March out on an errand, and I was just leaving myself, that's how I happened to be taking the call. Is anything the matter?"

"Not with me, doctor, but I am afraid there is terrible trouble across the river from me, and I don't know what to do about it. I sent the servants to the city shopping for me, and I'm here alone for the moment. They have a lot of errands and will be some time, I'm afraid, and *this* may be a matter of life and death. Doctor, *could* you possibly go right away and see? A little child came rushing across the ice to my door screaming for help. She said her mother had fallen down on the floor and wouldn't answer her when she called. She was half frightened to death, nearly frozen, and crying bitterly. She had come across the river without hat or coat and was blue with cold and shivering. Perhaps the woman has only fainted, but you know I can't walk over, and I thought someone ought to investigate at once, for maybe she is dying. The child said they had just moved here and didn't have a doctor. Can you take the time to go?"

"Of course. I'll go at once. Where is it?"

"Number ten Rosemary Lane, a little old red brick house across the river from our house. The name is Fernley."

"All right, I'll go at once. And I'll be reporting back to you afterwards. Don't you worry, and don't think of going out yourself. It would be suicidal for you. There is a glare of ice everywhere, and the wind is bitter. Good-by! I'm leaving immediately."

She turned from the telephone and hurried over to the window again, but the skater and the child had disappeared. She stood there a moment watching to see if the young man would be coming back, but the river was empty, no skater in sight either way.

With a sigh she turned away from the window, suddenly aware that she was very cold. She went to the hall closet and took out a warm soft old-fashioned shawl wrapping it close about her, remembering the little shivering child who had come crying for help.

Back at the window there was still no sight of anyone. If only Joseph and Hannah would come she would have them drive her over at once to find out what this was all about anyway. It was hard to have to be helpless and wait. And that poor woman over there dying perhaps. Was the young man staying in the house all this time, or could he possibly have gone by while she was getting her shawl? She could see the river perfectly from the telephone and she had been watching the window every minute. She hadn't been a second getting that shawl. Probably he was doing something for the sick woman. Of course. Reviving her perhaps, if it was a faint. But would he know how? Not every young man was versed in First Aid in such an emergency. This young man was at the age when he would have recently been away to college. They didn't have much time to study up First Aid in college, did they? Although if they were in athletics they might have some experience. Of course her own boys if they had been here would know what to do; at least enough to keep the woman alive if she was still living. And this young man looked like a wise fellow. He had intelligent eyes. Who was he, anyway, and how had he happened to know her name? Had she ever seen him before? The boys nowadays grew up so fast. And then of course she hadn't been around among the young people of the neighborhood so much as she used to be when her own boys were at home and had the house full of friends all the time.

How the years raced by her in panorama as she anxiously watched the icy pathway of the river! Oh, if she only hadn't sent Hannah and Joseph off this particular morning! They could have gone later just as well. What could that skater-boy do anyway for a desperately sick woman, even if he did know enough to bring her back to consciousness?

She wished she could see the little brick house more clearly. The big elm tree in her back yard almost hid its front door. Was that somebody coming out now? Probably if she went out on the kitchen porch the vision would be clearer. But no, she musn't, the wind was very sharp. She shivered now at the thought of facing it again as when she had called the young man. She mustn't risk getting bronchitis again. No, she couldn't go outside without fixing up very warmly, and that would take a lot of time. Likely she would fail to see the young man if he came back. But that surely was a car parked by the side of the little brick cottage. Probably the doctor had arrived. And, ah—there was the young man, coming cautiously down the snow toward the river, just as he had walked up her lawn. And now he was dashing out on the ice and skimming along. Probably she had made him late to something, asking him to help. He might be a worker in one of those munition places, and would be late arriving, maybe be docked in his pay, or even lose his job. But what else could she have done? She had to call someone, and he was the only one in sight. And he was a gentleman, she was sure of that. He had it written all over him, even in a leather windbreaker. He would never let her know she had inconvenienced him.

If he was late he wouldn't likely stop to speak to her now, though he had said he would be back. But, perhaps the doctor had understood, and promised to stop and let her know.

Then she saw him coming, and suddenly he whirled to face her house, and came dashing up, stepping in his same footprints as if they were stairs.

She opened the door and stepped out anxiously, but he called:

"Don't come out, Lady Winthrop. The cold is something fierce. I'll come in. The doctor sent you a message."

She stepped back into the house, and he was beside her almost at once, taking care, she noted, to keep his skate-shod feet on a rough mat at the door.

"She's a pretty sick woman," he said as he closed the door behind him. "It took me some time to bring her to, but the little kid brought some water, and told me where to find aromatic ammonia, and when I got a few drops of that down her throat she began to rouse. I got her on the bed and covered her warmly, rubbed her hands and feet. They were like ice. We put a hot blanket around them. They had a good warm radiator in the room. That helped to heat the blanket. But we couldn't find a hot water bag. The doctor said did you have one or two you could lend him, and a couple more blankets. Their goods haven't all come yet. And the doctor asked if you would please telephone his office boy and ask him to bring over his other medicine bag, and get hold of Nurse Branner and bring her right over to the house?"

"Why surely. There's the telephone, suppose you call the office and talk with the boy while I get the blankets and things. The number is 75-J."

As she hurried away she heard the young man's efficient voice giving directions to the doctor's office boy, and rejoiced that she had so able a helper. This young man was going to stand right by as long as he was needed. Then she heard him coming down the hall after her, walking very carefully, not to hurt her floor.

"Can't I help you?" he asked, and he stepped gingerly up and took the blankets from her, then reached for the two hot water bags that were set so neatly together on a high shelf in the bathroom.

"Thank you," said the old lady. "And now suppose we fill these bags from the teakettle in the kitchen. I happen to know it is full of hot water and standing over the simmerer. You can wrap the blankets around the bags and that will keep them hot and save a lot of time."

"That's a good idea!" said the young man. "You've been through a lot of sickness in your lifetime and you know what to do."

"Well, I couldn't have done much if you hadn't responded to my call. And it couldn't have been easy walking up that hill with skates on, either."

The young man grinned, and, turning, was soon plunging down the hillside, the big blanket-wrapped bundle held firmly as he sprang out on the ice and went skimming away again. What a fellow he was! How wise and brisk and efficient!

Lady Winthrop found she was quite weak with excitement when he was gone, and she sat down suddenly to rest and get her breath.

"Well," she said aloud to herself, "to think all this would happen the first time I sent Hannah and Joe away at the same time, when I was alone. If Joe were only here with the car I'd have been over there myself long ago seeing what I could do to help that poor woman. And now here I am, just a go-between. But perhaps that's needed just now more than anything else, to do the telephoning."

Then she got to thinking about that little brick house up the river and the people who had just moved in. Would they have plenty to eat? Food fit for a sick woman? The sick mother and the baby girl who had come across the icy way alone. She must see what food was quickly available in the refrigerator, in case somebody came back again. At least she could send it over by Joseph when he got back. Neither the woman nor the little girl would be able to do any cooking, of course.

There was a good bowl of chicken soup Hannah made last night. She always made enough for two or three days. And there would be some breast of chicken of course, there always was. She decided to fill one thermos bottle with the hot soup, and the other with hot coffee. So she went to work, making delicate little chicken sandwiches, heating the soup and the coffee, and working happily in her own kitchen, where her faithful servants had not allowed her to lift a finger to work for years. It was fun, she told herself.

Yet all the time she was watching out the kitchen
window, looking for somebody to come down the river.
She worked swiftly to be ready if anyone came. And
then she saw her young knight come out of the brick
cottage and down the icy pathway, and she hurried
into the living room to be ready to open the front door
for him in case he came up again.

He came. With that grave competent smile on his
face.

"She's recovered consciousness fully now," he announced as he stepped inside the room and shut the
door after him. "The doctor isn't sure yet how serious
it is, but at least she is able to speak. He says it looks
to him as if it might be merely a case of exhaustion
from having worked too hard on too little food. Of
course the heart might be more affected than he can tell
at present, but he hopes it isn't serious. And the first
thing that woman said when she came to herself was,
'Don't let my daughter know I fainted. Please don't!
She'll be so worried, and she mustn't lose her job! I'll
be all right now.' The nurse got her right into bed of
course, and she's warm now. The nurse is going to try
to make something for her to eat, but there doesn't
seem to be much that's suitable in the house. The doctor told me to ask if you can spare a little milk for immediate use. The child says her mother ate no breakfast this morning."

"Milk? Why certainly! Here's a whole bottle. Wait,
I'll get a basket. I have some other things ready. Coffee
and chicken soup in thermos bottles, and some chicken
sandwiches. I thought that mother had been too used
up to do much cooking. And here, put in a loaf of
bread and a carton of butter. Some oranges too might
come in handy."

"That's great, Lady Winthrop, I'm sure they'll all
come in for use and everybody grateful, including the
nurse and doctor. I don't think the people are exactly
poor, just pretty hard up for the present, moving expenses and the like. The daughter has a job down at
the first munitions plant. She hasn't had it but a week or
so, and I judge from the few words the mother said that

she's afraid she might lose it if she came home to look after her mother."

"Poor child!" said the old lady. "I wish I might go over and help. I will when my car gets back. You see I had a bad fall, and sprained my knee and strained my ankle and I can't walk very far, especially on snow and ice. I have to go everywhere in my car. It is providential that you came along. You've been wonderful!"

"Oh, I haven't done much. I'm glad you called me."

"Yes? Well you see I was watching for you. I've seen you go skating by on the river for several days. I knew you hadn't gone by yet but it was your usual time, so I just watched for you. I hoped maybe you'd come. Who are you, anyway? Ought I to know your name? You seem to know mine."

The young man smiled.

"No, you wouldn't remember me. I'm Mrs. Haversett's nephew, Val Willoughby. I stayed here with my aunt Mrs. Haversett for a year when I was a kid, while my mother was taking treatment with a specialist in Vienna. I've been here several times since for a few days at a time. But I'm not surprised you don't recognize me. It was a good many years ago. When mother came back we went to the west coast to live, and my trips east since have been brief and hurried."

Lady Winthrop was studying the young man's face, and gradually comprehension came to her eyes.

"Willoughby! Oh, you were little Valiant Willoughby, weren't you? Yes, I remember the sturdy little boy with the round eyes and wide grin. It was your eyes and your grin that made you seem familiar when you came up the hill. And what are you doing here now? Visiting your aunt again?"

"Well, not exactly visiting. I'm staying at my aunt's of course, but I'm here for work now, not fun. I have a job down at the airplane factory."

"Oh, you have! Well, aren't you going to be very late to it? And it's all my fault of course."

"Well, yes, I'll be later than usual. But I'm in a way my own boss. Nobody will say anything. I'll explain of course that it was an emergency, though I'm not really answerable to anyone but myself. But I guess I had better get going. They'll be needing these things across the river, and then the doctor thought I had better stop and tell the daughter. She might blame us for not letting her know. The doctor feels it might be serious later perhaps, although he thinks when the woman gets something to eat she may rally and be really on the mend. He says she's probably been going on her nerve for several days. Perhaps longer. Well, so long! I'll be seeing you again. I'll let you know tonight how things go."

She watched the young man striding down the snowy way on those treacherous-looking skates. How nimbly he trotted down that crusted slope! How skillfully he skimmed out upon the glassy surface of the river and went on his way with the basket balanced so easily on one arm.

She watched him out of sight, till presently she saw him returning, and when he neared the foot of the hill he lifted his cap in a courteous bow, and pointed on down the stream. He was hurrying now to the city.

She opened her door and waved a frail hand in acknowledgement, and got another wave from the cap in his hand as he turned and sailed off toward Hemlock Rocks.

Chapter 2

WHEN FRANCES FERNLEY was ready to go to her job that morning she turned back and looked at her mother.

"Oh, mother, I wish you'd promise me something. Promise me you won't do a stroke of work until I get back. There are hardly any dishes, and Bonnie can do those. I promised her she might, and you know she's very careful handling them. Besides, the ones we are using are just the old cracked ones anyway, and even if one broke it wouldn't be much loss. Now mother, you will go right upstairs and lie down and get a real sleep, won't you? I'm so worried about you. And you know I can't keep my mind on my work when I'm worried. If you would just promise me I know you wouldn't break your word. Please, mummie!"

"All right," said the mother with a weak shimmer of a smile on her tired, worried face.

"You know the rest of the goods will probably come late this afternoon," went on the girl, "and we all want to be fresh and rested to get things in apple pie order before we sleep. You know you can do a lot more if you are really rested, mother. And there isn't so much that needs doing now before the other furniture gets here. You take a good long nap on your bed, and then about eleven o'clock you and Bonnie run over to the store and get what we'll need for dinner. That's enough for you to do today. Will you *really* do that, mother?"

"Why, yes, surely, I'll rest. Now run along quick, Frannie, or you'll be late for your work."

So the girl had stooped and kissed her mother, and then gone carefully down the wooden steps to the ice, stopping to make sure the lacing of her skating shoes was fastened firmly, then went skimming off down the ice, looking back to wave good-by and blow a kiss to Bonnie at the window.

As she went skimming along in the bright morning air her thoughts were with her white-faced mother whom she realized was working too hard. It was all too evident. She tried to think how she might make these few hard days at the beginning easier for her. Of course, she could have stayed at home today and helped more, but she had a good job with an amazing salary for such a young beginner as she was, and both she and her mother felt they must not trifle with it, especially not now right at the beginning of things. A little later when she was sure of herself, and could take some time to help get settled, perhaps she could find a young girl who would come in to do some of the heavier work, or a stronger, older woman to take the burden from her mother. For the mother had warned her that they must not spend any more of their tiny capital in hiring help until it was absolutely necessary, and until Frannie was sure she was going to be satisfactory to her boss and that her job was dependable. She must not take success as an assured thing until she had been tried out by her superior.

So, against her strong intuitions she had gone away that morning, hoping that all would be well until she got back, and resolving to enquire around and find out whether there was a woman she could get who would be right for them. Maybe some of the women who lived in those smaller houses over in that far row. And yet those houses must of course be filled with people who had money, for they had to be *bought*. They were not for rent. And that took money, more downpayment than they owned. The little tumbledown brick where they lived was quite old, and just ready to fall apart, or they would not have been able to rent it.

Another thing that worried her was that they had no very near neighbors. Those houses in that far row were at such a distance that she was not sure if they were even finished. Maybe nobody lived in them yet. That made her a little uneasy to leave her mother and sister alone all day. Suppose something happened! There would be nobody nearby to go to for help. But of course nothing would happen. Not in the daytime. And pretty soon they would get in a telephone so mother wouldn't have to go to the store for groceries. The store was five blocks away. But they had been so delighted at the idea of living near to the river. It would be so lovely in the summer. And now too, all frozen this way, it was wonderful, and it was saving her carfare too. She was going to get Bonnie a pair of skates and teach her to skate. She was not too young to learn. When she got home this evening she would look in some of the big boxes that had come yesterday and see if possibly her own first skates weren't there somewhere. The ones her dear father had taught her to skate on so very long ago.

So she hurried along, over the smooth ice, so glad the

way was clear, so glad it had not snowed in the night.
It was wonderful weather; five whole days, ever since
they had moved, there had been clear cold weather. Of
course it couldn't last much longer, and then she would
have to start earlier to walk to the bus that would take
her to the plant.

She sighed at the thought. It was so much pleasanter
going this way, no crowded buses, no stuffy air. Just this
grand cold snap in the tingling crisp air and sunshine.
It made the blood simply dance in her cheeks, and gave
her such a free feeling, almost as if she were really
happy again, the way she used to be before her father
died, and there were not so many burdens to bear.
Mother looking so worn and sad, so worried at her having to go off into the world and work. Oh, of course
mother didn't mind her working. But she did hate to
have her go off into conditions that were all strange
and new to her. Mother had old-fashioned sweet ideas
that a girl ought to be guarded, and not have to go and
work in offices among men. Mother wanted to know the
people herself among whom her daughter worked all
day. Well, poor little mother. Some day perhaps she
would understand that it wasn't bad. It was really very
nice and orderly, and the men among whom she
worked were kindly, pleasant, most of them real gentlemen, in spite of the fact that many of them wore rough
working garments. And then there were a number of
boys, just like the high school boys with whom she had
so recently been associated. Some young college men
too, who had been debarred from military service because of some physical defect, or weakness. They were
fine and kind and she had a feeling that everybody in
the plant was wonderful.

She had come out into the world of business with
the idea that she must be on her guard wherever she
went. But she was gradually coming to feel that attitude
had been a mistake. All the men she met were so help-
ful, so ready to tell her what to do when she asked a
question, that she gave her sweet shy smile in return
without any withdrawal, and gave to all who came about

a sense of her wholesomeness and friendliness and willingness to serve. It gave her a happy satisfied feeling. She must make her mother understand how kindly and in earnest everyone was, and that perhaps would keep her from her constant worrying.

So it was with an almost light heart that Frannie sat down on the snowy bank to remove her skating shoes, and slip on her other shoes for the day, and then tucking her skating shoes into the ample pockets of her old coat, she ran lightly up the steps that led to the door of the building where she worked.

As she went toward her desk two young men stood at the end of the room and talked, watching covertly the different people in the room.

"There she comes," said one with a weak face, and pale eyes. "Isn't she a honey? Gosh, she's a sight for sore eyes. And look how she walks. She arrives on skates by the river! And can she move? Just like some little bird! Boy! I'm telling you!"

"Yes, she sure is a smooth little number," said the other, who went by the name of Spike Emberly, "I think I'll make a date with her for tonight and try her out as a dancer."

"Not on yer life you don't," growled the other. "She's my find. You keep hands off or you'll be sorry!"

"Oh, *will* I?" leered the boy with the mop of dark curly hair and bold eyes. "How do you know but *you'll* be the sorry one? Well, here goes! Watch me!"

He strode ahead and fell into step with Frannie as she walked toward her desk. She looked up startled into the bold black eyes.

"Hello, beautiful!" he greeted her with the kind of grin that did not belong in her social stratum. "I've been waiting for you. Want to make a date? How about going places tonight? Take you to a swell joint fer dinner. Good eats, good drinks, and then we'll go a-dancing. That okay with you?"

Frannie gave him a frightened look and lifted her chin with gravity.

"Thank you, no!" she said with finality. "I am busy this evening."

"Then how about tomorrow evening? That'll give me more time to make arrangements."

"Thank you, no. My evenings are all occupied!"

"Say, now, that's too bad. You really ought to take a day off now and then. Your health won't stand that kind of life. A little fun now and then is what you need. Tell me where you live and I'll call for you. You wouldn't know what you're missing till you try it. Come on, you try me out once and see if you don't have the time of your life. Where do you live? I'll call for you about seven-thirty, or eight. How's that?"

"Definitely, *no!*" said Frannie, turning sharply toward her desk.

And then the pale-eyed boy stepped up on the other side.

"What did I tell you, Spike, a dame like this one wouldn't be seen with a guy like yerself. She's *my* girl, I told you. You lay off her, Spike Emberly. She's going places with me. We have a previous engagement, haven't we, lovely?"

Frannie gave a frightened glance around and saw that the head of the department was just entering the room at the far end, so she settled down quietly into her chair and ignored the two, her cheeks growing white with annoyance. So, this very morning when she was so sure that all the young men in the plant were perfect gentlemen, here had come these two to disprove it. Well, she certainly would have to make them understand that she wanted nothing to do with them. Utter strangers! How upset her mother would have been if she had overheard what they said. Not, of course, that there was anything actually wrong about it, except that free-and-easy intimate way that seemed to be the vogue these days among young people. Perhaps she was growing prudish, but she certainly didn't like the way they had talked. Like picking her up on the street.

But the young men had cast an eye toward the doorway too, and noted the manager coming in their direction.

"Well, good-by, dolling," said the one called Spike. "Here comes the big boss. I better get on with my job," and he vanished out the opposite door. But the other lingered, his eyes on her face impressively, his voice lowered to confidential tones:

"Just in case you're interested," he said, "my name is Kit Creeber, and I'm meeting you down on the ice at closing time. So-long baby, till t'night!" Then he made the tour of the room, stopping to speak to three other girls on the way, as if he had messages from someone in the office for them.

Frannie was engrossed in polishing her typewriter, and seemed not to be aware of his presence, but she was exceedingly annoyed and no movement of his escaped her notice. Now, what was she going to do tonight? How could she get away without meeting him? But meet him she certainly would not do, no matter if she had to go out the front way and take a taxi home to avoid it. Of course that would cost a lot, and she didn't know the vicinity well enough to find a bus going home. Perhaps some of the other girls could tell her at noon. She looked despairingly around on them. There wasn't one that she felt friendly with yet. Perhaps that was her fault. Her mother had always told her that she was far too shy and retiring. She must overcome this and make friends of course, but how she hated the idea of those two fellows who had approached her this morning. Was she just silly? Perhaps she ought to have laughed them off, but somehow she just couldn't. The boys at her old home had never treated her that way. They were polite. But there! She must forget this and plunge her mind into her work. Perhaps at noontime she could ask a few questions about how to get home by bus, just casually of course. She wouldn't let anybody know that those boys had been fresh with her. Perhaps they wouldn't think there was anything wrong with what they did anyway.

Then the buzzer on her desk sounded and she picked up her pencil and pad and made her way to the inner office for dictation, and the two impudent young men passed out of her thoughts for the time.

The man for whom she was taking dictation was a kindly, reserved, elderly man with iron gray hair and a stern face. He wasted no time in his work, and Frannie's fingers flew to keep pace with his gruff voice. When at last she went back to her machine she was fairly breathless with the speed she had been going. She sat down at her typewriter and began to work, determined to finish all these letters before the noon hour.

She had been working nearly two hours at top speed when she became aware of two people coming straight toward her desk. One was Mr. Chalmers, her chief, and by his side a strange young man. At least she had never seen him in the plant before.

"Miss Fernley," Mr. Chalmers said, "this young man has a message for you, from your mother, isn't that it, Mr. Willoughby?"

The young man bowed, but Frannie turned white.

"Oh, my mother?" she exclaimed, springing to her feet, one small hand fluttering to her throat. "Has something happened?"

"Please don't be frightened," said the young man. "Your mother isn't very well. But she's resting now, and I'm sure she's going to be all right. She didn't want you to be told, but the doctor thought you might be upset if you were not told at once. He told me to assure you that at present there is nothing for you to worry about, and he will see that you are notified if there is any need for you to come home."

"But—I don't understand—!" said the girl frantically. "How did she get a doctor? She was all alone with just my little sister, and she's only a baby yet."

"Well, she's *some baby!*" said the young man emphatically. "When your mother fainted she ran across the river on the ice and told Lady Winthrop, and she sent her doctor over, so everything is all right now. We put your mother on the bed and the doctor brought his pet nurse along, so your mother isn't alone now, and you don't need to worry. She was most anxious that you *do not* come home until the day's work is over."

"Oh, that will be all right," said the chief kindly. "I can excuse you right away if you are anxious to go to your mother."

"Oh, but I *must* go!" said the girl frantically. "We

have just moved in there, and there isn't anything in the house to eat yet. I must go and see that she has food. I'll just finish that important letter you wanted to have go at once, and then I'll go. It's almost done!" She turned toward her typewriter with a quick nervous little movement, but young Willoughby put out a detaining hand.

"Listen!" he said. "You needn't worry about food. Mrs. Winthrop sent over a thermos bottle of chicken soup, and another of coffee. She sent bread and butter and chicken and a quart of milk too. You needn't worry at all about something for them to eat. They have plenty. I took it over myself. Mrs. Winthrop knew you had just moved in and thought you might not be prepared for illness, so she sent over some things that were suitable for an invalid and a child. You don't need to worry at all. And your mother was most anxious you should not be told. It was the doctor who felt you ought to know, as you might wish another physician called or something. So I agreed to tell you. But I'm sure your mother is in good hands. When I left she was eating spoonfuls of chicken broth and they were telling her she was to stay right there in bed and get a good rest. The nurse is staying of course. It just happened that she left a case this morning, and was glad to get a place where she could be useful until her next case comes on."

"Oh!" said Frannie, struggling to keep the tears back, "that is all very kind and wonderful. But I'm sure I ought to be at home. Mother will be so unhappy having strangers have to come in and look after her."

"No," said young Willoughby, "she will be much more troubled if you do anything to upset your job just now. I know for I saw her face when she begged them not to tell you. In fact the doctor told me he was giving her something to make her sleep for a little while, and by the time you get home she'll be just waking up and won't think there was anything much the matter perhaps."

"Oh, you are very kind and thoughtful. But we have never had to be such a lot of trouble to strangers."

"Well, don't think of us as strangers, call us neighbors," said the young man with a confidence-inspiring smile that somehow loosened the tightness around the girl's heart, and made it possible for her to breathe again. She wavered a pale little white smile in answer.

"You see, I'm sure you can trust the doctor. He's very skillful. He is Dr. Ransom, Lady Winthrop's own physician. And besides, he promised me he would go back again just before noon, and then will go straight to his office and from there telephone me how things are going. I am sure he will do that. And I promise to telephone you here immediately. May I do that, Mr. Chalmers?" He looked toward Frannie's chief, who bowed assent graciously, and Frannie began to feel as if the reeling ground beneath her feet was gradually steadying.

"Oh! That will help a lot," she murmured. "But— the movers will be coming this afternoon with the rest of our furniture, and there will be nobody to tell them where to put things!"

Her practical young eyes had taken on their frightened look again.

"Mother would never lie still and let that go on. She will get right up and go to work unless I'm there!"

"Not with Nurse Branner there!" laughed Valiant Willoughby. "You don't know her if you think that could happen. But I do. She nursed me through a broken leg once and believe me there isn't a thing that woman doesn't understand and can't take charge of. You'll find she'll ferret out the most suitable spot for every article and have it placed there right on the dot, and no patient of hers will get out of bed and go to work. She'll see to that! Now, will you be good, Miss Fernley? And I give you my word of honor to phone the latest news from your home at noon or know the reason why. Does that satisfy you?"

"Thank you so much. That will be wonderful. Now I can go back to my work."

Then Mr. Chalmers interrupted.

"Miss Fernley, I'm afraid it is going to be a strain on you to finish those letters I gave you this morning. If you like I'll call Miss Dart and let you read them to her and she can take them down and type them, and then you can go home."

But Frannie's business pride rose to the front. She clutched her precious notebook firmly and shook her head.

"No indeed, Mr. Chalmers, I'd rather do them my-self. You explained so fully what you wanted in some of the letters that I would hate to have you have to do that all over again. No, I'm sure since Mr. Willoughby has been so kind, that everything will be all right. I know that my mother would much rather have me stay here and make good than to rush home, since she has a good doctor and an efficient nurse. I would be silly to worry about her. I'll bring the letters to you when I have them finished, and if there are any changes to be made I'll have plenty of time to recopy."

"Well, if you are sure you won't worry—"

"No, I won't worry," promised Frannie with a grave, capable smile.

The two men glanced at the girl with approval.

"Well, good-by Miss Fernley," said Willoughby. "I'll be calling you around noon. And thank you, Mr. Chalmers, for your courtesy to us both."

The young man walked away, and the chief gave one keen look at his secretary, and then slowly made his way back to his own office, while Frannie settled down to do some of the most tensely careful work she had ever done in the line of typing. She somehow felt that her skill was in question, she was being put to the test, and she must not let even her anxiety for her beloved mother steal her thoughts away from the duty of the moment. This must come first, even before her mother. She *must* make good here if she was to be able to carry on and keep the little family together.

So with resolute will she turned her thoughts from the picture of the precious mother lying on the floor unconscious, and the little carefully-guarded baby sister flying alone across that great expanse of ice to call a stranger to help, and put her mind entirely on her work.

Valiant Willoughby, walking swiftly down the flagstones of the street that ran between the plant where Frannie worked, and his own headquarters which were about a quarter of a mile farther on down the river, was thinking of that girl, that sweet fine young girl! With what charming self-control she had taken the startling news he had brought her, though it was most evident that it had shocked her tremendously. How sweet her eyes had been as she lifted them with that frightened, almost pleading look. Grave, lovely eyes, they were, though she seemed not much more than a little girl.

And how quickly she had rallied to see where her first duty lay! Though it was plain it had been a struggle, because her heart was bidding her fly without delay to her sick mother. She seemed to be a rare girl, and really beautiful, though she was plainly dressed, with no pretense at the make-up and painted finger nails of most girls. Strange he should notice that in such a time, when he was not considering the girl as a girl at all, only as a human being, a young working woman with a family to support!

Well, he hoped the doctor would be on time with his news from the sick room, and that there would be something in his message that would give a possibility of cheer to that brave little girl when he relayed the message at noon.

So he went on to his own place of work, and was presently immersed in duties that were fully as engrossing as Frannie's. And the hours pranced on swiftly as hours have a way of doing when one is working hard, and noon not far away.

And then, before she realized how late it was, for she had not been keeping her mind on the time, but looking ahead to see how much work was still to be done, there came a summons from the office boy, "Miss Fernley, telephone! Mr. Chalmer's office!" and Frannie with her heart beating wildly hurried to the office. Oh, would there be bad news? Should she have gone home anyway? And then as with trembling hands she took up the instrument, there was that pleasant reassuring voice of the young man.

"Good news, Miss Fernley! Your mother is sleeping

quietly, a natural sleep. The doctor did not give her the sleeping tablets after all. She took the nourishment well, and fell right to sleep. Perhaps she was just very tired. The doctor says her pulse is decidedly stronger, and you have nothing to worry about. The nurse says she is glad to have a place to stay till her next case, so you can just trust her to look after things till your regular time for returning."

"Oh, that's wonderful!" breathed the girl softly. "I can't thank you enough for taking all this trouble."

"It wasn't trouble. It was a pleasure," said Willoughby. "And now, what about the return trip for you? Can I help in any way? I can easily get the car and take you back, much faster than if you went on the bus."

"Oh, no, thank you. You've taken too much trouble already. I shall get home all right."

"Why, it wouldn't be any trouble. I'd be glad to help you in any way I can. What time do you get done there? I didn't think to ask Mr. Chalmers."

"Why, we usually go out at five, but Mr. Chalmers said I might go as soon as I finished the letters for the day. However there were a great many letters. It was a heavy mail this morning. I can't tell how long it will take me. But *please* don't trouble any more about me. You have been very kind already. And I have my skates. It doesn't take long to get home on the ice. Thank you so much for all your kindness."

Skates? So she was a skater! He couldn't help but admire her independence.

"Well," he said in a genial tone, "run along then and get done as quickly as possible. I'll be seeing you later."

Frannie hurried back to her desk with a warm glow on her cheeks. How nice it was of that young man to offer to take her home. How wonderful it was that people had been raised up to look after her mother in her stress! But she simply must not think about it or she would get to crying. Poor dear little mother all alone with strangers!

And now what would mother think they ought to do? Perhaps she would have to give up her job for a while—until mother was better. Mother wouldn't like the idea of strangers in the house, even kind strangers. And as for that nurse, well, even if she was *very* nice, they couldn't afford a nurse. Nurses were very expensive. But she must not go into that now or she would get it all mixed up with the letters she was writing and would lose her job by careless work, and that would be worse than giving it up.

So she resolutely put it all out of her mind and went to work again. With no thought whatever of lunch, she plunged into her job and did her level best, though she had a neat little bundle of crackers and cheese and an apple tucked away in her locker, that might have helped out a little. But her only ambition was to get done and get home, home to her mother and her little sister and find out what she had to do next.

Of the two boys,—the *very* young men,—who had endeavored to gain an acquaintance with her that morning, she hadn't even thought all day, not since the tall young stranger had come down the aisle with Mr. Chalmers and brought her word about her mother. And if she had thought of them they would have been like the passing of a bad dream. They were nothing to her. She felt years beyond them. Even her dread that they might try to annoy her had passed beyond her memory.

So she worked on, now and again an eye toward the clock that loomed like a sentinel at the far end of the room. She was running a race and the clock was her judge, her arbiter. Breathlessly she worked, with strangely perfect precision, all keyed up as she was, not daring to turn a particle of thought away from the matter in hand. It was as if her whole life depended upon the outcome of her work that day.

Occasionally she drew a weary breath, and pressed cold fingers to tired eyes.

Then she slid another sheet of paper into her machine and typed on, her fingers in perfect rhythm with the timing of her goal.

And at last the final letter was typed, letter perfect, and ready for inspection.

Her eyes went to the clock again that ticked solemnly on with no evident intention of finishing the afternoon just yet. It was twenty whole minutes to five! She had finished! There was time to take the letters to Mr. Chalmers, and find out if he had other orders for her before she left.

Quietly she put her materials away in the machine drawer, covered the typewriter, and rose with her sheaf of letters in her hand, walking over to Mr. Chalmer's office. And just a moment later the two young men, Kit and Spike, strayed casually across the hall and paused in the open doorway, lingering long enough to look down toward Frannie's desk, and note that it was empty.

"She's gone," said Kit. "I bet you scared her off."

"Scared? That baby?" said Spike, "Not her! She's only independent. Or perhaps she's got away early to steal a march on us and laugh at us tomorrow. Come on. It's near five. I'm going down and get my skates on, and be ready for what happens. There's no need hanging around here."

"It isn't five yet," reminded Kit. "I already got so many marks against me for getting out early I can't risk getting in bad with old Jimsey. Let's go back to the room and make like we're awful busy."

"Okay! Go if you like. I'm getting my skates on. I'm not taking any chances on losing that little number. She's a honey and no mistake."

"Oh, well, if you think we can get away with it, I'm agreeable," said Kit, and discreetly they stole by devious ways to their lockers, stealthily procured their skates, stuffed their caps in their sweater pockets and vanished out the basement door. They chose a sheltered spot to attire their feet with gleaming runners, and then struck out on the ice, far enough away from the plant not to be noticed by any chance watcher.

"I'll tell you one thing," said Spike wisely, "that gal won't appear till the stroke of five. She's not one to slide out of things. She'll stay till the last minute or I miss my guess. She's conscientious. When you fall for a conscientious dame you've got to get wise to her ways, and go slow and easy. She won't break the tidy little rule she's got in her life, not even if she falls for you,

so you better go slow and easy. She's got to think you're
a nice guy like her own folks, or she won't look at you!"

"Oh, you don't say so!" said Kit. "Who taught you
all that, I'd like to know?"

And just then Frannie walked out of the basement
door, her skating shoes on a strap over her shoulder,
and sat down on the wooden step to put them on!

With wary furtive glances about to make sure the
coast was clear of anyone who could make trouble for
them, the boys struck across the ice and circled up to
her, Spike dropping neatly down on his knees before her
and boldly putting out intimate hands to the small shoe
she was attempting to lace up.

"How about me doing that for you, beautiful?" he
said, smiling boldly into her frightened face just above
him as he grasped her foot.

"No! No thank you!" said Frannie, pulling her foot
away and trying to rise. She clutched her other shoe in
her hands and held it almost as a weapon. "Please
don't!" she protested. "I *prefer* to do it myself!"

She tried to put dignity in her frightened voice, but
the bold young bully held her foot like a vise, and she
had to drop back again on the step.

"Let go of my foot!" she said sharply, and lifting the
other shoe with its skate she brought it down smartly
on the bold fingers, making Spike howl in protest.

"You little hell-cat!" he shouted. "What do you think
you're doing?" and with his smarting hand he came at
her angrily, and tried to seize the shoe from her, but
she realized her danger just in time, and hit him a
sharp rap again across the knuckles, which caused him
to howl still louder and dance angrily about on the ice
holding his bruised hand in the other one and shouting
to his companion to help him.

"Hi, there, Kit, get that shoe away from the little
fiend. Come on, we'll make her skate home on one foot.
We can do it. You grab her on one side and I on the
other. I guess she won't be so high hat any more with
us. Grab her now before she has a chance to strike
you! Pin her hands behind her! *Quick!* Don't let her

get another clip at you. Hold her elbows! That's it! Now, I'll wrench this skate out of her hands and then she won't have a chance, and will have to do just what we tell her. Take it easy there, girlie. If you don't fight you won't get hurt. We're not going to hurt you, girlie. We're just going to show you a good time. There, there, now take it easy! Don't try to yammer. We'll take care of you, beautiful!"

With a final yank he tore Frannie's skate from her tense fingers, and she let out a piercing scream. Then suddenly a voice spoke thunderously: "What do you fellows think you are doing?" and Spike was lifted from behind by his collar and wafted through the air in a circle that sent him hurtling on his back across the ice to a safe distance, where he lay, stunned, utterly astounded that this should have happened to him. Why, he was the big bully of his neighborhood! Nobody ever got *him*. What happened anyway? He tried to lift a maimed hand to pass it over his bleared eyes. Who was that guy, anyway? What wouldn't he do to him when he got up out of this!

But he wasn't out of it yet, and where was that Kit? Was he punishing the guy that butted into their frolic? And what had become of the girl? She couldn't go very far with only one shoe and one skate on. Where was the other?

He wanted to look around, but somehow he was too sore in his muscles to turn around and look. He had to lie still a minute longer.

"Kit! Oh *Kit!*" he murmured, and wondered why his voice didn't seem to carry farther. He tried again. "Kit! Oh, I say, *Kit!*" Nothing happened. Then he tried his piercing whistle that always waked the echoes, but the whistle didn't seem to pan out right. His lips were stiff and wouldn't work. Did that girl get away after all?

At last he managed to roll over, raising himself on one elbow to look around him. Blinking into the late afternoon sunlight he made out two figures skimming together far upstream, but look as he might he could not see Kit anywhere. He must have made good his escape.

Chapter 3

MARIETTA HOLLISTER was considered a beautiful girl. She wore severely tailored tweeds in the daytime, and affected the latest hair-do and make up, though she tried never to go to extremes. She considered herself very conservative. She kept the length of her finger nails within quiet bounds, and of late their color had resembled more the seashell pink of a young rosebud, rather than drops of blood. Perhaps it was because a young man she much admired had expressed dislike for the bloody looking hands of many girls of the day. Some of her friends considered her eccentric, but she went on her way serenely.

She took a deep interest in war work of various kinds. She attended class in First Aid religiously, offered her services as an ambulance driver, got up entertainments for the soldiers' camps, and was put on numerous committees for the various defense activities, patriotic and otherwise, to say nothing of keeping up her social obligations. She was a very busy and eager young woman, ready to set everybody right on everything, and in such a lovely way that they were not antagonized. She lived in the big colonial house on the hill, on the estate to the left of the Haversett House, where Val Willoughby was staying with his aunt and uncle. She was considered one of the most desirable and charming girls in the neighborhood.

Marietta had known Valiant Willoughby when they were children. Whenever he was in the neighborhood they had played together and taken each other for granted. She had just discovered his return, having not seen him during the four years he was in college.

It was that same morning that Marietta got up with a new plan in her mind. As it involved Valiant she proceeded to call up his aunt's house as soon as she had had breakfast.

"Oh, good morning Nannie!" she called as she recognized the old servant's voice answering her. "Nannie, is Val there? Oh, has he gone *already?* Why, I supposed he went down on the eight thirty train. You mean he goes this early every morning? What? You say he *skated* down? Why, how ridiculous! I should think it would tire him all out for the day. Well, he's gone then, and I can't speak to him. Does he come home to lunch? No, of course not. That would be too long a journey, wouldn't it? But Nannie, let me speak to Mrs. Haversett, please. That is, if she isn't busy. Oh, good morning, Auntie Haversett! This is Marietta. I called to speak to Val but Nannie tells me he is already gone. Can you tell when he will be home? Not till five? How provoking! I wanted to talk something over with him. I wonder if he would come over and take dinner with us tonight, then I can have time to talk things over with him. Do you think he will come?"

"Well, my dear, I'm afraid I can't say positively. Sometimes he has to stay all the evening at the plant. It depends on whether they are finishing some army order or not. I didn't have any talk with him last night. He was late coming home, and I was just going out. And this morning he was off before I got up. I am afraid he is very uncertain just now, my dear. But I'll tell him of course when he gets back, only it won't do to count on him too much. He is most uncertain. You know war work comes first."

"Why, how perfectly horrid!" said the girl indignantly. "I thought Val was in charge of a department or something. Can't he arrange his own hours?"

"I'm afraid not, my dear. He is in charge of something, I forget just what they call it. But nobody can arrange his own hours just now. The government arranges those matters, and we'll just have to be patient until the great work of defense gets going thoroughly, and it becomes apparent just what is the best method of working."

"Well, it's all wrong, I say, to waste time and good

men that way," said the girl. "A man can't keep on
working indefinitely without his proper rest, and he
needs a little play time too, time to do just exactly
what he pleases. Don't you think so, Auntie Haversett?"

"Well, in ordinary times, yes, I should think so," said
the older woman thoughtfully. "But in these times of
stress, my dear, people who have charge of important
matters have to put aside their own wishes you know—"

"Oh, certainly, I know that as well as you do, but it
isn't the way to run things, and I should think if Val is
in charge of things he could regulate his hours according
to common sense."

"Well, I don't know how much power he has yet.
Perhaps those things will work out. But in the meantime I'll tell him what you want, and I'm sure if he can
make it he will come."

"Thanks awfully, Auntie Haversett. I'm really planning something quite important. It's a scheme to raise
money to get shelter places ready for the children
down near the munitions plants—in case of raids, you
know. There are a lot of little children living down
there on the flats near the plants where their fathers
work, and there should be refuges with fully trained
nurses in charge, ready for sudden needs. You know
those places down there would be the very first spot
an enemy would bomb in case of a raid. And I thought
if we were to get up a series of dances for the younger
set, the ones who aren't really doing anything much
yet, and charge plenty for tickets, we could get quite a
lot of money in no time. There's nothing like a dance
to get the youngsters interested. And of course we
regular young set would be there to run things for the
kids. I'm quite sure it would be popular. That's what I
want to talk over with Val. If he will help me start it
I'm sure it will take like wild fire. Don't you think he
would be interested? And don't you think the project
seems fairly inspired, Auntie Haversett?"

"Well, I don't know, my dear. It sounds as if you
were planning a lot of hard work and a lot of fun for
somebody. But as for Val, I'm not altogether sure how
the idea would strike him. I really haven't seen enough

of him since he has been here on that job to know how
he reacts to such things any more."

"But he always was so ready to help in any good
thing," said the girl positively.

"Yes, I know he was. But these war times are un-
predictable times, and there is no telling how anybody
would react to any proposition. And of course there are
so many things that defense workers are not free to discuss that might make a difference, too, in any plans."

"Well, I can't see how such a thing as that could
possibly carry any objections, can you?"

"Well, no, it doesn't seem so on first sight, does it,
dear?" said the older woman thoughtfully. "But, as
I say, I don't seem to be able to judge just what reaction *any*one will have to anything any more. And of
course Val is changed in some ways. He's a lot quieter
than he was. By the way, Marietta, did your mother go
to the club meeting yesterday? I was wondering what
they did about the special war fund? Did you happen
to hear her say whether they were going on with their
plans for that play, or were they just going to ask for
voluntary contributions? Of course everyone is begging
for something now, and it does seem as if it was hope-
less to try to sell tickets to any more things."

"Why, no, I didn't hear mother say anything about
the club meeting," said Marietta, "I haven't been at
home much in the last day or two, but it does seem as
if something that has been planned and looked forward
to for so long ought to be carried out, don't you
think so? Of course I know some of the actors have gone
to camp, and Jason Allenby can't be here. He went to
England by clipper plane yesterday, you know. But
surely there will be somebody who could take his place.
I think Val would be a wonderful substitute to take
that part. I'll remember to suggest it to him tonight.
I'll suggest it to the committee, too. Well, Auntie Haversett, you'll be sure to tell Val to call me up as soon as
he gets home, won't you?"

"Yes, I'll tell him when he comes, dear, but you
mustn't be surprised if you don't get a response right
away. He may not come home till very late."

"All right. But, Auntie Haversett, isn't there some way to call him up at the plant?"

The lady looked troubled.

"I'm afraid not, Marietta. That is, one could of course, but it isn't expected, except in emergencies."

"Oh, I see. And you wouldn't think this was an emergency?"

"Well, I'm afraid not, dear."

"Of course I could drive down there and ask to see him," said the girl speculatively.

"Oh, my dear! Is it that important? If I were you I would just forget it. Because really, I think Val is so extremely busy and so absorbed in his work just now, that it isn't in the least likely he'll have time for social affairs until things get going. You know the government is urging intensive work."

"Oh dear! Well, I suppose we'll have to put up with it for a while, but I don't see why other work isn't just as important. Well, good-by for the present, Auntie. I must be getting back to my work. I'm on a new committee this morning and I must hurry."

So Marietta went to her new committee which was at nine o'clock, followed by another at ten, and a third appointment at eleven, but her eager and prolific brain had already solved her problem. That afternoon at a quarter to five with determined mien and assured voice she called up Val Willoughby's plant.

But Val Willoughby was not in his office.

"Has he gone home yet?" demanded the efficient voice.

"I couldn't say, Miss," answered the man who was detailed to look out for phone calls.

"Well, you know whether he is coming back to the plant, don't you?" asked Marietta impatiently.

"I couldn't say, Miss. Mr. Willoughby is a very busy man. He doesn't tell us where he is going. He may be back tonight and he may not. He doesn't have to tell us what he does. He might be outside in the yard. He might be over to the other building. Or he might be gone into the city to see somebody. I don't know. He comes and he goes."

"Well, really!" said Marietta. "I shouldn't think that was very efficient work. Well, if he comes in will you ask him to call me? This is Miss Hollister. The number is Cliveden 725. Will you write that down?"

"Oh sure! But I ain't sure I shall see him. I'm going off duty now, and the other man hasn't come in yet. I'll write the number here. Mebbe he'll see it, I don't know."

And, desperately, at last Marietta hung up.

But Val didn't call her. He was out on the ice dealing with the two young bullies who had set out to play a joke on a girl they thought was too stupid and too young to get it back on them.

Spike came to somewhat while Willoughby was helping Frannie on with her other skate which he had retrieved from a distance whither it had slid at Kit's last frantic yank before he had sighted the enemy coming toward them. He had given the girl's shoe a quick fling across the ice, and then suddenly vanished in a way he knew and had often practised in his early youth. So when Willoughby returned with the shoe in his hand enemy number two had disappeared from off the face of the earth.

Val dropped down before the girl and helped her put her skate on. Then taking her hand he set her upon her feet, and looked her over.

Her hair was awry, the little green cap sat crazily on her brown curls, there were tears on her white cheeks, but not in her eyes, and with brave determination she was holding her trembling lips fairly still.

"Are you sure you are able to go on home this way?" he asked her, looking into her wide eyes that had been so frightened when he first came up.

"Oh, yes," she said, with a catch in her voice. "Yes, I can go on! I'm so sorry I made you trouble again! How wonderful that you should have come along just now! I don't know what I should have done!"

He smiled.

"I'm glad I was here. Who were they? Do you know them? Have they troubled you before?"

"No, I never saw them before till this morning. They

stood in the hall when I went in and were awfully fresh. They asked me to go dancing, and when I told them no they insisted they would meet me out here at closing time. I didn't answer them, and I forgot all about them, or I would have gone out the front door and taken to the river down beyond the next street. I never knew any boys like that."

"There are a lot of tough fellows down in this neighborhood of course," said Willoughby, "but I don't fancy they will trouble you again. Perhaps we had better curve over in the direction of that one and see if he is coming to, or whether I ought to send someone to look after him."

Then still holding Frannie's hand protectively he set out slowly at first, watching the prostrate form of Spike sprawled across the ice.

"He's coming to," said Willoughby. "I saw him move his arm just now. Didn't you? There! He's turning his head. He'll be himself presently. I'll just stop at the next corner and tell the plant night watchman to take a look at him, and send for an ambulance if necessary, or a taxi, if he can't navigate himself. I wonder where his companion is."

"He won't come back while you are here," said Frannie in a low trembly voice. "He's a coward. I watched his face when you took the other one off and flung him out on the ice. He was scared to death. And I don't think he has any very great love for his pal either. He won't want it known that he was mixed up in this affair."

He looked at her and smiled.

"You certainly are a brave girl," he said fervently. "I watched you defend yourself while I was sprinting to the spot and you never flinched once. I was afraid you might faint."

"I don't faint," said Frannie seriously, as if it were a thing to be deplored. "I just don't know how."

"Fine! That's wonderful. There are not many girls who could claim that. But, aren't you feeling pretty well broken up after all this? I think we had better steer in to shore at the next street and take a taxi."

"Oh, no, please! I'm all right. Just a little shaky, but I'll be steady in a minute or two. Skating isn't any effort."

"Oh, isn't it? Well, that may be so at times, but after a brisk fist fight such as you've been through I can't think it is the best thing. We'll just steer for that corner, and take the next bus."

"Please, no," said Frannie frantically. "It rests me to skate. It really does. And I should be frantic hanging around waiting for buses and changing from one to another. You don't understand. It does steady my nerves to skate."

He studied her face an instant.

"Oh, very well," he said, "but you're going to let me help steady you. Here, cross your hands. I think we can travel faster and easier this way." He took her mittened hands in a firm clasp, and they sailed off together. It was easier that way, of course, and she gave him a thankful little smile.

"You're being very kind to me, a stranger," she said. "I can't ever thank you enough."

"Don't try," he said with a smile. "And besides, you're not a stranger, merely a neighbor. Now, let's forget it, and have a good journey. That will rest you more than trying to be grateful. See that color in the sky, and how it reflects from the ice. It's like sailing into a pavement of rubies."

"Yes, isn't it lovely? That's one great reason why I like to come this way. It's so beautiful, any time of day, especially morning and evening. I dread so to have the weather change and spoil the ice."

"Yes, that's right. Weather has a good deal to do with it. I feel that way myself, watching the sky every morning when I wake up. Rejoicing when the sky is still clear and bright. But say, where did you people come from when you moved here? Was it from far away?"

"No," said Frannie. "It was only about seventy miles north, but it was in the country. We went to stay with my grandmother after my father died. Grandmother was quite ill and needed us. But she died three weeks ago, and mother and I felt we should come down here where I could get a job. I think I was most fortunate in finding such a good job, just by answering an advertisement in the paper. We came from a little place called Bluebell, and that is the reason our goods are coming in sections. There wasn't a regular mover to be had, and so an old farmer, a friend of my grandmother's, is moving us, a little at a time. That's why you found our little house so bare. But I think the rest of the things are coming today. The farmer borrowed a larger truck and is bringing his son with him to help, so we can soon get in order, I hope. He thought they might get here before dark tonight."

"Well, perhaps they'll be there when we arrive. I'd like to stick around awhile and help a little if I may."

"Oh, but you've already done too much!" said Frannie.

"It seems to me that I've somewhere heard that there's a kind of law, perhaps it's in the Bible, that the reward for doing something is that you get the privilege of doing something more a lot greater. Anyway that seems a pretty good rule to me. I've enjoyed what I've done so far immensely."

"That's a beautiful way to look at it," said Frannie wistfully.

"There are other compensations, too," said the young man with a smile. "I feel that I have made some very lovely friends, besides renewing the acquaintance of one whom I knew several years ago when I was a youngster. I mean Lady Winthrop. It was she who called me from the river and sent me to your mother. I want you to know her also. I know you will love her."

"Oh, yes, and I shall want to thank her, too," said Frannie eagerly. "Tell me about it again please. That is something I shall not want to forget."

So he told her about it, more in detail, as they skimmed along on the sunset-colored ice, her mittened hands held firmly in his gloved ones, his strength steadying her balance. And the way did not seem long in such company.

And then they were in sight of the little brick house,

and saw that two trucks were drawn up by the sidewalk.

"Oh, the furniture has come!" cried Frannie. "I'm so glad. Now mother can have her blankets and pillows. I'm afraid she wasn't warm enough last night."

"Oh, but Lady Winthrop thought of that too, and sent over some blankets with the first load I took across."

"How dear of her!" said the girl, her face brimming over with gratitude. "I'm eager to know her. She must be wonderful!"

"She's all that!" declared the young man, guiding the girl to the steps. "Well, here we are! Now, let me unfasten those shoes and put on your other ones. And may I suggest that after the shock, and the unusual experience you had this afternoon, you save yourself as much as possible? I'm going in and help, and I want you to give me orders instead of doing things yourself. Will you? Please promise me, for I shall be worried that I let you skate home if you don't."

"But I feel quite all right, *really*. You made the journey so much easier than it would have been if I had skated alone."

"Well, I'm glad of that, but I want your promise all the same, because if you don't keep it I shall have to tell your family what you have been through, and I know you don't want that just now. Anyhow not till your mother is well and up and around."

"Oh, no, I wouldn't have her know it for anything. She has been awfully worried lest I would get in with a tough set, and I'm afraid she wouldn't want me to go to work any more, and would worry all the time I was away. Please, you won't tell her, will you?"

"Not if you keep your part of the contract. You've just got to sit down as much as possible, and get to bed as early as possible, or you certainly won't be able to go to work in the morning."

"All right, I'll be very careful. And thank you so much for all you've done."

"Oh, but you've already thanked me. Now, let's go in and see what we can do to get this household settled for the night. And by the way, if the morning is clear and the ice still good, are you going to skate down to work again?"

"Oh, yes, of course."

"Well, then, may I have the pleasure of accompanying you?"

"Why, that would be lovely, but—you mustn't feel that you've got to take me over as a continual burden."

"Oh, it wouldn't be a burden. It's nice to have a skating companion, and it certainly helps to eat up the miles. Now, here we are, and the door is wide open for us. The furniture seems to be mainly inside the house, doesn't it? Just a few more pieces. Here, I'll help with this couch. It's a little awkward for two to handle. And then in a minute I'll hunt up the nurse and introduce you."

And so at the doorway of the little brick house they parted and Frannie rushed up the stairs to find her mother.

At the closed door she paused, startled. Her mother's door! Had something dreadful happened this afternoon? Was her mother worse? Oh, she ought to have come home before! She knew she should not listen to the persuasions of strangers, not even to the voice of caution for her job. She should have come at once.

Softly, cautiously, with trembling fingers she grasped the doorknob, firmly, and turned it ever so softly. Why, it didn't open! It seemed to be locked! What had happened? She glanced wildly around, and then called softly.

"Bonnie! Oh, Bonnie!" And then in a desperate wail: *"Mother!"*

Suddenly she heard small footsteps downstairs, Bonnie hurrying to answer. Bonnie at the foot of the stairs, her important young face bright with grown up responsibility.

"Here I am, Frannie," she whispered, "Mother's asleep. You mustn't wake her up."

"Oh, Bonnie *dear!*" grasped Frannie, the tears rushing to her eyes. "How is she? Is she worse?"

"No indeed!" said the little girl with childish gravity. "She's a great deal better. But Nurse Branner is trying

to keep her quiet till the men are gone so she won't
try to get up."

And then suddenly the key turned in the lock and the
door was opened by a pleasant-faced nurse in full uniform.

"Oh, this is Frannie, isn't it?" she said in a low clear
voice. "Come right in. Your mother is awake now and
has been asking for you. Don't let her talk too much.
She wants you to give directions to the movers where to
put things. Just be as quiet about it as you can, and
smile a good deal!" She gave Frannie a knowing look
that changed Frannie's tears into sunbeams.

"Of course," smiled Frannie, giving a quick wipe to
her wet lashes. Then she stepped to the side of the bed
and knelt beside her mother:

"Oh, mother dear! To think you've been sick and I
wasn't here!" she whispered, but there was a bright
smile of relief on her face as she said it. "But you're
better now, mother dear, aren't you? And what wonderful neighbors we have! Bringing a nice nurse and
a doctor. I was so happy when I got the message that
you were being taken care of. I wanted to fly right home
of course when I heard you had fainted, but they said
you sent word I mustn't, so I stayed. But mother, I did
a lot of praying all day."

Her mother smiled peacefully.

"Yes, dear, there wasn't any need for you to come
home. I was perfectly all right. Just a little faint. I was
only tired, and perhaps some worried about your going
off alone on that dreadful ice."

"Oh, mother dear! But the ice was lovely, as smooth
as glass."

"Well, I'm glad you're safely home again," sighed the
mother with a smile of relief, "and I suppose I'll get
used to it. Only really, my dear, I didn't need to be
put to bed. I could perfectly well have kept up and
gotten dinner for us, I'm sure."

"Why, yes, of course you could," smiled the nurse
cheerfully. "I told you that when I was putting your
nightgown on, don't you remember? You *could* have
got up and gone to work, of course, but since I was here

and there really wasn't anything important to do all
day but what Bonnie and I could do, it didn't seem
worth while, did it? You know, Miss Frannie, I
wouldn't have felt comfortable to stay here without doing something to help pay my board," and she gave a
merry little twinkle of a wink toward Frannie. "So you
see, Bonnie and I got everything fixed up as well as we
could without bothering your mother, and just let her
have a rest. And then that nice Lady Winthrop sent that
lovely lunch over to us, and we certainly were in fine
shape to enjoy it. Your mother ate a whole cup of the
chicken broth, and we put some in a cup in the tin pail
with snow around it, and had enough for her this afternoon when she woke up. She really enjoyed it a lot,
didn't you, Mrs. Fernley?"

The mother's eyes assented with a sweet smile.

"How lovely that was, mother," said Frannie, catching the idea of cheerfulness from the nurse. "Wasn't it
grand of Mrs. Winthrop to be so thoughtful? You
thought we would be so lonely among strangers for a
long time, and you were going to miss the dear Bluebell people. But even Bluebell couldn't have been any
kinder."

"Yes," said Bonnie who had come upstairs importantly to join in the conversation, "there was hot water
bags, and a n'ice bag, and blankets and soup. It was
grand!"

The mother lay there looking at her children and
smiling almost hopefully now, relaxing on her pillows,
realizing after many hard days that someone was caring
and helping, and she could lie still and get rested before
she had to get up and go on with her troublous life.

"And now, Mrs. Fernley," said Nurse Branner,
"what were those things you wanted your daughter to
look after when the movers came? They have brought
in some of the larger pieces and I did my best to have
them placed where you said, but maybe she had better
run down and see if everything is just as you planned.
I think you've talked long enough for a little while, so
you take a nap while she goes, and Bonnie and I will
get the kitchen to rights. I saw them bring in the barrel

of dishes and we can rinse them off and get them in the cupboards so we'll be all ready for supper. You shut your eyes and be real rested when the doctor comes back before supper, won't you? I want him to think we've done a good job of nursing you, you know, so you can get up sooner."

"Oh!" said the sick woman with a troubled look. "I really ought to get up now. I'm feeling quite well enough," and she lifted a frail hand and tried to raise herself to her elbow.

But the nurse gave her a soft little push back to her pillow.

"No, you don't pull any tricks like that on me, my lady!" laughed the nurse. "I promised the doctor I'd keep you perfectly quiet in bed until he came back to-night, and I mean to keep my promise or he wouldn't let me nurse for him any longer."

So the nurse puffed the pillows up, drew the blanket a little closer, opened the window just a crack, watched the tired eyelids droop down, and the sick woman's breath come softly, steadily, until she knew she was on the way to sleep again. Then she slipped away to see what Bonnie was doing in the kitchen, and whether the movers were anywhere near through their work.

Chapter 4

DURING THE DAY Marietta had more or less perfected her plans for the defense of her country. After all she would be the one to plan, and she expected it to be an easy matter to bring Val Willoughby to her way of thinking. Of course he hadn't always been easy to move. He never by any chance saw things, even the things of mere play, exactly as she did. But he was polite. She could always count on that. And in things that did not seem to him to matter he always gave in to the lady. He

had been trained that way. Though she could recall
times, a few of them, when he had stood out against her
in the matter of what he called fair treatment to someone else, even someone whom she disliked very much.
He never would consent to let anyone be put out of the
game for some trifling matter. He always insisted that
one child was as good as another, even if the one was
the small meek daughter of the cleaning woman, who
had to come along with her mother because there was
no place for her to stay alone while her mother was
working. Marietta saw no reason for that child to be
called into their game, but Val insisted that she should
be asked. Val used to be queer that way. He said little
Annie was lonely, and he took special pains to teach
her how to hide so that she would not be too easily
found, how to run to the base when opportunity came.
Marietta never had liked that in him. She felt that it
somehow took from her some of the prestige that
should have been hers. She wanted all the attention herself. She felt it was her due.

Marietta was not unduly proud, though she was well
aware that she was beautiful and better dressed than
most of the other girls. On the strength of all that she
assumed a precedence for herself that gave her the right
to rule, to order the lives and goings of her companions,
and such menials as should be related to their in-
dividual groups. And when an occasion arose in which
some unfortunate friend balked her plans, either in-
tentionally or otherwise, Marietta usually dealt out a
punishment in the form of cold words and sharp looks;
sometimes followed by honeyed forgiveness and res-
toration to high favor if they were duly repentant.

Val Willoughby formerly was one of her most de-
voted subjects at the age of ten to twelve years. But
advanced prep school and then college had removed
him from her immediate neighborhood, and she had
had little contact with him of late, except for a few
isolated hours now and then when he stopped off on his
journeys for a brief visit with his aunt. But now that he
had come back to be with his aunt indefinitely, or at
least "for the duration," Marietta fully expected to take

over again, and this "defense plan" as she called her scheme of a series of dances, was the first move in that direction. She was therefore greatly annoyed not to be able to get in touch with him at once to make him aware of his part in the activities.

So it was with a deeper frown than mere annoyance would have caused that Marietta turned from the telephone at last and wondered what to do next. She wasn't often balked so fully and so continuously as this. Surely, *surely* Val would come home to dinner presently. She would wait a little longer and call again. Then she interviewed the cook and had their own dinner hour delayed a half hour, just to allow time to get hold of Val.

Meantime Val was helping the Fernley family move in, and watching Frannie as she went capably about, directing the arrangement of furniture, putting dishes and pots and pans away in the cupboards, showing that she had calculated to a nicety just where everything would fit and be convenient.

He watched her gracious young face as she thanked her former neighbors for bringing their goods so safely. She urged them to stay a little while and let her get them some supper before they would begin the long drive back to Bluebell.

"No, Frannie," said the older man speaking for them both, "we gotta get back. I promised mother I'd get back along the edge of dark, and she'll be worrying till we get there. And don't you worry about us. Mother, she put up a lunch for us, and she sent you some of her raisin cookies you like so much. Here they are. I calculate you'll have enough to do to get supper for your own family without any of us added to it, so if you're sure that is all you need we'll just be hurrying right along. We'll be back some day next week with the pianna. Then that's all your things, but don't forget, if you should need anything else of us, don't hesitate to write us, or telephone my son's house and he'll let us know."

So they were gone, and Frannie turned to thank the

young man who had helped her so materially all day. "You've been just wonderful!" she said again.

"Nothing like that," said he smiling. "I've been having the time of my life. It's fun to help other people get settled. Say, this is going to be a real handy little house, isn't it? I never dreamed there would be so much room here. And now, what do we do next? Don't we have to get supper? And by the way, how did you find your mother?"

"Why, she seemed really bright, although I could see she is still very tired. She has been through an awful beating, it's true, and I suppose we didn't realize what it was doing to her, although I'd been terribly worried about her. But she really is getting a good rest. She went to sleep when the nurse told her, like a tired little child. I'm so thankful for that lovely nurse. I can see she knows how to manage mother. If I'd been here alone with her I'm positive she'd have gotten right up and tried to get supper. But isn't that a car stopping at the door? You don't suppose those men have come back, do you? Perhaps they forgot something."

Willoughby looked out of the side window.

"That's the doctor," he announced. "I'm glad he's come. Now we'll know just how your mother is. I was hoping he would come before I left. Shall I open the door? You know he won't be surprised to see me here. He and I really opened this hospital together this morning, you remember. Come in, Doctor Ransom. This is Miss Fernley."

Frannie looked up to meet the kindly eyes of the old doctor and her heart gave thanks at the instant confidence he gave her.

"Oh, is my mother very sick?" she asked him, her keen young eyes on his face, a sweet wistfulness in her voice.

"Why, I trust not, my dear," assured the hearty voice of the old doctor. "I thought she was doing very well when I was here at noon. How does she seem now? Where is the nurse?"

"She's upstairs with mother. Will you go up? The

movers have just gone. I hope the noise wasn't too much for her!"

The doctor smiled at the anxious young face.

"Why, I don't see why that should harm her," he said. "Suppose we go up and see. I think your mother is simply tired out and needed a little rest. I'm sure she's going to be all right very soon. Val, suppose you wait here till I come down. I want to see you a minute."

"Yes, sir, I'll do that," said Willoughby.

Very quietly the doctor entered the sick room, and Mrs. Fernley's eyes opened instantly, as if his coming were what she had been waiting for even in her sleep. The doctor's presence was like a ray of sunshine in the little room. He came over and sat down on the chair by the bed with a cheery smile.

"Well, little lady," he said, "how are you feeling by now?"

He peered keenly into her eyes, and put a fine soft hand over her wrist with a friendly motion, searching for the pulse which had been so weak that morning. Then he looked up at the nurse and gave an almost imperceptible nod of his head.

"Yes, Nurse, this is a good strong pulse," he said decidedly. "You've done a good job of nursing here today. I think this lady will be coming around in a very few days. What do you think?"

The nurse smiled at Frannie.

"Yes, I thought she was getting along nicely," she said happily.

Frannie's heart rose, and her joy was reflected in her happy eyes.

"Oh, I'm so glad!" she breathed. "I was so afraid I should have come home, even though you did send me word it wasn't necessary. I knew those movers were coming, and I knew mother would worry about that."

"Yes, but my dear child, you didn't realize that your mother was too ill at first to worry about anything, except that you should not be disturbed. And then as she got a little rested, there was the nurse, and she didn't take long to get acquainted."

"No, I didn't know all that," murmured Frannie

gravely with a bit of a sigh. "But you see I knew mother, and how used she was to worrying."

The doctor gave her a quick glance of comprehension.

"I see!" he said understandingly. "Well, we must fix it so that she won't do any worrying, at least not for a while."

"Yes," said Frannie with a suddenly troubled look in her eyes. "But that won't be so easy to arrange."

"Oh, I think there'll be a way to arrange that," said the doctor comfortably. "You leave it to me. I'll find a way. Now, nurse, how much of that medicine have you got left? I see. Well, I'll give you something else to go with it."

It was quiet in the room while the doctor was preparing his medicine, and giving now and then a crisp direction to the nurse. Frannie listened with a growing confidence. Then he rose and looked down at the patient.

"Good night, Mrs. Fernley. I hope you will eat a nice little supper, and then go to sleep and sleep until morning. I shall expect to find you greatly improved by morning when I run in again, but remember, if you want to get well quickly you must do just as the nurse says."

"But doctor," said the invalid, "I should have told you. We are really poor people. We can't afford to run up doctor's and nurse's bills. I'm sure I shall not need you again in the morning."

"There, there, my dear, we're not running up bills. This is just a neighborly visit on my way home, so you needn't worry. In fact I like to be good friends with my patients, and I like to run in and get acquainted with them now and then. Now, Nurse Branner, is that all, or do you want to ask any questions?"

He stood a moment at the door talking with the nurse, and Frannie stole near to her mother and softly kissed the frail hand that lay on the pillow.

The mother smiled, and murmured, "I'll be all right, dear child. Don't you worry!"

"No, I won't, mother, if you do just as you are

told. Now I'm going down and hunt some supper for you."

"Just some milk will do," said the mother softly. "Don't go to any trouble for me. I'll be all right."

Frannie kissed her again and stole downstairs after the doctor.

"Don't worry about her supper," said the nurse softly as she passed her at the door. "I saved a cup of that chicken broth for her."

Frannie flashed her a grateful glance and sped on after the doctor, who was standing in the room below with his hand on young Willoughby's shoulder, and a comradely look on his kind, benevolent face. They might have been talking about personal affairs, or business matters, or even political and defense programs, but in reality the doctor was saying:

"My boy, I wonder if I can rely on you to keep me in touch with how things are going in this family. That little mother has gone just about as far as she could go, and not slip over the border entirely. And yet I believe that with reasonable care she can snap out of this trouble entirely and recover her normal health. But there has got to be somebody watching for at least a few days, or maybe even weeks, and so I am hoping they will let the nurse stay here awhile—just as an accommodation to her you know, that is, ostensibly—and keep a watch out. You see it happens most fortunately that Nurse Branner has just come off a year's case. And the people with whom she formerly boarded have suddenly gone to California. Of course we would take her into our home if necessary, but my wife's sister and her daughter are with us this winter, and it makes it a little crowded to take in another at present, so she has really been expecting to look for a new abiding place. But she is enough of a Christian, and enthusiastic enough as a nurse, to get interested here and stay awhile, as long as she is needed. So the matter of money does not need to come into the picture at all. So then, could I depend on you, Val, to see what you can do with the family to see this thing straight, at least until the mother is out of danger? I know you haven't much time, but are you so situated that you could run over here early in the morning and then phone me how things are, so that I won't have to leave home until after my office hours are over? They ought to have a telephone here, but of course that can't be done tonight, and I ought to be in a position to get word from the nurse early. Can you do that?"

"I can," said Willoughby with a pleasant ring to his voice. "I'll be glad to help in any way I can. I think they are unusual people."

"Yes, you're right, my boy. Well, thank you. I'll be depending on you," and with a smile of reassurance at Frannie the doctor strode out to his car and was soon driving away.

But as Frannie and Val lingered for a moment watching him, another car drew up before the house and stopped. It was a big, old-fashioned car with plenty of room, a shining exterior, and an old lady sitting on the back seat alone.

The chauffeur helped the old lady out, and she started up the walk.

"Why, Val Willoughby!" she said. "I wondered if you would happen to turn up around here again. That's nice. You can introduce me to my new neighbors, can't you?"

The young man came quickly to her side and offered his arm.

"I surely can, Lady Winthrop. I'll be delighted. This is Frances Fernley. I think they call her Frannie. She is the young lady, I believe, whom you have admired so much, skating down the river."

Frannie looked up surprised, and flashed a shy smile at the old lady.

"And you are the wonderful neighbor that came to our assistance when my mother was taken sick, aren't you?" said Frannie. "I've heard all about you and I'm so glad to be able to thank you. I know my mother will want to thank you herself as soon as she is able to see anybody. Won't you come in? We're not really in order yet. Our things have just come. I don't know what we would have done without those blankets you sent, so few of our own came in the first load. And the hot water bags! And the food! I was so relieved when I heard you had sent my mother that wonderful chicken soup."

The old lady held the girl's soft hand in a warm clasp.

"You dear child!" she said. "I was so glad to know of something I could do. And your dear little sister! Is she all right? I was so afraid she would take cold going out across that awful ice without a coat."

Then Bonnie appeared smiling.

"I'm all right," she said shyly. "That soup and chicken you sent over were just *grand!*"

"Were they, my dear?" said the old lady with a pleased smile. "Well, I've brought you some things for supper. One couldn't be expected to get meals when there is sickness going on, and moving too. Here, Joseph, are you bringing the basket?"

"Yes, Madam, I'm right here!" said the old serving man walking up behind her. "Shall I just take it inside to the kitchen?"

"Oh, yes. Bonnie, you show him the way to the kitchen. And now I'll sit down for a minute so I will feel I know you, and then I must go." Lady Winthrop dropped into a big chair by the door, and looked around her smiling, taking in every little detail without in the least seeming to do so.

"This is a very attractive house," she said. "I can't see it well from my windows, but I think it might be very lovely in the summer. You'll need some vines. I have plenty of ivy slips. If you want them in the spring I'll send them over. I think a brick house always looks lovely with English ivy growing over it."

"Oh, we would love to have that," said Frannie eagerly, "and I know mother would be delighted. The only objection she made to the house was that it looked so bare and stark. Mother loves trees and vines and flowers."

"Well, that's interesting. I'm sure she and I will

have a lot in common. Only I'm not able to go out and work among my flowers any more. I had a fall and it left some of my joints and muscles rather stiff and balky, though Joseph knows how I like the garden, and he fixes it the way I used to have it. But soon the spring will be coming again and you can see it for yourself. Do you like flowers?"

"Oh, I love them," said Frannie with eagerness in her eyes. "Mother used to have an old-fashioned garden up in the country where we've been since father died, and it was lovely. Mother seems to know just how to make flowers grow. She charms them into bloom."

"Well, I want to get acquainted with her just as soon as she is better. And now, my dear, I think I had better go, because I want you to eat that supper while it is nice. I want your mother to have that milk toast right away while it is still hot. It's well covered in a hot dish, and the nurse will understand how to fix it. I put in a couple of little bags of tea lest you hadn't had time to go to the store yet. Well, good-by dear, and don't you worry. *You* can't afford to get sick, you know, not till your mother is well anyway. Now, Val, are you coming with me? I want to talk to you a few minutes. How would you like to eat dinner with me? It was all ready to put on the table when I came away, and I told the cook I might bring you back with me if you were here. It won't take you any longer to eat with me than if you went home, and I won't hinder you if you want to leave immediately after we finish."

"Why, delightful! Of course I'll come," said the young man.

Then he cast a quick look and smile toward Frannie. "Are you sure you don't need me for anything before I go?"

"Oh, no," said Frannie shyly. "You've been wonderful. I couldn't think of troubling you any longer. And really there's nothing more to be done."

"All right, good night then, and I'll be seeing you in the morning. You heard me promise the doctor. And besides, if you are planning to skate down we might as well keep each other company, if you don't mind. It looks as if the weather was going to be all right for the ice at least for another day or two. Good night."

Frannie stood at the door a moment and watched the big car swing away up the road to the bridge. There was a warm feeling around her heart. How nice and pleasant they all were! How glad she was for their friendship. How nice it had been for the young man to protect her down at the plant, and come home with her. And how he had helped the movers.

She went into the house with a smile on her lips and hurried out to the kitchen to investigate the big basket that had been left there. She found Bonnie and the nurse already there looking at it.

What nice things they found in that basket! Milk toast made out of homemade bread, light as a feather, browned just right, and with that delicious cream dressing over it, piping hot.

The nurse had the cup of tea already made, and they lost no time in conveying it to the invalid, who ate hungrily, appreciatively, and dropped sweetly to sleep soon after.

Down at the dining room table, which Bonnie had been setting to the best of her ability, the three sat and ate the meal that had been prepared for them. Broiled chops, enough to have some left over for the next day, chopped creamed potatoes cooked to perfection, spinach and peas, a dish of applesauce and a small delicious custard pie. How good everything tasted, and how grateful they all were!

"And now," said the nurse, assuming charge of the little household, "you two girls run upstairs and make up your bed. I didn't know where to find the sheets or I would have done it. Don't worry about me. I've taken that cot the movers brought and put it in your mother's room. If you've got an extra blanket and quilt or something just lay them out and I'll be fixed fine. I want to watch your mother and give her the medicine through the night, you know. And you girls ought to get to bed right away. You said you had to start early in the morning, Frannie, and there'll be breakfast to get.

I saw some cereals among your stores on the pantry shelf. Would you like me to start some oatmeal? You ought to have a good hot breakfast, Frannie, before you go to work. I can start it while I wash up these few dishes. And I'll squeeze a little orange juice, too. I see there are some oranges here."

"That will be lovely, Miss Branner. But I could do all that," said Frannie.

"No, we'll work together," smiled the nurse. "Run along and get that bed ready."

So in a very short time Nurse Branner had martialed the little household into bed, and except for a dim night light in the sickroom the little house beside the silver way was in darkness, until late that night when the old moon dropped over the brow of the hill, and reaching down for a brief space gilded the edges of the mossy roof, and glinted for a few flashing seconds from the window panes behind the gaunt hemlock tree.

The weary little family who slept behind those modest old brick walls felt great content at the refuge they had found, deep gratitude to the God who had provided it for them, and dreamed pleasant dreams of a comfortable future.

But out on the dark frozen river there stalked two figures. One, a tall man in a warm sumptuous overcoat, furred to his chin, hands in his pockets, rubber shod, had his hat drawn over his eyes. The other was short and thick set in a heavy sheepskin-lined windbreaker, rough shoes spotted with plaster, and a soft hat that had seen many years of service.

"There it is," said the tall man, "right behind that line of houses. As neat a piece of land as you could get for the job. And I should think it ought to be had for a song. The house is just ready to drop down anyway. But suppose they won't sell."

"Oh, they'll sell all right," said the other, commonly known as Mike.

"But there's somebody living there, isn't there? I'm sure I see a light. A blue light."

"Only renters," said Mike. "I seen 'em move in last week. Only had one truck load of stuff as far as I could see. They might even be only squatters. I don't think they're anything to worry about, Mr. Granniss. It would be dead easy to drive 'em out."

"Not if they have a contract. You couldn't do a thing if they have."

"Oh, they wouldn't have a contract. Not plain folks like that. And besides, if they have, it would be dead easy to get the house condemned, and then the owner would have to tear it down, and he'd be glad enough to take what's offered him, in a case like that."

"H'm! I see!" said Granniss. "Well you go ahead, Mike, and see what you can do about it. It certainly would be a convenient place for our powder plant, right on the river and all. I suppose perhaps there might be a kick from some of those grand residents across the river, who think they own the earth with a gold fence around it, having a powder plant so near, but they wouldn't be able to do a thing about it of course after we had bought it. Don't let a word get out about this, Mike, till we get it all settled."

"That goes without sayin', Boss. And you wouldn't have trouble with those swells over there anyhow. They're too far off. And besides, they don't even look over across the river. They wouldn't touch one of those people on the other side with a ten foot pole. They're too snooty. But say, Boss, did you take notice to them new houses going up on our side? They'd be just the place for our workers to live. And only two of 'em is rented, so far. That'd mean you could house your workers right off the bat after you got your plant built, and that don't take any time at all these days."

"That's so, Mike! Well, suppose we walk over past the brick house, and get a little closer so we can see it better. And we'd better not talk while we go by. Some one might hear us and report on us. You can't even trust a sleeping woodchuck these days. Then we'll get back to my car and go get some sleep. Meantime you get in touch with your owner. Better do it by long distance phone. This thing has got to be settled at once if it is going to be any good to me. And tomorrow

night, same time, same place, you'll find me. Let me
know how you come out."

"Okay!"

Then the two figures shuffled silently across the
river, and up nearer to the river bank, even pausing a
moment at the very steps where Frannie had sat to take
off her skates, and looked up at the house a moment.
The house with the blue light in the upper front window, and the silver edges to the old mossy roof. Then
they turned and shuffled away to the car that was
parked on a side street back of the half-finished houses,
higher up the hill.

Chapter 5

VAN WILLOUGHBY WENT to supper with Madam Winthrop. He had always admired her, even from a child,
and he felt that what she had done for these stranger-
neighbors was a beautiful act. She was going to be a
good friend to the newcomers, and somehow he was
very glad of that. For some unanalyzed reason he had
taken a deep interest in these Fernleys himself. He
hadn't thought it through for himself yet, but he was
glad they would have such a friend as this gentle-
woman. Moreover she had two sons whom he used to
admire, both older than himself. He must find out about
them, where they were and what they were doing. So
he accepted her invitation with alacrity. He was too late
for the formal dinner at his aunt's house anyway, and
might as well enjoy himself. And it wouldn't be necessary for him to let his aunt know. She understood that
he often had to stay late at the plant, and would not
have waited dinner for him.

The dinner was delicious of course. All Hannah's
dinners were. And they lingered talking for a long time.

Lady Winthrop was telling of incidents of her sons' experiences in camp, telling where she *thought* they were located now, and how she wasn't sure just when or where they would be moved. They spoke briefly of the terrible things that were beginning to happen over the world, of the possibilities if the war should come nearer, the safety regulations.

"We have a wonderful storm cellar, of course," said the old lady. "Not that we've ever used it for storms in our time. The grandfather who built the house came from the west where they had so many tornadoes, and he insisted on a storm cellar. So, in a way, I suppose we are prepared for raids. I had them come and inspect the foundations and they are solidly reinforced. So I've had supplies taken down there, in case there should be a need. Of course I don't suppose a quiet country house like this would be the object of a raid, but I thought we might be able to help others who have no refuge. And I've provided rolled up black shades which can be quickly adjusted for a sudden blackout. I think we must comply with the requests of those in charge of course, but it is hard to realize that such terrible things could actually come to our peaceful land."

"Yes, that's right. It surely is," said the young man seriously. "It doesn't seem possible that such a state of the universe can possibly fit in with the Creator's scheme of things for the world, either, does it? But perhaps He's just disgusted with us all and has given us over to do our own ways. Weren't there some old fellows in the Bible times who had to have a lesson to teach them how they had abused their privileges? I don't really know much about such things, but lately when I've been spending my days planning instruments of punishment for our enemies, I've been wondering what God thinks of it all. I guess my mother's way of teaching me when I was a kid has made me think such thoughts. What do you think about it all, Lady Winthrop? You used to know my mother, and I have a kind of memory that she thought you were the best Christian she knew. Have you reasoned it all out?"

"Why, no, not *reasoned* it out exactly. I never was

enough of a Bible student to do that. I think it is better just to *trust* it out. I believe God has it all planned though and there's a reason for everything that happens. Some of it undoubtedly must be warning to sinners if not actual punishment for unbelief."

"But there are a lot of good people suffering through this war, aren't there? How do you account for it that God lets so many of what you would call real believers suffer? Do you mean you think some of those who *seem* to be such good people are really sinners in secret?"

"Oh, no, I didn't mean that. Though there might be some of course. But don't you remember the story of the blind man when you went to Sunday School? Don't you remember how the disciples asked the Lord, 'Did this man sin, or his parents, that he was born blind?' And you remember the Lord's answer, 'Neither hath this man sinned, nor his parents; but that the works of God should be made manifest in him.' "

"You mean," said Willoughby, his eyes bright with thoughtfulness, "that perhaps this war is in some way going to show that God is working through it all? Going to show that God isn't dead, and hasn't forgotten?"

"Yes, I think it may be something like that. God is using these evil nations and their ungodliness, and hatred, and especially their hatred of His chosen people, the Jews, to show the world that He means all He has said in the Bible. And I think we are going to discover pretty soon that everything that is happening in the world, all that is in the newspapers, and on the radio every day, has been written long ago in detail, in the Bible."

"You don't mean it!" exclaimed Willoughby. "Do you mean to say that the Bible has anything to say about this present war? About the things that are going on all over the world today?"

"Why of course. Didn't you know that? We have a wonderful class that meets here once a week and we've been studying about that."

"I'd like to come and hear about it," said the young man. "Would that be permissible?"

"Wonderful!" said the old lady with sweet satisfac-

tion on her face. "I've been wishing we could get some
of the young people to come, for I know they would be
interested if they could just hear even a few minutes of
it. It is fascinating."

"That's great. Surely I'll come. If there is anything in
the Bible that shows God is aware of this awful war I
would like to know about it. You know, Mrs. Winthrop, I think this war business has made us all think
more seriously about what we're here for."

"Well, maybe that is one of the good things about the
war then," smiled the old lady. "They say so many of
the young people are just going on gaily as if life was all
a game, and had no end. I'm glad if a few of them are
beginning to think. I knew my boys were, but they are
older than you are."

"Yes, they are older and they are doing great things
in the service. I only wish I could be over there where
they are."

"Don't say that, Val. You are probably just where
the Lord meant you to be. You're doing most valuable
work where you are. I just heard about your plant today. Mr. Strong, the head of the committee for war
plants, told me that your plant is one of the most
valuable in the country, and they were especially favored in having a young man in as responsible a position
as you are, who had your training and ability. He felt
you were doing far more there than you could have
done in any other capacity, and I was proud to say that
I knew you."

"Oh, thank you, dear lady. That means a lot to me.
It's almost like having my mother send me commendation, because I know you were her friend, and she
honored and loved you."

Presently she took her caller into the library and
showed him some letters and pictures her sons had sent
her, and then some of the books on prophecy that her
class had been studying.

"That one is written by a friend of our teacher," she
said. "He has made quite a study of prophecy, and I
think he is one of the most fascinating writers we have.
Take it along with you and read it if you like. I've

finished reading it. Do you have any time to read?"

"Well, a little, now and then, when I'm not too late coming home at night," he said taking the book and opening it interestedly. "Thank you. I'd like to read it. It looks interesting."

"Oh, it is!" said the old lady enthusiastically.

And so, while Marietta over in her own home, ate a belated dinner, and hovered uneasily near the telephone until it was time to go to an engagement, waiting and expecting Val to call her, Willoughby was discussing prophecy and war probabilities with a lovely lady four times Marietta's age, and enjoying every minute of it. Before Val went home they talked a little about the new people who had come to reside in the plain little brick house across the ice, and what could be done for them.

"You and the daughter came home together, didn't you? You both skated home, didn't you? Do you know, I was watching for you although I didn't know that that girl was the Fernley one. I never saw where she came from before, only noticed her as she went skimming by, and admired her. She seems quite an attractive little thing, doesn't she? Was she much worried by the news you brought her?"

"Yes, she was," said the young man. "She wanted to drop everything and hurry right home, until I finally made her understand that the doctor did not think it necessary, and had promised to telephone at noon just how things were, and that her mother was very insistent that she should not be told lest she would think she had to come home and perhaps lose her job. Her boss was very kind and offered to let her go at once, but that seemed to bring her to her senses, and she braced up and stayed. She seems to be a girl with a good deal of character."

"Yes," said the old lady. "Of course I only saw her a short time, but she impressed me as being very sweet besides being pretty. I do hope her mother will soon get well. That little Bonnie is a darling child, but she's too young to be left alone with an invalid. I'm glad the nurse is there."

"Yes," said Willoughby, "they certainly need her.

But I'm not so sure they will keep her long. I think even now they see through the excuse that she needs a place to stay, and they are very proud. But I guess they cannot afford to pay nurses' prices."

"Well, there'll probably be a way to work it out till she is better, and in the meantime they'll get very much attached to that nurse. She's rather wonderful, you know."

"Don't I know! She nursed me once, and she's swell! But say, is that clock right? Don't tell me I've stayed here all the evening, wasting all your time! I ought to be hanged at dawn. But I've enjoyed every minute of it, and I hope you'll let me come again sometime."

"I certainly will, and I hope you'll come often. Though when you get really settled down to this part of the country again I expect there'll be so many girl-rivals that I shan't see much of you," smiled Lady Winthrop. "But I shall cherish the memory of this evening, anyway."

"Girls?" said the young man with an indifferent shrug, "don't worry! I don't waste much time with them. That little skating girl today is about the most sensible one I've seen since I was a kid. But I don't believe she has time to use socially, and she might not care for my society if she did. She's a most independent little lady. Besides, she lives on the other side of the river, and when the ice is gone that makes a wide barrier for people who haven't much time to themselves these strenuous days."

"Well, that river was anything but a barrier today. I don't know what would have happened if that child hadn't crossed the ice. Not many of those houses near them are inhabited yet."

"That's true," said Val, "I was thinking myself how none of that today could have happened if the river hadn't been frozen."

"Yes," said the old lady with a soft little contemplative sigh, "it's a great river! I call it my street. It has always reminded me of the words 'And the street of the city'—the Heavenly city, you know, 'was pure gold, as it were transparent glass.' And evenings when the sun is setting I always think of the 'sea of glass mingled with fire.' "

"Say, that's beautiful, Lady Winthrop! I feel I am greatly privileged to know you."

"There, young man, don't go to imagining I am anything unusual. It's just some fanciful ideas that came to me from time to time when I was reading my Bible, or looking at my river. They are not my ideas at all, just a sort of vision the Father gave me. Perhaps I should have kept them to myself. But I'm alone so much I get to thinking out loud."

"Heavenly thoughts!" said Val in a grave sweet voice. "I shall like to catch the vision with you. I'll be thinking of that when I go skating down your 'street of the city.' Well, now I must go home! Do you see what time it is? You are more fascinating than any people I know —Around here, anyway."

And after he was gone the old lady stood thoughtfully a moment looking at the chair where he had sat.

"Nice boy!" she said softly. "Almost like one of my own. I wonder if he will really ever come to a Bible class. Maybe just once. He's very polite. He might think that necessary. Well, he's a nice boy, anyway. And how he has fitted into the need of the day! I hope he comes to see me often."

Meantime Marietta was making another angry attempt to reach Valiant Willoughby. He heard the violent ringing of the telephone as he unlocked the front door of his aunt's house, and no one seemed to be answering it. The servants must have retired, and his aunt was out on one of her endless committees which had succeeded her former endless bridge parties.

He stepped over to the telephone and his clear impersonal voice came like a draught of ice water to Marietta's angry spirit.

"Yes?" he said.

"Well, for pity's sake! Are you actually there at last, Val Willoughby! Where on earth have you been keeping yourself all day and all the evening? I've fairly been driven to call out the police to search for you."

"Oh, it's Marietta, isn't it?" he said amusedly.

"It certainly is. Did no one tell you? I left messages that you were to call me the minute you came in."

"Well, I just this minute entered the door, and came immediately to the telephone. Is there something I can do for you?"

"Yes, there certainly is. In the first place I invited you to take dinner with me. I had something to talk over with you. Something quite important. Do you always stay as late as this at the plant?"

"No, not always," said Willoughby. He was not one who told all that he had been doing to everyone who asked.

"But do you mean that they actually keep you at the plant till all hours of the day or night? I think that's outrageous. Something ought to be done about it!"

"No, not usually. Not unless there is something important to keep me there," he said. "I'm sorry about the dinner invitation, but as it happened I had another invitation to dinner, and I didn't come home at all until just now. But what else was it you wanted of me, Marietta? You know I'm not my own master all the time now, and can't be depended upon to be always at home at my usual hours."

"Well, that's absurd! You can't be a slave to your work. You've got to have a little time for yourself. I think you ought to make a stand for that. If you don't *I'll* have to get to work. I happen to know some of the head men interested in that plant of yours and I shall certainly tell them what I think of the way they are treating you."

"Listen, Marietta, you'll do no such thing, do you hear? I'm in no need of your fine official hand in my affairs. I know what I am doing, and these are strenuous days you know. This is no time for a man to baby himself and cry out for playtime when the world is at war. My work has to do with government defense."

"Well, so has *mine*," said Marietta loftily. "And that's why I want your help. I know you are utterly loyal to our America, and would be a grand one to take hold of this plan of mine, and help me make it a great success. It's quite an important matter, and I want to talk it all over with you and get ready tonight to start right in and do something really worthwhile."

"Well, Marietta, that sounds very interesting of course, and it would probably be interesting to work with you, but I really couldn't promise to get into anything that involves much time or thought. I'm *busy*, Marietta and can't count on my hours at all. What is this scheme of yours, and just how do you want my help?"

"Oh, I can't tell you over the phone, Val," said the girl impatiently. "Can't you come over *now* and I can outline it for you? I don't want to waste any more time."

"*Now!* Why girl alive! Do you know what time it is?"

"Oh, what difference does that make? We've stayed up much later than this at parties, many a time!"

"Not me, lady! I never was one of those late birds. My work means a lot to me and I have to be early at the plant tomorrow morning!"

"Now Val, don't be stuffy! Come on over now, this minute. It won't take so long for me to explain, and I'll have a nice little snack for you to eat while we're talking. Good eats and good drinks. Come on! An hour or two longer won't make any difference in the long run."

"I couldn't do it, Marietta. I'm a working man and have to save my best faculties for my job."

"Now Val! I didn't think you'd stand me up that way! I tell you this is important work. It's for the good of your country!"

The young man was silent for an instant, considering.

"What's the nature of your scheme," he said. "What is it you are so anxious for me to do?"

"Why it's a perfectly wonderful scheme for raising money and furnishing entertainment for the soldiers in camp. It's something I know you can do. I've practically got the thing all thought out, and if you'll just run over a few minutes I won't keep you long."

"Nothing doing, lady," said Val. "I've got to be in

my little bed within the next ten minutes. And I wouldn't have time for raising money and getting up entertainment. Sounds childish to me. What do you mean, get up games for the soldiers? Seems to me they ought to have brains enough to get up their own games."

"No it's not that, Val! Don't be stupid! It's to do some really serious planning to have a steady income for such things. You see I'm planning to get up a series of dances for the younger set, with a few of us older young folks to sort of sponsor and chaperone them. I just know it could be made popular among the young crowd, and we'd get a lot of money. Of course we'd make them pay a good price for their tickets. And it would be awfully popular among their parents if you and I and a few others of the really solid set of young people were sponsoring it. You were always popular everywhere, and just your being in the scheme would give it a boom right off at the start. The kids would be crazy to join it and there would be enough of our own set to have really a good time for *us*. Don't you see? While we are carrying on something worth-while for the younger ones, helping *them* to do defense work, too, you know. And *you*, Val, you need something really restful and relaxing once a week at least."

"Hold up a minute, Marietta. Do I understand that you are proposing a series of dances once a week for which I should be partly responsible? Well, right at the beginning, lady, *nothing doing!* I never was interested in dances in my life, and I don't propose to stop my man-sized job now and start in playing with kids. Seriously, Marietta, you don't seem to know what this war is about."

"Oh, now Val, you don't really understand. Do come over a few minutes and I'll make you see what a perfectly swell plan it is."

"Not possibly, Marietta. You'll have to excuse me now. My time is up and I'll have to hang up. Sorry to disappoint you, but you picked the wrong man for a thing like that. I've grown up since you and I used to play prisoner's base, and fight who should be allowed in. Good night, Marietta. See you sometime soon for a few minutes when I get a chance, but I can't say just when it will be."

Valiant Willoughby hung up the receiver and went upstairs with a bound. Was Marietta really as silly as she sounded? What had life done to her? Was she as much of a snob as she used to be, or had she acquired a semblance of courtesy? Her voice didn't sound like it, but maybe he was mistaken. He really would have to run over some time and renew his acquaintance. But, how would she compare with that little girl he had brought home tonight? Getting herself a difficult responsible job; going there on skates; fighting her way against those two bullies; coming home to take the responsibilities of a family upon her frail young shoulders. Marietta: well educated, rich, not a responsibility in the world, and all she could think of to help her country's necessity was to get up a series of dances, where she could have a good time among her kind. Bah! Well, maybe he was misjudging her. He would go and see her sometime and give her a chance to prove herself, whether she was worth-while.

And then the very next afternoon about closing time she appeared on the scene at the street door of his plant, in her gorgeous sport car, wearing becoming furs of sable, her gold hair in a long sleek bob with the ends duly curved in the latest twirl. She sent a boy to Willoughby's office to say that she had come to take him home, and would he please come out to the car *at once!* She wanted to see him about something important.

Chapter 6

BUT VALIANT WILLOUGHBY had just gone out the back way and was hurrying up the frozen river to the plant where Frannie worked. He didn't intend she should run any further risks tonight.

And so while Marietta waited impatiently for the office boy from the front office to go all over the plant hunting for Willoughby, he was kneeling on the ice fastening Frannie's skates, and hadn't even seen the beautiful vision in her sport car who had set all the office boys around the place agog with envy of "the young boss." At last the boy came back apologetically and said they couldn't find Mr. Willoughby. They thought he must have stepped out somewhere.

"But that's the same tale you had for me yesterday when I called him on the telephone," said Marietta impatiently. "Isn't he *ever* here?"

"Why, yes ma'am. He works here. That is, he's all over the place usually. We never know just where to put a finger on him. He's been here all day, more or less. He just keeps track of every worker under him and never gives you a break if you get tired or lazy. He's right on the job. But you know a fella can't just do that and be in one spot all the time. For after all he's the young boss. He *works,* you know."

Marietta stared at the youth who had a comical grin in one corner of his mouth. She couldn't believe that just a common workman was capable of sarcasm, but somehow it sounded that way, almost the way Val had sounded last night. Well, there was such a thing as being almost too patriotic, perhaps. Certainly Valiant Willoughby was taking his obligations seriously. She must do something about this.

"I'll wait," she said resignedly, and sat back luxuriously. "As soon as he comes in you tell him I'm here," she added crisply.

"Okay!" said the youth with a polite grin, and bounded up the steps to the office.

So Marietta sat in her car, the admired of all the workers from all the shifts as they came forth from building after building. She even carried on a mild flirtation with a couple of the young fellows she knew who lived in her neighborhood and were filling in the time until they were called to the army or navy by taking a temporary job.

"Doesn't this place ever shut down for the night?" she asked them petulantly.

"Shut?" they exclaimed in a breath. "I should say not! Nothing shuts down any more. Didn't you know that, Marietta? This country has gone mad on work. We work when we ought to be sleeping, and we sleep when we ought to be working, and when we get almost used to that they lay us off. I suppose that's good for our moral characters, but somehow I can't see it. What are you waiting for? The young boss? Well, he's hard to find. You know there are times when he works all night as well as all day. He's a kind of superman, you know. But I think he went home early tonight. I heard him asking one of his subs to take over for him while he went somewhere. I don't believe he's coming back to-night. You might as well call it a day and quit. But I'll tell him in the morning that you were here for him. That is if I can get speech with him. He's a hound for work. He doesn't hang around much talking."

So at last Marietta decided to take the two young men to their homes and then stop at the Haversett house, hoping to find the lost Willoughby there.

But Valiant Willoughby was putting up curtains for Frannie Fernley, and hadn't turned up at his home yet. And though she waited until after time for her Red Cross class, he did not come. She began to wonder on her frantic way to her class, if by chance this could be intention and her old playmate could be evading her? But she didn't really think that seriously, for she had a fairly good opinion of herself and her charms, and would find it hard to believe that any young man would not be glad to go with her anywhere.

Frannie hadn't seen anything of her two tormentors at the plant that day, and as she was intimate with none of her fellow-workers she heard nothing of them. Besides, they were employed on another floor from the one where she worked, so she did not know that they were both at home nursing black eyes and bruises. And she was so well cared for that she had no fears of a repetition of their annoyances.

"You really mustn't go out of your way to look after me," she protested when she saw Willoughby come sailing up as she came out of the lower door with her skates in her hand. "I truly am not afraid of those boys. I haven't seen anything of them all day. I think they had enough yesterday."

"Yes? Well, I hope they retain that impression," said the young man. "It's just as well they should see you have friends who will protect you."

"Thank you! That's awfully kind of you," said Frannie, "but you know you can't go around being a daily nursemaid to me. An utter stranger! And of course I must learn to fight my own battles!"

"Well, it was very evident yesterday that you are quite able to do that, but I don't want those hoodlums to think you're entirely on your own. So now for a few days while this ice lasts we might as well take the trip together."

On the way they talked about the war, and about Frannie's life.

"You've been to college," said the young man, giving her a quick look when she spoke of classes in some advanced studies.

"Yes, I had a year and a half till father died, and then we came to this part of the world and I had to hunt a job."

There was just the breath of a sigh on the girl's lips, but there was no cloud in her eyes.

"You didn't mind?" he asked.

"Why, yes, I minded. But it couldn't be helped of course, and I was only too glad to be in shape to work. I had to take care of my family, you know. Mother wanted to work and make me stay at college of course, but she wasn't well enough. As it was she wore herself all out taking care of grandmother. That's why I wanted to get them down here where I would be near them and could see that mother took it easy."

"That was pretty plucky of you," said Valiant pleasantly. "But you must look out now that you don't work too hard," he warned. "You can't afford to get sick, at least not till your mother gets well."

"Oh, no, I won't work too hard. Why, you ought to see the way Nurse Branner watches over me. She made us all go to bed last night the minute supper was over and the few dishes washed. And she made oatmeal for us. She's great! I wish we could afford to keep her on for awhile. But of course I know we couldn't, even if we had a lot of money. She's an important nurse. Other people need her."

"Yes, I suppose she is," said Willoughby. "But she'll be there for a little while, anyway, the doctor said, and that will help. You haven't much more to do to get settled, have you?"

"Why, no, not so much. We're going to put the curtains up tonight and a few pictures, and then we'll feel like living. The rest can be done a little at a time, or not at all if we don't want to."

"Ah! I see! That's where I come in. I was wondering where I could work into the picture."

And so, in spite of her protests, Val walked into the little brick house, saluted the nurse who appeared in the kitchen door smiling, and said, "Now, bring on your curtains! I'm the man they sent up from the interior decorators to put up draperies and hang pictures."

"Well, Mr. Willoughby, that's nice," said the nurse. "Frannie says the windows are all washed. It certainly will be fine to have your help. You've got such nice long arms. But how about sitting down with us and having a little bite of supper first? I made some soup this afternoon, and it's grand and tasty if I do say so as shouldn't. Doesn't it smell good? Carrots and onions and barley and potatoes, and tender meat from the soup bone. It's cooked all the afternoon."

"Well that's great!" said the young man. "I'm hungry as a bear. The menu sounds very alluring."

"Better sit down now," said Miss Branner. "Everything is ready to put on the table. You sit here, Mr. Willoughby, and Frannie, you take the head of the table and pour the coffee."

It was good soup, and Val Willoughby was hungry. So was Frannie. Such a pleasant, friendly, merry time they had eating it, just as if they had known one another for years. And then there was a luscious apple pie, and delicious cheese they had brought from the country.

When the nurse went upstairs to take the sick woman her tray and settle her for the night, the two young people jumped up and began to clear the table.

"Oh, but you mustn't do this," said Frannie in horror, as she saw the young man gathering up the dishes in an orderly manner as if he had been doing it all his life.

"And why not, I'd like to know," said Val, fitting the four plates neatly together, gathering the silver by itself. "Haven't I eaten here, and should I not help to put things back into place? You see I want to get at those curtains right away, and we can't do that until our consciences are free from these dishes. Is this the dish pan? I'll wash and you dry and put them away, for I don't know where they belong."

"But truly, you don't need to do this. There aren't many, and I can do them in no time after the curtains are up."

"Yes, but that's exactly what I don't want you to have to do. You see I'm concerned about you, all you went through yesterday, and then going to work so early again today. How did you get through the day? Weren't you all shaken up? You're such a little thing, and you took quite a beating from those two boys you know. And I wasn't at all sure you wouldn't have more trouble with them today. They are not the kind who give up a fight. Don't relax your vigilance. They'll try to catch you unawares. They may lie low for a while though, for it's my opinion that one of them had a pretty good case of black eye and wouldn't want to appear in public, not for a while, if you ask me."

"I hate to be the cause of any workman losing time," said Frannie with a troubled look.

"They deserved it," said Val, setting his lips in a stern line.

And so they worked together and soon had all the dishes washed and put away. Then Frannie produced the curtains.

They went to work chattering pleasantly, getting well acquainted and feeling like old friends.

And there went another day when Marietta couldn't find her old playmate to take dinner with her. Even though she had gone to the plant to find him, and then called up the Haversett house. Strange, she thought. He hadn't been at home to dinner for two nights. She would certainly have to go and have it out with Auntie Haversett, for she was determined to get Val to help her with her plans.

But Val was showing his skill at putting up curtain rods, and advising about which curtains would fit best in certain places. He was really having a good time at it. This little girl he was helping was so much in need of help, and so utterly free from superficial airs and graces that he felt the atmosphere was just easy, pleasant, unrestricted. He hadn't thought of Marietta since he talked with her on the telephone the night before. He assumed that she had gone elsewhere for help. Marietta was seldom at a loss to find somebody to kowtow to her beauty and her father's wealth.

About that time out on the ice two figures walked again with their eyes toward the little brick house.

"Well, how did you make out, Mike?" asked the tall man whose name was Granniss. "Get in touch with the owner?"

"No, not yet. He's gone west on business. May be back tomorrow or next day, they weren't sure."

"M-m-m! Well, we haven't any time to spare, Mike."

"I know sir. I tried to find out the man's address. I meant to wire him, or find out what train he might be on, but nothing doing. Nobody knew where he'd gone or what for. But they said his brother-in-law was coming home tomorrow and he might know, so I'll try again tomorrow."

"Better make it snappy, Mike, for I got wind of another place I might get if this one fails."

"I'll do me best, Granniss, devils can't do no more you know," and Mike snickered apologetically.

"Yes, I know, but you've got to do better than any

devil if you want to work for me, Mike. Understand?"

"Okay," said Mike sullenly, and tried to think what he should offer next as an alibi.

"Say!" said Granniss. "Isn't that the house over there where that light just went on in the front room? Why, there's a man standing up at the window doing something to a curtain. I thought you said there weren't any men in the family, just two women. I thought you said that was the reason we wouldn't have any trouble working this racket."

"I didn't hear of no man there," said Mike. "Mebbe it's just some workman they hired."

"If they are poor people as you thought, they wouldn't hire a man to put up their curtains, would they? They'd put them up themselves."

"That's right," said Mike, perplexed. "Well, mebbe it's some neighbor, or the grocery boy or something. Mebbe it's some man works at the plant where the girl works."

"That's bad," said Granniss, "her making friends so soon. We don't want any man in on this, not if we're going to carry it through quickly. A man might block things and hold us up."

"Well, I couldn't say who he is. I never heard about any man. Mebbe some more of them movers come back to bring something."

"Well, there's no time to waste," said Granniss determinedly. "It seems to me you could have found that owner somehow, or his agent. I don't believe you half tried."

"Say, looka here! I guess it's as much to me as it is to you to get this thing started quick."

"Okay. See you get a hustle on and get some action. I ought to have things under way by the end of this week."

The two men drifted by on the far side of the river, and when they finally turned to go back again, the front room of the little brick house was dark, and a skater shot by them and disappeared into the shadows up-river, but the memory of a man putting up window curtains in the distance stayed in the minds of those two men as they went on to find their parked car, and caused the man Granniss to call to the other as he left him that night:

"You make sure you find out something about that lease, even if you have to go to the owner's office and pump his office boy, or his secretary, for information. There's always a way to find out things if you just know enough to pave your way with a little dough. I've surely given you enough to use that way, and I want it *used!* Understand, Mike?"

"Okay!" said Mike heartily.

Val Willoughby got back to his aunt's home a little after ten o'clock, and was presently called to the telephone by the butler who was still on duty. Again it was Marietta's indignant voice that challenged him.

"What's the idea?" she demanded haughtily. "Are you trying to avoid me? Here I've spent another whole evening racing after you. I even went so far as to drive down after you at the plant at what I judged to be closing hours, and waited endlessly without success. Nobody knew where you were nor when you would return, if you did. Now I should like to know where one finds you? Are you always completely evanescent?"

"Why, I'm sorry, Marietta. Nobody told me you were looking for me. Where were you? What time?"

"I was parked right outside your office door for at least an hour, from quarter of five on, and then I chased you everywhere I could think of. What on earth do you do with yourself, and when do you usually leave the office?"

"Why, I don't have any special time. But usually around five unless there is a stress of work. Sometimes, I told you, I'm needed there nearly all night. But I'm not always in the office. I'm here and there and everywhere."

"So I understood," said the girl coldly. "Just where were you tonight?"

"Tonight I was out on an errand," said Val firmly. "It took more time than I had expected. But now, Marietta, what was it you wanted? I'm sorry I should have been so

unavailable when you wanted to get me. Is there anything important, that you were so anxious to find me?"

"There certainly is," said the girl haughtily. "I was
delegated by our district committee to contact you and
find out if you would undertake to organize and be
warden of the air raid group in this neighborhood. You
were unanimously chosen to do that, and when they
found I knew you, they asked me to give you the
papers and tell you what was wanted of you. It certainly
hasn't been an easy job locating you. As this is a request
from the citizens in our neighborhood, and not a
private plan of my own, I suppose you'll be a little more
affable about it than you were about my request last
night."

"Well, Marietta, I'm sorry I wasn't affable last night,
but what you asked was utterly out of the question.
And as for this, it is equally impossible. I am a worker
you know, under government orders, and my time is
not my own. I would seldom be available at the times
when a warden was wanted. Remember my work is
defense work!"

"Well, I certainly think that is perfectly ridiculous.
You can't be busy *all* the time!"

"Not all the time of course, but enough of the time
so that I could not be depended upon for any other job
that was important. But really, Marietta, don't you do
anything but go around contacting people for jobs?
Isn't there some small favor I could do for you for old
time's sake that would make you understand I am not
merely trying to be rude?"

"Why, yes, there is. I'd like you to take me to the
orchestra concert tomorrow night. Then perhaps we'd
have a little time between numbers to talk seriously."

Val made a wry face at the telephone, but answered
in a pleasant voice:

"Well, now that's a simple request. Yes, I could try
to do that. Of course you have to understand that if a
stress should come I might have to get a substitute at
the last minute. But I'll really try, Marietta, and you
know I enjoy symphony concerts extremely. It ought to
be a very pleasant occasion, and I'll do my very best to

appear at the right time. I'll ask my aunt if I can borrow her car."

"Don't bother," said Marietta. "I have a new one of my own that I want to show you. I go everywhere in it, semi-officially you know. And as I want to talk over some of my defense plans I shall count that a trip for the country's good. All right, Val, and get here at quarter to eight. That'll be plenty of time. Now I'll say good night and let you get some much needed rest, or you'll fall asleep at the Academy of Music. Good night!"

He turned from the telephone with a sigh. So, that was that! He'd be as nice to Marietta as possible, but he would make her understand that he had no time this winter to attend her on her various activities. He could still hear her insistent voice ringing in his ears as he went about preparing for rest. And it flashed across his mind that there was a vast difference between her and that little Frannie who was so gay and sweet, and so free from demands of any sort. Was that the reason why he enjoyed helping her so much, and why the picture of the simple little home lingered so pleasantly in his memory?

Chapter 7

BUT MARIETTA DID not dismiss the subject of the conversation she had just held with the young man as easily and quickly as he had done. She flung herself down on her luxurious chaise longue with a petulant look on her face. She had won, it is true, a whole evening to herself with Val Willoughby—with reservations —for she didn't at all feel sure of him even now, since he said he might have to call up and cancel any engagement he made. But what was one evening? For he seemed perfectly capable of talking around a thing without once coming to the point to say anything but a decided no. And what was it all about anyway? The excuse he gave of work seemed to her altogether too trivial for a young man from his class in society. He might have an important job, yes, but he wasn't a day laborer, was he? He surely could get someone else to take his place when there was need. And wasn't courtesy and precedent in the class of real need? It was just unthinkable that a nephew of Mrs. Robert Haversett should be so tied down to any kind of a job, even for defense, that he couldn't take time off for social duties, and she didn't mean to accept that excuse any longer. She would go to some man of importance in the defense world and find out just how much Val's talk really meant. But of course there was some other reason. Could it possibly be a girl? Another girl than herself? She couldn't believe that. If she chose to run after a man and honor him with her smiles, of course he would prefer herself to any other girl. That went without saying. She had grown up in that belief, and had never seen reason to doubt it. Well, if it was another girl, she must find out the girl and deal with her. There was usually a way. But of course the main thing was to make herself important to the man. She would have to work fast and well if she had only this one evening to start with, and that cluttered up with music, besides. He would likely be stuffy about talking while the music was going on, too. Well, she would have to do her best. She must just keep him on her mind until she found the way to conquer him.

It was the next day when she was talking with one of her friends at a committee meeting that she began her work. Deborah Hand was one of those girls who always asked questions and managed to find out a great deal about this and that, so Marietta began to talk about the old crowd, but didn't mention Val Willoughby herself. She knew better than to begin that way if she wanted to find out anything really worth while about a person, and also retain her own prestige and importance. But it wasn't long before Deborah got around to think of him herself.

"Do you see much of Val Willoughby since he came

back to our neighborhood?" she asked and fixed her keen gray eyes on Marietta knowingly. She and several others of their group had spoken of it a number of times lately, wondering if Marietta had renewed her attentions to Val, and if he was succumbing nicely.

"Oh, yes," said Marietta casually, as if it were to be expected. "I see him or talk to him almost every day. He's looking awfully well, don't you think? But he's so horribly busy he can hardly ever get off. Isn't this war simply horrid, driving some of our men to the ends of the earth, and keeping the rest of them so busy you can hardly get speech of them."

"Yes, I suppose the war is responsible for the lack of young men these days," sighed Deborah. "Well, let us hope it will soon be over."

"Yes, it will be a relief when it's over," said Marietta, "but you know I've been really interested in what we are all doing. It makes quite a change from the regular monotony of life. And then the uniforms are so becoming to some. I just love mine. And it's awfully interesting to be doing something really important. Something men respect you for doing, don't you think?"

"Oh yes," said Deborah listlessly, "but somehow I'm not so awfully interested. I just loathe making bandages, and studying all those First Aid things. I never can remember whether you stand up a person who has fainted or lay them down, and it's gruesome to have to lie down and let them bandage you up as if you had been hurt. I had to do that the last time, and I thought I should expire before they finally undid me and let me act like myself. Personally I think it's silly, don't you? I never would even *try* to revive somebody who had fainted. I'd just ring the bell for my maid and make her do it, or send for a doctor and a nurse."

"Well, you know if there was a raid you couldn't always get your maid. She might even be hurt herself. Really I think it's a good thing to know what to do. You could at least tell somebody else what to do."

"I suppose you could," said Deborah. "Well, personally I hope it's soon over, though if the people in charge want to keep on playing the game I suppose it

will last as long as they want it to. But to go back to
the crowd. I'm glad Val Willoughby is looking well. I
haven't really seen him close enough to tell. Only twice
skating on the river with a girl. I thought perhaps it was
you till they got nearer to the house and I saw she was
smaller than you. She's a tiny little thing, graceful as a
wand, and skates like a bird. Do you know who she
is? They go down in the morning together and skate
back around five or five-thirty. At least I've seen them
twice now, and they do skate divinely together. Last
evening I happened to be up in our attic looking down
the river at the sunset, and I saw them coming back.
They went to a red brick house on the opposite bank. I
thought I'd remember to ask you the next time I saw
you who the girl was."

Marietta had fine control over her facial muscles. She
never by so much as a flutter of an eyelash gave evidence that she was astonished at the news she was receiving. The smile on her face was one she often locked
there on occasion, not to be lifted till called for, and
she turned an imperturbable serenity upon her friend
Debbie.

"Why, could it have been one of the Haversett
nieces? You know they are growing up fast, and they
perfectly adore their uncle Val. Even when they were
almost babies they fairly dogged his steps, everywhere
he went. I used to think they were a perfect nuisance,
myself. You never could go anywhere with Val but
they were underfoot."

Deborah looked thoughtful.

"Oh, perhaps it *was* one of them," she mused, "but
—he stooped over and unfastened her skates, and she
went up the steps and into that little brick house that
has been empty so long. He went up the steps too and
went in. You know someone is occupying that house
now. Some working people, I suppose."

"Oh, very likely they were going after a cleaning
woman then, for her mother."

"But I thought those nieces were off at boarding
school somewhere."

"Why, yes, they were," said Marietta calmly, "but

they often come home for the week-end, or for a party here among their set, or something like that, you know."

"Oh! Well, that might have been the explanation. But if you ask me, that girl didn't look like either of those nieces. She seemed older, more sophisticated. Well, perhaps not sophisticated, I wouldn't use that word for a girl that lived on that side of the river—not in a little tumble-down house like that brick one. However, I saw him go skating with her twice, and that wouldn't be likely to happen with his nieces *twice*, would it, and have them stop at the same place? Well, I don't know. I always thought Val Willoughby was a pretty decent sort of a fellow, with such an aunt and all, but of course boys do go wrong and get silly over a pretty face. Of course I didn't *see* this girl close by, and she might not be pretty at all, but I did think his attitude looked very attentive."

"Nonsense!" said Marietta sharply. "Val Willoughby isn't at all that sort of fellow. I know him too well. He hates anything sordid like that. I've heard him say so. And besides, remember how well I've known him since childhood. That would be practically impossible, for Val to have an affair with a common sort of girl."

"Yes—well, I *thought* you knew him pretty well, and that's why I mentioned it. I knew you would know whether it could be so or not. And then of course if he was tempted by some pretty face that works in his office or something, I thought perhaps we ought to rally around him and keep him out of temptation. We might get up a skating party and go down to meet him nights or something. I fancy that would drive away any little cheap girl that was attempting to interest him."

"I don't fancy that will be necessary in the least, Deb. I tell you *I know Val!* And anyway if one attempted to break up anything that way and take him by storm it would simply work the other way with him. We'd have to be very subtle about anything we did. He's keen, Val is, and he'd see right through anything like that and resent it. No, Debbie, I'm certain there's some very simple explanation to all this. I'll try and find out about it myself. I'm going out with him tomorrow night,

and I'll ask a few simple questions that will bring the
situation out in the open. If there's anything going on
I'll nip it in the bud, and don't you worry about it. I
know Val too well, and he knows better than to try to
deceive me. We've known each other too long and too
well."

"Well, I shall be just dying to find out who it was he
has been skating with," said Deborah Hand. "But I'm
not so sure as you are that Val isn't capable of a little
sly flirtation now and then. That holy look he wears so
much would crack sometime if he didn't have any
chance to relax now and then."

"You're talking as if Val were a hypocrite," said
Marietta, "and he's anything but that. It shows you
don't know him very well." Marietta's tone was cold and
indifferent in the extreme.

"Oh, well, you needn't take that tone, my dear," said
Deborah indignantly. "One would think it was a personal matter with you and I never thought you cared
enough for him for that."

"Of course not," said Marietta with contempt in her
voice, "but you know really, he is a very old friend, and
I don't like to hear him maligned."

"Well, I didn't malign him, my dear. I just said I saw
him with a strange girl and I wondered who she was.
But of course you know Val Willoughby always was
kind to every stray kitten he found in the alley. Always
insisted they had a right to play with us all as much as
if they were one of us. Don't you remember that child
of the scrub woman who always had to play hide and
seek with us on Wednesdays because Val thought she
was lonely? But you know, Marietta, that's a dangerous position for a young man to take. If he carries that
out in his life his wife will certainly have plenty of
heartaches. And somebody ought to warn him. He'll get
into something very unpleasant if he doesn't look out. A
breach of promise case, or something like that. You
know those cabaret beauties are utterly unscrupulous."

"Oh, for heaven's sake, shut up won't you, Debbie!
I simply won't hear you talk that way about a friend

you've known for as many years as I have. I'm ashamed
of you. Val has sense enough to look out for himself,
I'm quite sure, and what's more he's principled against
such sordid things."

"Well, principles don't always save people from bad
breaks. I think if you're a good friend of Val's you
ought to warn him!"

"How about doing it yourself, if you think you know
so much about him? As for me I don't believe any such
tales as you're trying to spread, and I'd rather not talk
about it any longer. Suppose you tell me what they did
at the class last night. I simply couldn't get away from
home. I was waiting for a long-distance call from New
York, and it didn't come till very late. Who did they
use for the victim last night? Clara? My word! She must
have been a handful to roll over after they got her
bandaged. Aren't these First Aid classes simply a
scream? I always enjoy them, and I'm learning a lot,
too."

And so no more was said about Val Willoughby,
but neither girl forgot the matter. Deborah had watched
her victim sharply as she insinuated some things that
she did not really know, or see; and Marietta with all
her nonchalance resolved to search this matter through
and find out just who that girl was—if there *was* really
a girl. She didn't half believe it. For Val had been
known for years as the boy who never had had a crush
on a girl.

Skating! Could that be where he went, that he disappeared so utterly just before closing time from his
office?

And if so, could it be some secretary, or some worker in his plant with whom he went up the frozen way?
But she had always understood that there were no
women in that plant, even as secretaries. She had made
particular inquiries about that, thinking she might even
apply for something herself. Not that she was fitted for
anything really practical, in lines needed in an office.
That was the trouble with Marietta. She thought she
could succeed anywhere, just by being her lovely self,

wealthy, popular and beautiful. She felt that of course she would be an asset to any business to which she condescended to lend her exquisite presence.

But this skating girl, she really had to be tracked down and investigated. She couldn't have any common girl poaching on her preserves, and Val certainly was that. She could remember Auntie Haversett telling her to give the dear little boy a sweetheart kiss, just one little sweetheart kiss, baby dear. And she could remember the stolid look on the face of the little boy during the transaction, for even at that age Marietta registered definitely those things which had to do with her popularity. She could still remember the challenge in his angry red face after her kiss had been administered, for he had not received it graciously. Indeed he had jerked away and said, "No! No! I don't wanta!" and he had rubbed his fat red cheek indignantly with a crumby black hand, that erased even the memory of her delicate touch. So, ever since, she had been in the position of setting the seal of her rights upon the reluctant young man.

Certainly this skating girl must be investigated!

So Marietta set herself to investigate.

The little old run-down brick house! She cast an eye across the frozen river. The little brick house was over there down river from where she lived. It had been there always, but she had never given particular attention to it. It was dark now, save for a tiny blue light in the second story front window. Why should they have a light like that? A night light? Was the girl sitting up reading? But one could not read by a blue light of that sort. She must find out about this. Perhaps it was a spy who lived there, and that light was a signal. Marietta had fantastic ideas sometimes, especially if someone she disliked were connected with it. If she could only prove that that girl was a spy, and was trying to find out some secrets from Val about his plant, her way would be clear before her. For Val was loyal to his country. She was sure he was. He wouldn't have anything to do with a girl who was a spy, if he knew it. So she stood for a long time looking out her window and trying to think out a plot by which she could rid Val of the girl, when she didn't even know the girl by sight yet. But underneath it all was a boiling rage that Val should dare refuse to go places with *her,* and yet take up with a girl of "this sort." Of course she did not know just what she meant by "this sort," as the whole thing was made of her imagination. But she decided not to let another day go by without finding out about that girl, and she spent a good deal of her brain energy studying out just how she was to go about it.

In the end she decided to go to the house on some one of the canvases connected with defense drives. Selling bonds! Could she get these people to feel that they must buy some bonds of her?

The Red Cross. That would be a good number to urge, and when she once got into the house she would be able to find out a lot of things. Marietta was not shy about prying into others' affairs, especially if they belonged to what she termed "the lower classes." And of course these people, or this girl, whoever she was, belonged to the lower classes or she wouldn't be living in a little old ramshackle house like that. And on the "other side" of the river too. The only thing she couldn't seem to fathom was Val's taking up at all with a girl from the other side of the river. He was aristocracy, and had no right to as much as look at a girl from the other side of the river. Not when he had plenty of nice girls to choose from on the right side.

So Marietta got up early the next morning and wrote out all the plans she had made the night before. She intended to go at once to that little brick house across the river, and at least see that little sneak of a girl who seemed to think she could take over the really most eligible young man in the neighborhood. Scores had gone to camp and there weren't so many to depend on as there used to be.

After she had her list written out carefully so that she would be provided with an idea in a hurry that would fit any contingency, she arrayed herself in her most stunning uniform and started out in her shining new car.

Chapter 8

MARIETTA DROVE UP the road to the bridge and over the bridge to the despised "other side," turned down the old river road, past the tiny new houses that represented "the laboring class" to her aristocratic mind, and at last reached the little brick house.

She sat a moment in her car surveying the place. This was the place where that obnoxious girl lived! It needed painting terribly. Strange that even a laboring man should be willing to live in such a run-down looking house. If he was worth anything surely he could find a few minutes a day to paint at least around the windows and the door. The door was simply impossible. Dirty fingermarks and scratches as if heavy boots had kicked it for years. Well, of course no decent girl could come out of a house like this. Poor Val! What had possessed him to take up with a girl from a house of this sort? It probably was just another case of the scrub woman's child. Well, she would have to do her best. She turned to get out of her car and then looked back at the windows. Why, there were *curtains* at the windows! That was astonishing! Perhaps somebody in the house had ideas.

Slowly she went up the path and tapped at the door. She could hear hurrying little feet coming from the region of the back of the house. A child! Well, perhaps it would be as well to meet a child first, then she would not have to stand at the door in this cold wind and talk. Getting in would give her an advantage.

Bonnie opened the door and smiled up at the beautiful girl in the lovely fur coat, and a real uniform showing beneath. She was charmed with the haughty visitor, and opened the door a little wider. Marietta stepped in and looked about her curiously. Why, the curtains which had looked rather nondescript from outside, were clean and quite attractive, as if someone with taste had selected them. Probably some rich person for whom the mother worked, washing or scrubbing perhaps, had donated them. Or they might even have been stolen from some clothes line in the wealthy part of the city. Such things had been done.

"Won't you sit down?" said Bonnie politely. "We aren't in very good order yet. We just moved in last week." The child did the honors in a quaint old-fashioned way, and Marietta looked at her astonished.

"Is your—mother, or your—sister at home?" she asked sharply.

"My mamma is sick," said Bonnie. "She's been very sick upstairs in her room. The doctor said she mustn't see anybody yet."

Marietta instantly decided that the mother was drunk and this was probably an excuse.

"Well, haven't you a sister?" she asked.

"Yes, I have a sister, Frannie, but she has gone to her work in the city. She is a secretary down at a munition plant. She won't be home till supper time. She goes to her work on her skates. She's a very nice skater," and Bonnie smiled engagingly.

Ah! That was the girl. Then she did skate. Probably Val had been lured by her skating.

"Well, isn't there anybody here at all that I can talk to? Someone who is older than you are?"

"Oh yes, there's the nurse. She's very nice. She could talk to you, only I think she's giving my mamma a bath now. You could wait for her, or I will talk to you. I know more about the family than she does, because she's only been here since yesterday."

"A nurse!" said Marietta. "Do you have a nurse?"

"Yes, we had to, 'cause my mamma got so sick, and Frannie had to go to her job."

"Oh!" said Marietta, wondering what she had got into. Was the woman sick with some contagious disease, perhaps? Marietta had a good imagination, and could always go a step ahead of the facts. "What is the matter with your mother? Has she got anything that's

catching? Any contagious disease?" Marietta involun-
tarily stepped toward the door—her hand on the knob
—preparatory to escaping if necessary.

"Oh, you mean anything like measles and whooping
cough? Oh no, it's nothing like that. She just fell down
when she was clearing off the breakfast dishes, and her
eyes shut and she couldn't answer me. They said she
fainted. The doctor said she was all tired out and needed
a rest."

"Oh," said Marietta relaxing from her alarm and
dropping down in the hair cloth chair by the door. It
was then that she noticed that several of the chairs in
the room looked like simple old antiques. Could they
have been given to these people? Where did they get
fine old chairs? There was nothing to show that they
had money. If they had they would never have come to
live in this dreadful little house, whose wall-paper was
soiled and faded, and looked as if it had served large
families for a century or two.

"And you have a *nurse?*" asked the bewildered caller.
"Is she some relative who is living with you?"

"Oh no," said Bonnie with her sunny smile. "She's
just a nurse. The nice doctor sent for her and she came,
and she's wonderful. She knows how to do almost
everything."

"Yes, nurses usually do," said Marietta dryly. "But
this nurse, is she an old woman? Somebody without
any home?"

"Oh no," said Bonnie affably, "she's a nice lady and
she has a home somewhere I guess, only she's staying
here now because my mamma is sick and she wants to
help her get well. She loves to help people. She has a
pretty white uniform. It's not like yours, it's white all
over, and a pretty white cap, and she always smiles.
But say, are you a soldier?"

"Well, no, not exactly. I'm just a person who has
signed up to help in the war."

"But you have a uniform like a soldier. What do
you do? Go out and pick up dead soldiers and take
them to the hospital to be mended?"

"*Mercy* no!" said Marietta, shivering. "What put that idea into your head, you crazy infant?"

"Why, because our nurse said people in uniforms were all doing something to help the poor soldiers, and I wondered what you do to help them."

Then suddenly there was a step on the stairs and the nurse came down bringing a tray.

"Oh, Bonnie, have you a caller?" the nurse said cheerily. "Why didn't you call me? Was something wanted?"

"Why, I don't know," said Bonnie. "I forgot to ask that. But I did tell her to sit down. Was that right?"

"Yes, that was right, dear. Why, Miss Hollister, is it you? Aren't you lost over on this side of the river?"

"Well, almost," laughed Marietta unpleasantly. "But I might ask the same thing of you, Miss Branner. You don't usually nurse over on this side, do you?"

"Why, I nurse wherever I'm needed," said the nurse calmly.

"But isn't it unusual for people in these walks of life to be able to pay a nurse of your class?"

"Well I really couldn't answer that question, Miss Hollister," said Nurse Branner with dignity. "I've never happened to see any statistics in that line. Is there anything I can do for you? Whom did you want to see?"

"I understood there was a young girl living here," said Marietta haughtily. "I came to see her."

"Yes, Miss Fernley lives here, but she is not at home at present. She does not usually return until a little after five."

"Oh! Every day?"

"Yes, every day."

"Very well. I'll call again."

And so Marietta took herself out of the little red house angrily, as if it was definitely someone's fault that she could not attain her object at once. But she did not dismiss her plans. Instead she began to turn over new ones which should further her investigations.

Why, for instance, shouldn't this dance program that she had proposed, work out for girls like this? If the girls of her crowd thought they were really doing something to uplift other girls less favored than themselves they might even be moved to give larger sums for the furtherance of the idea. That would be the very thing! Invite a favored few of these working girls to the dances and entertainments, and give them the privilege of seeing how the wealthy and aristocratic girls lived. And they, the promoters, could go on and have their own good time while the guests had the privilege of watching them. Of course there would have to be a few young men of the underprivileged class to provide partners for their guests. It would have to be worked out very carefully, or the outsiders might take advantage and make unpleasantness, but she was satisfied she could work it out. So she went to her committees and told some of the other girls about her idea. But she did not find a very enthusiastic response to her suggestions.

"Oh, forget it, Mari," one girl said. "Haven't we got enough unpleasant things to do in this war-torn world without your dragging in something like that? Who wants to do good to every green awkward girl in the county? When I go to a dance I want to have a good time myself and not have to worry about any forlorn wallflowers who don't know what it's all about anyway."

"And there's another thing, Hollister," sounded another dissenting voice, "they won't come if you do invite them, those freaks who haven't any social life of their own. They don't want to be patronized and told how the other half lives. They think they are as good as anybody, and a little better than some. It wouldn't be a success even if you did try it. I'm against it, Holly! Don't do it!"

But Marietta was of the type that always grew stronger under opposition, therefore she determined to go ahead with her plans.

"It all depends on the approach you make when you invite them," she said contemptuously. "You've got to sell them the idea of coming in the first place. Make them see it will be a privilege to come. I know one girl that I'm certain I can bring, and I'll make her dig up some others."

And so, without having even seen Frannie Fernley, Marietta determined to make her the center around which she would organize the whole scheme.

She spent most of the rest of the day in perfecting her plans. In bullying enough of the girls into contributing money for the initial expenses, getting lists of names of young people who were eligible material on which to begin their uplifting work, in hunting up a suitable hall for their gatherings, and inquiring prices; also interviewing orchestra leaders and getting them down to a price commensurate with the amount pledged. Oh, Marietta was most efficient when it came to carrying out her own way. And all this just to find out and nip in the bud this girl who had dared to be seen with Valiant Willoughby.

And Marietta did not waste any time in interviewing Frannie Fernley. She was on hand at the little brick house quite before five o'clock, sitting in the dim little front room filled with the dusk of the evening, and listening to the high-pitched sweet voice of Bonnie in the kitchen talking with the nurse while they prepared the pleasant evening meal that was sending out such delightful odors: the delicious mingling of molasses and butter and a bit of fat browning over the top of a pan of baked beans; the tang of a fresh raw onion cut across a salad of lettuce, green pepper and tomato, with lemon in the dressing; the rich spicy fragrance of cinnamon on the top of a custard pie just being taken out of the oven.

Marietta sat back in the old comfortable chair, in the gathering dusk of a room lighted only by a single dim lamp, and realized that she was both tired and hungry. Those things they were cooking smelled good and tempted her. She didn't try to identify the different smells, but they certainly seemed like an expensive dinner, here in this little tumble-down brick house. What did it mean? Had the neighbors sent in these things because the mother was sick? But then she remembered that the laboring class always were good eaters, and probably insisted on having plenty.

It was almost dark when Frannie at last came home. Marietta had been watching occasionally out the window for her arrival, but a great drowsiness had come upon her, for she certainly had worked hard all day. So Frannie glided up to the wooden steps and changed her skate shoes to her house shoes, without being seen or heard. She entered the house by the kitchen door left on the latch for her.

It happened therefore that she had a moment or two to smooth her dark curls, straighten her collar, and wash her hands and face before she entered the front room to speak to the guest, whom Bonnie and Nurse Branner had had no opportunity to describe to her. And the big beautiful car had been parked across the street where Frannie could not see it as she entered from the river side of the house. So without any warning, except Bonnie's soft whisper, "There's a beautiful lady waiting for you," she went in to meet the girl who had prepared to hate and humiliate her as far as she could.

But there was about Frannie a grace and gentleness that gave a natural loveliness to her movements, and she was not self-conscious. She had no reason to dread this caller, perhaps just some kindly neighbor like Lady Winthrop, she thought. So the two girls met in the dim room.

"Oh," said Frannie, "you are sitting almost in the dark. And are you warm enough? That fireplace is always needing another log." She stooped in passing and flung a small stick on the dying coals, and it presently blazed up and flung lights and shadows through the room, and over the faces of the two girls. "You are Miss Hollister, they said. I'm sorry, that doesn't tell me anything because I am almost a stranger here."

Marietta stared at the girl she had come to patronize, and then answered coldly:

"Yes, my name is Marietta Hollister, and I understood you were a stranger. That's partly why I came. You see we are getting up a scheme to socialize this side of the river, and give the people living over there a chance to see some of the amenities of life, and to learn how to behave when they go out among really educated, cultured people. An opportunity, you know, to mingle with young men and women of your own class and have a place where you can have really good times."

Frannie cast a puzzled glance at the imperious young beauty with the glow of the firelight on her long golden bob. Was all this meant for kindness, or did it smack of condescension?

"Why, that's kind of you, I'm sure, to think of other girls and try to help them," she said hesitantly, uncertainly. Was it really kindness, she wondered? "But—I'm afraid I would not be in a position to benefit by anything of a social nature—"

"Oh, well, that's all nonsense of course. Everybody has got to have recreation. I suppose you have a job and you think you can't spare the time, but you owe it to yourself to have some enjoyment out of life. You'll do better work if you relax now and then. You see we're proposing to have a series of dances, and we'll have some suitable young men there who will ask you to dance and will be attentive to you, and in that way you will get acquainted with some really suitable young men. We shall take care to inquire into their characters and shall sponsor no one who is not respectable and steady and dependable. You know, many girls who are employed have no opportunity to meet young men of their own class, in respectable places, and that is one reason why there are so many unhappy marriages. The girls often cannot meet men anywhere except on the street, and they do not have a chance to get to know them. We are trying to provide places for you girls to meet men who would make good husbands by and by."

Frannie suddenly broke down and giggled.

"Excuse me!" she said, suddenly sobering. "I'm afraid I wouldn't be interested. I'm not looking out for someone to marry. I have a job to do and my mother and little sister to care for, and I have no time to waste on such things."

"But that is utterly senseless," said Marietta. "You want to marry and have your own home. Every girl does. Let your family take care of themselves. There is always the Welfare for the family if they need it. And then you know there are Homes where dependent people can go and be cared for, if they cannot live on what welfare they can get. You have a duty to yourself, and we want to help you with it."

Frannie grew suddenly white and rose to her feet:

"I'm sorry," she said coldly. "You are wasting your time! I wouldn't be interested in anything you have to suggest." And then, with as much dignity as her gentle self could summon, she added: "And now if you will excuse me, I think I will go up to my sick mother. I've been away from her all day. I think that is about all you and I have to say to one another."

"But you don't understand," said Marietta rising to the occasion and putting out a detaining hand. "I have something else to tell you and it's really very important. It's something you ought to know."

Frannie stopped, her head up, her lips and eyes suspicious, and looked her visitor over quietly, with much the same look that she had given to Spike Emberly and Kit Creeber not long ago. The very tilt of her chin showed that she was not in a receiving mood.

For an instant even Marietta was a bit abashed. This wasn't just the way she had planned her approach. Then she flung up her arrogant beautiful head and went on.

"It seems that you—at least I have been told that you have picked up an acquaintance with a young man who is not at all of your class, and that you have been seen skating with him, more than once, holding hands in broad daylight! I felt I ought to warn you that it isn't safe for you to do a thing like that. Not only would you bring disgrace upon yourself, but there would be actual danger. For it happens that the young man you have selected to play up to is quite an important member of our social order, far above you, and his friends and relatives would certainly rally around him, and pay you back for daring to attempt any such bold-faced flirtation with him! It might mean actual bodily harm to you if you keep on having anything to do with him. You probably do not know this, but young men of respectable families do not give *serious* attention to girls from this side of the river, and you might as well understand at once that such an acquaintance could never come to anything with you. Besides, he is already practically engaged to a girl of his own class, and though he might play around with you a few days it could never bring you anything but heartache! I mean what I am saying, and I'm speaking out of kindness for you, to warn you, for your own good."

Now Frannie had a large sense of humor, and just now it suddenly came to the front in a radiant smile, that was almost a grin.

"Thank you!" she said. "I'm sure you're trying to be kind to me. And now will you go, please? I have other things to do." Frannie reached out and swung the front door wide open, letting in a blast of the icy outside air. And there seemed nothing in the world for Marietta to do but go. Her resourceful mind could not think of another thing to say. And the worst of it all was that she could not make up her mind whether she had reached the real girl in the warning she had just uttered, or whether she was being laughed at.

And then, as she swung across the snowy road, there came a burst of more laughter, gay and sweet, from the little red house behind her. Walking into the dusky night, her cheeks were burning with a new kind of shame. This girl whom she had come to humiliate, had humiliated her. And yet she had not transgressed a single law of courtesy, nor once lost her temper, although she suspected by the look in the girl's gentle eyes that some of the things she had dared to say had cut to the quick.

So this was the girl Val Willoughby had been skating with! She was not going to be an easy one to dislodge. She must think up a better plan to get rid of her.

And tonight she would have the evening with Val, and would see what she could do with *him*.

Chapter 9

WHEN THE NURSE and the little sister who were tip-toeing around the kitchen getting supper ready, heard the front door shut and then a moment later that merry little gurgle of laughter from Frannie, they came cautiously to investigate. Bonnie opened the door a crack and peeped in, and then opened it a little wider, and whispered hilariously, "She's *gone!*" and then the nurse came near and there they stood watching. Frannie was sitting down in the big chair by the door, laughing.

But in a moment Frannie lifted her head, looked at their astonished faces, and laughed again. More quietly now, and softening down to a good-natured giggle.

"What is it, Frannie? What happened?" asked the nurse who wondered if Frannie was so tired that she was near hysterics.

"Oh nothing. Nothing. Only it was so very funny. She came here to invite me to a dance or a series of dances, so that I would meet some respectable young man I could marry and have a happy home," and Frannie went off again into a burst of giggles.

"Was that all?" asked the nurse with a relieved sigh.

"No!" giggled Frannie, "that wasn't all. She wanted to warn me not to take up with strange young men whom I met skating out on the river. She said they would have no serious intentions and I would only get my heart broken, or words to that effect, and maybe even my head too! She said someone had told her that I had been seen skating with one of the young men from the other side of the river, and she felt she ought to warn me that he was somebody important and his friends would never stand for it. But please, Miss Branner, don't tell my mother this! She would want to move away at once. She would be filled with horror that we had come to a place where people would meddle and gossip like this. She would think I was disgraced. Oh, I thought Bluebell was bad enough with its kindly folk-gossip, but this is a thousand times worse. It's so bad it's really funny."

"Oh, dear me! That girl is certainly a fool!" said the annoyed nurse. "I should have thought she would have known the minute she laid eyes on you that you were not that kind of girl. But I'm glad you're taking it this way."

"Well, why shouldn't I? She seemed to think the main thing that was the matter with me was that I lived on this side of the river. But if that's it I tell you it's *very* funny. I've heard of living on the wrong side of the railroad track, but this seems to be something a good deal worse."

"Yes. Absurd, isn't it? Well, let's forget her. Come, the supper is all ready, and I've just taken your mother's tray up. Let's sit down while the beans are hot."

"Oh, yes!" said Frannie. "And am I hungry! How good they smell. Everything smells wonderful! I noticed it the minute I opened the door."

So they sat down to the simple supper and enjoyed every crumb, and then they sent Bonnie up to talk to the mother while they washed the dishes and got things ready for breakfast.

"But don't tell mother anything about what that girl said, Bonnie dear. We don't want mother to worry."

"Of course not, Frannie. Don't you think I have any sense at all? I'll just tell her it was someone about some 'fense work. It was, you know. I heard her say the dances were for 'fense work, to get money to have 'musements for the soldiers."

"That's the girl," praised the nurse with a smile of commendation, "she's got good sense. She knows what not to tell her little sick mother. Run along, Bonnie, and don't talk any more about it than you can help."

So Bonnie hurried joyfully up to her mother and Frannie and the nurse went swiftly to work. But the nurse could see a little cloud of annoyance on Frannie's sweet face, and knew that in spite of her gay little laughter she had been troubled by her arrogant visitor.

"Frannie," said the nurse in her most cheery comforting tone, "if I were you I wouldn't waste a minute's thought on anything that cold-hearted selfish girl said. It isn't worth it. Believe me, I know what she is, and I've known her ever since she was a spoiled baby. When she goes around trying to do good, and uplift what she considers inferior people, it's always because she has an axe to grind for herself."

"Yes?" said Frannie with a troubled question in her eyes. "But I don't see what she would expect to get out of it."

"Well, that's the subtlety of her. You never know till afterward, unless you know her pretty well. And knowing her, I can guess what she was at when she came here and tried to warn you against picking up young men on the ice that way. She must have either seen you, or been told of your skating with Val Willoughby. And she would be very jealous of that. She thinks Val Willoughby, and all the rest of the eligible young men of the neighborhood, belong peculiarly to herself."

"Oh!" said Frannie with sudden enlightenment, "that must have been what she meant. She said the young man I had been seen with was practically engaged to another girl who belonged on the other side of the river."

"Yes, I thought it would be something like that. That sounds very Hollisterish. And what did you answer, Frannie?"

"Why, when she got through talking I didn't really answer her at all. I just said I guessed her plans wouldn't interest me, and if she would excuse me I must go up to see my sick mother."

"Good!" said Nurse Branner. "You couldn't have done better. Just keep up that kind of a front and pretty Marietta won't know what to say. She wouldn't be able to understand your not getting angry and answering back."

"Well, she made me get all weak and trembly inside," confessed Frannie, as she gathered up the knives and forks and placed them on the table for breakfast.

"Poor child," said the nurse cheerily. "You certainly

didn't show it when you came out to the kitchen afterwards."

"Well, of course I didn't want Bonnie to see how I felt. She wouldn't be able to keep it from mother, if she found out. She may be very wise, but mother's eyes are very sharp and keen. She would know at once if something worried Bonnie."

"Yes, of course. Well, now my dear, don't you worry one bit about this. It will all pass away and you'll forget it. That girl can't hurt you. You two don't live in the same world. She wouldn't know how to reach you. She couldn't understand you even if she tried. But if she comes again, don't give her any answers back. If she gets disagreeable come and call me. I'll settle her. Just give me the high sign, and I'll come to your rescue. I know all the answers."

"Oh, thank you, Miss Branner. You've made me feel a lot better. I won't worry about her any longer. But I don't think she'll come again. I think she was very mad at me that I didn't let her talk any longer. She probably thinks I'm the rudest girl she ever saw."

"Never mind what she thinks. Just forget it. Now run up and have a little talk with your mother before she goes to sleep. She's been a lot stronger today. Her pulse is definitely losing that thready consistency. I thought you'd be glad to know that."

"Oh, that's grand, Miss Branner. But—do you think it may get worse again?"

"No, not if she is reasonably cared for. She must be kept from worrying."

"Yes, and that's one thing I was afraid of, Miss Branner. If she should hear what that girl said about my skating with a young man she would die of shame, to think I had got to a place where I could be common talk that way. And there really wasn't anything wrong about it at all. He came after me with a message from the doctor and my mother."

"Yes, I know, dear. The doctor told me all about it. And anyway I know Val Willoughby. Nobody would dare say anything against him. It's just as she said, he has friends enough to rally around him. But the whole thing is that they wouldn't bother you. They would know that anything Val Willoughby did was all right, and that any girl he took up for, even if it was just to skate home from work with her for a while in order to protect her from any unpleasant boors, was to be treated with reverence. Anybody that is a real friend to that young man has to respect what he respects whether they like it or not, or else they will have to settle with Val Willoughby."

So, gradually Frannie's perturbation was quieted, and she was able to forget the unpleasant half hour with her beautiful visitor.

Willoughby had not come home with her that night. He had explained to her in the morning that he would have to leave the plant early in the afternoon and was not sure of returning until late. He had an engagement that evening that was rather upsetting his routine. He had asked her to be very watchful, and go up to another landing before starting to skate home, lest those boys might take advantage of his absence to annoy her again.

So Frannie knew that Willoughby would not be coming that night and was keen enough to realize that this was probably the end of his kindly espionage. Also, probably the end of her seeing him at all.

Which was as it should be, she told herself. He did not belong to her as an intimate friend. He had a different background, belonged to the aristocracy as that yellow haired girl had blandly said. He wasn't her rightful companion. She was a working girl now, and while he was a working man, still it was different with men. They were supposed to work. Even social life recognized that, and she might as well understand and accept it. Of course her own people were cultured and educated, and until her father died she had not had to work. But work was no disgrace, and while she would not for the world assume a social position that those around her would not concede, she had nothing to be ashamed of. Why, even the wealthy girls were running around now trying to find jobs and camouflaging them under the name of "defense." It was just a silly social notion, and she wasn't going to be bothered about it at all. But of course she mustn't let herself get any foolish ideas about this young man. Probably it was a good thing that that obnoxious girl came to warn her or she might, unaware, have become more interested in him than she realized.

So she resolutely put aside all thoughts of the young man who had for the last two or three days made such a bright thought in the midst of her hard-working hours. She made herself concentrate on getting the house in order. This was Saturday night and she had all day tomorrow to rest up and get herself organized for the life that was beginning before her, and she didn't need any of Marietta's dances either to give it a cheerful slant. She had her little home and her mother and sister, and was glad and thankful for them. Tomorrow, perhaps, she could find a church somewhere near enough for her mother to walk to when she got well. That would be one of the first things her mother would be wanting when she was able to go out again, the right kind of a church.

So Frannie went up and had a cheery little talk with her mother, telling her all the little pleasantnesses she could find in her day of work, describing Mr. Chalmers, and a few of the girls who worked at nearby desks, trying to make her mother see how really pleasant it was, with the frozen river outside making a path straight home when she was done her work. Not an unpleasant moment in the whole tale.

Then they discussed what kind of church they would like to find. Not a large one, the mother hoped, nor a rich one. Only a plain one where the Truth would be taught, and where they would have a good Sunday School for Bonnie. Then Frannie kissed her mother good night and went to wash out some stockings, and get her clothes in good trim for tomorrow and for the week that was to follow. So at last she came to the end of the day where presently she could lie down and go to sleep with a clear conscience, not having taken any time out to hate that interfering girl who had come around trying to humiliate her. She resolved she would not give a thought to it either while she was on the way to sleep.

It was while she was running the water and working away at her washing, that a low knock came at the back door downstairs. It happened that Nurse Branner had gone down to the kitchen to heat some milk for her patient before she went to sleep.

A little startled, she opened the door and looked out, wondering why anybody would come to the back door at this time of night. But she was not a timid woman so she had no hesitation in opening the door. She was, however, a little astonished as she saw a short heavy set man standing there in front of the door, his hat pulled down over his eyes, and his mouth set in a determined line.

"What do you want?" she asked in a cool voice, setting her broad foot in such a way as to block the entrance of anyone trying to get in.

"Good evening, lady. I was just wondering if you could tell me a few statistics. I been sent here to find out some things. I know it's late, lady, but my work kept me late tonight, and I had so many places to go getting these facts that I got delayed. This is my last stop, so if you don't mind, will you tell me, have your folks bought this house or do you rent it?"

"Rent!" said Nurse Branner crisply, and tried to think what Frannie had told her.

"Oh, you do! Well now, I wonder if you've signed a contract or was it just a verbal transaction?" said the man.

Nurse Branner was clever. She knew it did not do to hesitate.

"A contract, of course," she snapped. "Is that all?"

"Well, no it ain't," said Mike with an apologetic grin. "But if you'll just get me that contract and let me look it over I can get all the rest of the necessary data from it. It will save us both a lot of time."

Nurse Branner was on her guard, besides she had sensed a shadowy form down on the ice in the darkness of a lot of dead bushes. She was letting no one into that house tonight!

"Sorry," she said. "Contracts are kept in safety deposit boxes in the bank. You will probably have to go to the bank to get that information. Good night!" and she shut the door firmly, turning the key in the lock and then she shot the big iron bolt noisily across into place.

When she turned the kitchen lights out and took a peek through the tiny pantry window she saw two figures, a tall thin one and a short stout one, slipping stealthily away along the shore, and then climbing to a parked car higher up the stream. She began to wonder if after all this river site was so desirable for three lone women.

She went upstairs after a little, settled her patient for the night, and then watched out the window again for a long time, but saw no more stealthy shadows on the ice.

But after she lay down in her bed she couldn't get to sleep for some time, wondering what that man had really wanted. He didn't look exactly like a crook and yet he didn't seem to be the sort of man who would be sent out near midnight Saturday night to get statistics. She must warn Frannie never to let strangers into the house at night. Should she tell her about this strange caller at the back door? Frannie wouldn't have heard him because the water was running in the tub. But maybe she ought to tell her. Or perhaps she had better ask the doctor first, or Val Willoughby if he came over pretty soon. She would have to think about it.

And so the nurse slept, and the two men drove away again.

"I think she was lying," said Granniss.

"No sir, she was talkin' straight," said Mike. "I was there and you wasn't, sir, beggin' yer pardon. I can tell when a dame is talkin' straight."

"She was scared by our coming to the back door."

"No sir, she wasn't fazed in the least. Her voice was that pleasant, and she was one of them dames that don't get scared."

"But people in a house like that wouldn't have sense to demand a contract. Not people that lived in a ratty little old house like that. They probably don't know what a contract is."

"Mebbe they got better sense than the house they live in," said Mike with a touch of his native humor. "They do sometimes. And if you'd been near you'd have seen how quick she answered that 'of course' they had a contract."

"Well, I'd like to know why you didn't ask what bank that safety deposit box is in and what time she'd meet us there, then?"

"Well, because she didn't give me no time. She closed the door that quick, and then shot the bolt. And besides I think that owner will be coming home on Monday and then we won't have to run no more risks of gettin' pinched because we scared a coupla women. We'd cook our goose in earnest if that happened."

"That must not happen!" announced Granniss severely. "If anything like that happened you would find yourself on the spot. Do you understand?"

"Now, Granniss, you promised me that if I tackled this business I wouldn't be in no trouble at all," said Mike in alarm.

"Yes, I told you that, Mike, on condition that you would get this site turned over to me within the week, and the time is up now and you haven't got the initial move started. Another day or two and it will be too late. The conditions I'm counting on for working this deal will be off. Understand?"

"Well, just give me a coupla days more, Granniss, and I'm sure I can pull it off."

"Well, see that you make it snappy then," said the big man as he stopped to let Mike off at his house. "This is the last time I'm warning you. And meantime I'm going to look up a substitute go-between. You see, Mike, this ice is liable to get tacky, or crack or something and we've got to get our materials up here on runners in the night, so nobody will suspect what's coming till it's here, or there'll be a great hue and cry and you'll get the ladies on the other side of the river all stirred up about commercializing their precious river. We don't want that till we've got so far they can't stop us. Now, Mike, you get hold of that owner and report to me by Monday morning early or else I'm going places without you!"

So Mike and Granniss parted company, and the dwellers in the little brick house slept on unmolested.

Chapter 10

VAL WILLOUGHBY BARELY got back to his aunt's home from the business that had taken him away that afternoon, in time to change for the evening, and snatch a bite of supper from a tray he inveigled the butler into bringing him while he was dressing.

He didn't want to go to this concert. Not that he did not enjoy music, and wouldn't always be glad to hear it whatever he was doing. But he was not especially enamoured of the company in which he was going. He had nothing against Marietta, as a mere concert companion, except that she would talk all the time the music was going on, and not only spoil the delight of the whole program for him, but also bring down frowns and reproof from those people who had the misfortune to be sitting near them. Besides he was morally sure that Marietta had some ulterior motive in thus pursuing him. She was probably plotting in some way to involve him in one of her wild plans under the impression that she was doing a great deal for her country and democracy. He felt that his job this evening was smilingly to refuse her insistence, and pleasantly lead her thoughts to nice safe subjects, giving her the impression that she had had a lovely time. He was wondering as he brushed his hair, meantime humming a strain from the symphony he knew was to be played that evening, whether it would be at all possible really to interest Marietta in the music itself. Suppose he set himself to make her see something in the wonderful strains beyond just a big noise that it was smart to seem to enjoy. Why not try it? It certainly would be something worth while if it were possible.

Then out on the road in front of the house he heard a car drive up and an expensive sounding horn summoned him to begin the evening. He quickly swallowed the last drop of his coffee, swung into his overcoat, caught up his top hat, and went down to his task. He had not much idea he would succeed, but he certainly would find out once for all whether there was really anything to Marietta except a big will to have her own way.

And Marietta, down in her luxurious car, watched his room light go out promptly, and rehearsed in her mind the points she meant to cover for Willoughby's instruction during the evening. She had far more confidence of victory in her endeavor than the young man could muster for his own endeavor. He had tried different things on Marietta before, and always failed. But this time he meant to give her a real tryout.

So he climbed into her luxurious car with a fairly cheerful mind.

Then, they had no sooner started on their way than Marietta opened the conversation. Marietta never wasted any time in getting at her latest topic of interest, and she had decided that it would be as well to get the unpleasant part of her evening over first and then she could enjoy the rest. Not that she would own that even her first approach was going to be unpleasant. She had all assurance that she would win, and she perhaps enjoyed the thought of setting Val Willoughby straight. So she began as soon as they were well out on the main road to the city.

"Val, there's something I ought to tell you, and I may as well get it off my conscience first before we get to talking about anything else and I forget it."

"Yes?" said Willoughby, wondering what trick she was going to pull now. Marietta always had plenty of surprises, and he had not been unprepared for something in an unusual line this evening, but he had hardly expected her to begin quite so soon.

"Yes?" he said casually, looking at her perfect little lips with their unusual set of firmness, or spoiled-childness, which was it? He was not so much concerned about what she was going to say, because he did not intend to do anything she asked, and he had a pleasant "no" with plenty of alibis prepared for every request.

"Well, you see, Val, people have begun to talk about you, and I knew of course you weren't aware of it, and that you ought to be prepared."

Willoughby laughed. Strange that Marietta should be met in all her uplifting tasks by a laugh, but she was so intent she didn't notice.

"Talk about me?" he said with a chuckle. "Heavens! What difference does that make? Though I can't for the life of me imagine what they could find that would be of interest enough to say more than a sentence or two. Don't worry about a little thing like that, Marietta. It won't bother me in the least."

"Oh, but you ought to care, Val," said the pretty lips. "You really ought. It's important. It definitely is! If not for yourself, then for the sake of your friends. It isn't pleasant to have things that are not nice said about someone you've been close to practically all your life."

Willoughby gave her a puzzled look.

"Well, I see you've got something on your mind. Go ahead and tell me and let's get it over. What is it?" he said.

"Yes, I thought so too, Val," said Marietta with satisfaction in her face. "You see, Val, you've been seen skating with a girl from the other side of the river. They are saying that you picked her up, and implying that *she* picked *you* up, and *you let her do it!* And it doesn't do the least bit of good to tell them that you wouldn't do a thing like that. That I've known you all my life and you aren't sordid and horrid like that. They say, 'Oh, my dear, you don't know *men!*' "

"Oh, really, Marietta? And who is this person or

persons doing the talking? Anybody I know?" He said it in a casual tone as if it were a mere matter of indifference to him.

"Well, I don't think it's quite honorable in me to tell you who it was, but it was somebody that I knew told the truth. Somebody who was truly troubled that you should have done a thing like that, and she told me in the utmost confidence. She knew I was a friend of yours and she felt I ought to know. She hoped I would be able to explain it, perhaps know who it was that you went skating with and so perhaps there was an explanation that would leave you without reproach."

"And were you?" asked Willoughby amusedly.

"Well, I told her I thought perhaps it might be one of your nieces home on a holiday from school, but she didn't seem to believe that."

"I see," said Willoughby smiling. "Well, that was kind of you of course. But it isn't important, is it? It can't do any harm, so perhaps we'd better forget it. It doesn't seem worth while to bother about it, does it? Certainly not tonight when we are off on a pleasant evening."

"Valiant Willoughby, how can you be so utterly indifferent to a thing like this? Why, I supposed you would indignantly deny it, and demand that I help you do something about it. What do you mean?"

"Why, Marietta, what's the idea? Am I not to go skating any more, or ever speak to a girl that you and your friends are not acquainted with? I can't make out what awful thing I have done."

"But *did* you go skating with that unspeakable girl?" Marietta's big blue eyes searched his face with horror in her own.

"With *what* unspeakable girl?" he asked amusedly. "What is there unspeakable about her? And if she is unspeakable, why do they speak about it?"

There was a real twinkle in Willoughby's eyes now, and at one corner of his lips, and Marietta was enraged that he should take it so lightly. She felt that he was making a joke of it.

"Oh, Val, you are impossible! You are perfectly *mad-*

dening! You know why she is unspeakable. You know
she comes from a little ratty house across the river, the
other side of the river, Val, and that's enough to make
her impossible, if there weren't anything else. No girl
from that region would be a fit companion for you,
Valiant Willoughby!"

"Why not?" asked the young man, looking imper-
turbably at the impeccable girl beside him.

"Do you have to ask? Don't you realize that the mention of a girl from that side of the river implies ig-
norance, coarseness, boldness, irresponsibility, un-
couthness, lack of culture and of course entire lack of
ethics, unwholesomeness, even uncleanness, immoral-
ity—"

"*Stop!*" said Willoughby. "That will be enough! The
girl I know from the other side of the river is not like
that! She is not any of those things you have mentioned.
And as you have never seen her I don't understand
how you dare insult her by such talk."

"I certainly *have* seen her," said Marietta. "I have
some pity on girls like that, even if you do carelessly
make fools of them. I went to see her this evening, just
before dinner. I wanted to let her know what danger she
was running in picking up young men on the river just
because she was a good skater. I told her that young
men from the other side of the river had no serious
intentions ever toward girls of her class who lived over
there, and that she was likely to have her heart broken,
and lose not only her self-respect but her reputation. I
told her that I was warning her for her own sake, and
that I wanted to help her. I told her that people were
already beginning to talk about her, and that it was a
shame, because if she would behave herself everybody
would be glad to help her to know a few rightminded
young men of her own class, and that would be so
much better for her."

Marietta suddenly finished and Willoughby regarded
her solemnly.

"You say you told her that?" he asked sternly.

"I certainly did," said the girl vivaciously.

He was still a full minute, and then he asked:

"And may I inquire what answer she gave to that?"

"She *laughed!*" said Marietta haughtily. "She was even ruder than I had expected her to be. She *only laughed*. So you can see what she is. She only laughed and went away."

"Yes," said Willoughby thoughtfully after even a longer pause, "I should think she *would* laugh. I think she answered you very wisely. I feel like laughing myself to know what you have done to one of the loveliest girls I have ever known."

"Now Val Willoughby, you don't mean that. You are just saying that because you are angry that I dared to call you down, but I thought you ought to know just what people were saying about you. And now you are acting as if you didn't care at all! I never dreamed that you would react this way. You must have greatly changed since I knew you."

"Just how did you expect me to react, Marietta?"

"Well, I certainly thought you would be ashamed to think you had been caught and recognized. I expected you to be filled with repentance, and give some plausible excuse about her being sick or poor or something and you thought you had to help her out some way, like you used to do with that scrubwoman's child when you were an exasperating kid."

"Oh! I see!" said Willoughby coolly. "But I'm not ashamed, and I'm not repentant, and I do not feel that I have done anything disgraceful. So if people decide that I have, knowing nothing whatever about it except that they saw me skating with somebody they didn't know, I think we can let it go at that and not talk any more about it, can't we?"

"Well, I don't think we can," said Marietta. "I think that respectable people who had supposed you were one of their friends have a right to an explanation of your conduct."

"Why?"

"Because you have gone against all our traditions in having anything to do with a girl on the other side of the river, exactly as if she were as good as anybody!"

"And yet you, Marietta, not knowing anything of the facts of the case, presumed to go into that girl's home, and according to your own account of the affair, insult her! It seems to me that I have a right to demand an explanation of *your* conduct."

"Oh, indeed! Well, Val Willoughby, I like that! I didn't go there to insult her. I went there to help her. In fact I began by inviting her to a series of dances where I told her she could meet young men of her own class, who would be suitable mates for her. I tried to make her understand that all I was saying was for her own good."

The young man looked at her in growing amazement.

"And she laughed, did she? Well, I'm glad she had the grace to do that after your insults. But now, suppose we forget all this and stop talking about it. We've almost reached the Academy of Music and we certainly won't be in any mood to enjoy the evening if we keep this up."

"But aren't you going to say you are sorry for having gone with that kind of girl? Or at least offer some sort of explanation for your conduct that I can tell people who are inquiring?"

"No," said Willoughby, "I certainly am not. I did nothing out of the way. But even if I had it was none of their business!"

"*Val!* But you can't stop people's mouths by saying it is none of their business."

"Perhaps not, but you don't have to discuss the matter with them, and I do *not* intend to do so, not even through you as a go-between."

"Oh, Val!" exclaimed Marietta in a voice of despair. "How you have changed!"

"Now, look here, Marietta, are we on the way to a symphony concert to enjoy ourselves, or shall we go to a funeral parlor and see if we can find a place to mourn? I really haven't time to waste a whole evening if you are going to carry on like this about something that you know nothing about, and is none of your affair. Come, Marietta, snap out of it, and let's talk over the music we are going to hear."

"Well, if you'll promise me just one thing," said the girl in a melting tone.

"Not till I know what it is," he said in a matter-of-fact tone.

"Well, it's that you won't ever do this thing again."

"What thing?"

"Why, that you won't ever go skating with that outrageous girl again. That you will not have *anything* more to do with her in *any* way."

"No," said Val Willoughby sharply, "I will *not* promise that! If that is your condition you had better drop me out now. Perhaps you could take the tickets and find some more congenial companion to accompany you. I'm rather fed up with your conversation at present."

But Marietta drove on to the entrance of the Academy of Music, her head high, her mouth wearing the martyr-like downdroop of one who forgives with great effort.

"I'm greatly disappointed in you, Val," she said as the doorman came up to take the car to the parking space, "but I'll forgive you of course. You're one of my oldest and dearest friends. But I'm grieved to death about you," and with great obvious forbearance she took his arm and assumed her haughtiest stride.

Val Willoughby hesitated an instant as she took his arm, and then acceded to her evident wish to go on with their plans for the evening. But he walked silently with stern, set expression, and wished with all his heart that he had never embarked upon this undesirable expedition. However, it was to be got through with somehow, and he felt that before they took their seats it would be best to establish some neutral topic for the duration of their private war, or the concert. So as they stepped into the main hallway and began making their way to the door that led to the aisle where their seats were located, he bent his head and said in a low tone that could not be heard by the gay throngs about them:

"I suggest, Marietta, if we are to go through with this evening as first planned, that we select some neutral topic for what conversation we are likely to have, and confine ourselves to that. And since we are attending a concert of some of the finest program music that is to be heard anywhere, suppose we talk about that. The music, and anything relating to it."

"Oh, if you are going to be disagreeable," said Marietta in her most martyr-like tone, "I suppose we can do that. Though I don't see why you select such a dumb topic. You know I'm not awfully fond of music, and just because I thought it was my duty to try and show you what a great mistake you were making, you get angry and try to punish me by refusing to let me talk about anything I choose; I feel you are most discourteous. I didn't think you were so touchy, Val Willoughby! Didn't you *want* me to tell you the *truth?*"

"Not particularly," answered the young man haughtily, "especially as most of the things you were saying were *not* true."

She flashed an angry look on him immediately.

"I don't care to discuss this matter any further this evening," he went on. "Is that plain?"

"You're just plain *rude!*" said Marietta, tossing her haughty head.

"Sorry," said Willoughby. "I thought you were rather rude yourself. So you see it would be better to take a neutral topic. I've been reading some very interesting items about the symphony we are to hear. Would you care to have me tell them to you? Don't you think that would be better than to spend the whole evening in sulking?"

"Oh, I suppose so!" said Marietta in a furious tone. "But if you want my opinion *I* think *you* are acting like a *spoiled boy!*"

They walked the rest of the way to their very fine seats in utter silence. Willoughby had a grave, almost haughty look on his face, but he was utmost courtesy as he seated Marietta, adjusted her wraps and provided her with a program. But Marietta still had an angry frown on her face distorting its beauty into anything but charm.

For the first few seconds after they were seated the young man applied himself to the study of the program, and then quite casually began to speak about it.

"Have you read the description of the symphony?" he asked. "It certainly promises to be quite colorful."

"No, of course not!" snapped Marietta. "I never do. Why waste time doing that? The music is supposed to give you the full idea, isn't it? I never could see the sense of going to work to try to explain what it's supposed to represent. I think it's all nonsense anyway! As if a sound could represent people and emotions. You might as well try to explain a sky or a tree or any part of a landscape in words. It's there, isn't it? And what more do you want? Why be sentimental about it? I like practical things. This trying to mix literature up with art is ridiculous! It's enough to listen to a long program without having to torture your brains trying to tell what it means. Of course it doesn't mean anything but what your imagination makes it mean, and of course every person has a different idea of it. I think in these times of war they waste money printing a lot of stuff like that. It would be far better to save the money and the paper and put it into war bonds."

"Yes?" said Willoughby with an amused twinkle. "Well, that's an angle I hadn't thought of, but of course there might be something in it. Why don't you put that in writing and send it to the Board of Directors? But— now that it *is* printed, and put in your hands, don't you think it is up to you to see that it isn't wasted? What if you and I put it to a thorough test this evening and see if there is anything we can get out of it? Just read each description carefully beforehand and then listen with it in mind and see whether it makes the music any more enjoyable. Suppose we try it. Now this first movement. It starts with a darkening sky, and wind blowing the grasses and the leaves on the trees, you can hear the rising wind and then comes the patter of the rain as it begins to fall—!"

Marietta looked at her escort in astonishment. This was a new phase of Val Willoughby, eloquent and fanciful. Why did he waste himself talking such foolish prattle as this?

"I think that's fantastic!" she said with a sneer. But she listened and watched him while he talked, and finally forgot her annoyance at him in admiration of his handsome face. He certainly was the best looking one of the old crowd of men. How well he would look in a uniform! What a pity he had allowed himself to be tied up to a stupid factory when he might be in some position of high command!

But Willoughby was talking well, and Marietta was fairly intelligent when she allowed herself time off from doing the talking herself. Somehow the story of an oncoming storm began to take form in her mind and when he came to the maiden alone on a desolate road with the rain pelting down, and then the knight on horseback coming to the rescue, she gave over thinking her own angry thoughts and began to take an interest in the tale he was telling. Not that she had as yet any idea of expecting to get the picture again by the sound of music that she was to hear, but at least she was getting the background of the scene, and the hint of a love story, which perhaps alone would have been able to interest her.

Val Willoughby worked hard at the telling because he knew unless he could interest the girl enough to keep her quiet, the whole evening would be an awful bore to him. So now as he talked, and watched a small growing interest in the girl's face, he began to feel that perhaps it would be worth-while after all. If he succeeded in making Marietta take an interest in music, perhaps he might hope that it would keep her tongue still about her own schemes for a little while and let others enjoy the concert. So he put the same zest into this description as he would have put into some experiment in the laboratory, or some delicate execution of government devices to help win the war, and felt really encouraged as he saw her turn toward him and really begin to listen. If he had known however, that the supreme thought in her mind had been admiration of himself, he would have been disgusted and disappointed.

Yet, back of her observation of the way his hair waved back from his fine forehead, and the curve of his pleasant lips when he smiled, there was forming in her mind that picture of darkening sky, rising wind, lovely girl against an oncoming storm, the sound of horses' feet in the distance. Definitely Marietta would remember that picture when the music began, even against her will. Certainly it would be the first time she had ever formed a mental picture of music she was hearing. And Willoughby was at least comforted by the thought that so far she was listening to him. Perhaps she didn't even realize she was giving him her attention. She seemed to have had her interest caught unawares.

The people had been drifting in rapidly, until now the house was full, and though the young man had lowered his voice little by little until it was scarcely more than a murmur, Marietta had her eyes riveted to the tip of her companion's pencil with which he had idly been sketching on the margin of his program the outline of a mountain, a gnarled tree, and wispy tall grasses with bent heads. Val wasn't an artist. He was merely talking with his pencil for his own help as he went along. But the girl was watching, and making something out of the sketch even though it wasn't very good, as his low voice painted the scene of the music.

And now he was outlining a little bird on wing, flying toward shelter. Then suddenly the audience burst into wild applause. Looking up they discovered that the beloved orchestra conductor had arrived at the front of the stage and was being applauded.

With a deep breath Willoughby straightened up and sat back, feeling as tired as if he had been dragging a heavy burden up a hill. Well, at least he had kept her tongue still for a few minutes, and now, presently, he would have opportunity to discover whether his pupil had taken in aught of what he had been trying to demonstrate. For already the conductor was in his place, and the audience had settled into utmost stillness.

Then came the first soft notes sending forth the shimmer of the summer sky, spreading it out in the semblance of a perfect summer day.

"Listen!" spoke Val softly, but more by the form of his lips, the lifting of his pencil, than by any sound he spoke.

And Marietta was so far under the spell of his pencil that her eyes turned to the platform as if she expected to find that summer day spread out to view.

He watched her. Would the music hold her to the thought, or would she grow restless?

Then all unexpected in the soft summer sky came the distant rumble of thunder menacing, beneath the delicate thread of melody the wind instruments had brought into being, and then again and again, coming nearer each time and more insistently, and Marietta's eyes grew wide with wonder. Nobody had ever made her see anything in music before save a tune that didn't matter to her in the least. But this had caught her. And now Val's pencil touched the sky over the mountains with a smudge of growing darkness, more grass bending low, branches bending, just a line here and there, and that little frightened bird winging its way as the big drops fell, and the storm went on wildly in a tumult of sound.

On to the end of the opening number Marietta's interest held, unaware as she was that she was listening, and when it was over and the delighted applause came she turned to Val:

"I didn't know music could be like that!" she said, half vexed with herself to admit it. "Where does that girl come in?" Val's answer was with the tip of his pencil, for the silence had broken into music again with the theme of the maiden, and softly the pencil kept rhythm, till it seemed the girl was struggling, trying to breast the storm.

It did not require words the rest of the time, nor drawing, only a sort of thought-directing on through the story, and Marietta sat through the performance like one entranced. Only when the intermission came and everybody was buzzing and talking around them, and some were stepping out into the wide corridors to smoke and meet their friends, was there opportunity to talk, then Val found Marietta was studying her program, reading it all the way through.

By the time she had finished the conductor had returned and the music began again. Marietta listened, aware that here was something worth-while that she had hitherto passed by, annoyed at herself for not having known it before, wondering if all music were like this if only one understood how to listen.

They went quietly out with the throng, meeting now and then some they knew and nodding, but for the most part without speaking to one another. And because he knew she would expect it, he took her to a fashionable place for supper afterward, wishing in his heart this need not be, dreading lest now would be the time when she would start arguing again.

But Marietta sat for the most part silent, absorbed in her own thoughts. At last she roused.

"Well," she said, half crossly, because she always hated to own she had been wrong, "I suppose I'll have to thank you for opening my eyes, or rather my ears, to something great I have been missing. I certainly have enjoyed the evening for its own sake, and I hadn't expected to enjoy it for that reason at all. I think you have a wonderful way of teaching something if you once make up your mind to do it. But watching you all this evening, and seeing how skillful you are with a few crude pencil lines, and how eloquent you are with just the right words to sway my mind to listen, I still feel that I cannot bear it that you should waste your talents amusing yourself with a cheap little ignoramus like the girl you go skating with. I know you made a condition that I say no more on that subject, but the evening is over now, and I can't bear to leave you without your promise to quit her."

Willoughby's lips took on their firm line again, but

he smiled indulgently, and was still for a moment. Then he said quietly:

"I have not changed my determination about that, Marietta, and I do not wish to discuss it further tonight. Sometime perhaps I shall have the pleasure of making you see the loveliness in the character of that girl you despise, just as I have had the pleasure of opening your eyes to the beauties hidden in the music to which you never really listened before. Sometime perhaps I can introduce you to the girl, and make you understand what I mean."

"Never!" said Marietta with the ugly prejudice coming out and sitting plainly on her face. She seemed a different girl from the one who had listened raptly to lovely pastoral strains that evening. "I shall *never* care to meet her as an equal."

"But you know, that is almost what you said about the music when I asked you if you had read the program through. Sometime perhaps you will learn that prejudice often blinds people to some of the rarest things in life. I often wonder if we don't miss out that way in trying to learn about God and things of the other world."

"Oh, for Heaven's sake, Val Willoughby, *stop!* You make me shudder! Don't spoil the whole evening by talk about such gruesome things! I hate solemn stuff like that!"

So they went out to the car and drove home in a strange silence, Val greatly relieved that his evening was over and in a few minutes he might say good night and be free once more to think his own thoughts and go his own way, with no further obligations toward this girl, with whom he had surprisingly been able to spend a pleasant evening listening to thoroughly classical music.

So he rode to her home with her and left her at her door. Said good night gravely, received his thanks, but declined to come in and talk.

"I've given you all the time I can spare tonight," he said pleasantly. "Perhaps some other time we can have a talk about something else we don't agree on, but it

won't be very soon. I've an engagement tomorrow night,
and the next night, and I don't know but I may have to
go to Washington next week on Government business.
Good night." He walked down the pavement to his
aunt's home, catching occasional glimpses of the frozen
river with the late moon glinting it with silver touches,
and wondered if he had utterly wasted this evening.

Chapter 11

SOMETIME DURING THE pale hours when the dawn was
beginning to steal into the sky, and rosy lights touched
the river of ice, Nurse Branner woke up and decided
what to do. There ought to be a telephone in that
house, and she decided that she would see that there
was one. She would tell Frannie that it was necessary
for *her* business that she be within call at any time of
the day or night. That she had several "cases" in the
future, and one woman in particular had asked her to
let her know just where she was, so that she could call
her up in a sudden emergency. Frannie might think it
queer perhaps, but Frannie didn't know much about
nurses' emergencies of course, and she felt she could
make her story quite plausible. And it was true that
several old patients were in the habit of calling her
occasionally, and her own sister always complained
when she allowed herself to be more than a day in a
house without a telephone.

Besides, Frannie had been saying that she meant to
have a telephone, so she would just tell Frannie that
she was presenting her with the initial cost, and if she
didn't want to retain it when the nurse left, she could
always tell them to take it out. So that was settled. She
would have it put in the first thing Monday morning.

Next, somebody who could do some responsible investigating ought to know about that man who had

come to the back door so late, and the two shadows that had moved in the dark across the ice. This problem would not be quite so easily handled as the other. Besides, this was going to be Sunday morning pretty soon, and Sunday was a different day from the rest. People didn't go around and put in telephones on Sunday even in emergencies, unless some very great person ordered it. And there was no one whom she could call upon to do any investigating or protecting, who would actually have the right to do it, but the police, and did did she have a right to go to the police? This wasn't her house, and the householders didn't even know she was worried.

So she lay there and thrashed her brains until she finally remembered the big burly policeman whose baby she had nursed a couple of years ago, and who had told her that if there was ever anything he could do for her please to let him know. She would go to officer Rowley and tell him all about it. She would go that very morning. Frannie would be at home, at least unless she wanted to go to church around eleven. Yes she would tell him all about it. She knew she could trust him to see if any special vigilance was needed.

So after she had taken the breakfast tray up to her patient she came down and said to Frannie:

"My dear, I wonder if you and Bonnie could take turns sitting with your mother for about an hour or an hour-and-a-half this morning? I want to run over to a friend's house for a few minutes on an errand. I won't be long. No, sit still and eat your breakfast. I'll get my hat and coat. I drank some coffee and had some toast before you came down, to save time. Now, will you mind, dear?"

"Mind?" said Frannie. "Of course not. We'll have a lovely time talking to mother, and take beautiful care of her. You stay just as long as you want to. We'll be all right. I didn't mean to go to church this morning anyway. I thought I would stay and talk with mother. She wants to ask me a lot of things about the place I work. But don't you worry, I won't tell her anything to trouble her. I realize she needs real rest for a while.

And by that time she will be used to seeing me come home safely every day."

So Nurse Branner hurried away. She had carefully planned her campaign for the shortest possible time, so she did not waste a minute. Bonnie, watching out the window, saw her turn to cross the bridge and sighed. She wished the nurse had asked if she might go with her. But Frannie heard the sigh and came with a smile.

"What's the matter, dearie?"

"I was thinking how quick Nurse Branner walks," said the little girl wistfully. "She went right across that big bridge up there. I'd like to go across that bridge."

"Well, you shall, little dear," said Frannie. "I'll take you for a walk myself across that bridge. Perhaps this afternoon, if the nurse gets back."

"Oh, Frannie! And can we walk over to my pretty lady's big white house? I want you to see how pretty it is."

"Why, perhaps so, if it isn't too far."

"Oh, but it isn't too far, Frannie. I runned it across the river when mother was sick."

"Yes, I know. But we'll walk around by the bridge if we go today. Now come on upstairs and let us make the bed and then we'll go in and talk to mother a little while and see how she feels."

So they hurried through the brief housework, Bonnie bustling about with a dustcloth and making a great show of being very busy. Then they had a nice talk with the mother, who seemed brighter, and quite cheerful that morning, glad of the sunshine that came in her window.

Meanwhile Nurse Branner took a taxi to the home of her policeman friend, and as she rode along the sunlit street she was praying in her heart that he might be at home, or at least somewhere that she could reach him.

It was a neat little gray house to which she finally drew up, not more than a mile and a quarter from the bridge, and she could see the round bright face of the little girl who was the baby she had nursed a little while ago, looking out the window, pink cheeks aglow with health, red curls atoss.

She kept the taxi waiting while she went in to see if the man she sought was there.

"Oh, Nurse Branner!" cried Mrs. Rowley in great delight, as she opened the door and welcomed her. "I've been hoping sometime you would come, and now you are here! And see, baby, *see,* this is the nice nurse that saved your life!" Mrs. Rowley seized the baby at the window and brought her forward for the nurse to look at.

"Isn't she wonderful, Nurse Branner? Jim he can't be thankful enough to you. He's always saying he wished he could do something for you, who did so much for us. Sit down, won't you, and let us look at you. It's good to see you again. We love you so much."

"Well, that's very nice, Mrs. Rowley. I'm glad to be here. And I've come to ask your husband's advice about something. Is he here, or could I find him at his station?"

The woman gave a quick glance at the clock.

"Oh, he'll be here in just ten minutes, unless something hinders him. He always comes about this time for his Sunday morning breakfast. He likes fish balls for Sunday, and he wants them piping hot, so he tells me about what time to expect him, and he'll be that glad to find you here. Excuse me just a minute, I think I smell the fish balls burning. I'll just turn down the blaze a bit."

When Mrs. Rowley came back from her neat little kitchen Nurse Branner had the baby in her arms, and was talking to her, and the baby was looking up at her charmed.

"Oh, but she's remembering you!" exclaimed the mother. "She's that bright, Nurse Branner, you'd be surprised. But I'm sure she remembers you. Look at her cuddle down contented, smiling."

And then in the midst of it all in walked the big policeman, with his breezy welcome, and hearty voice:

"Well, bless my soul, if there isn't our Angel-nurse Branner! Isn't this something to honor the day? Did I ever dream to have the blessing of your presence in our humble home again?"

After Nurse Branner had laughingly received his voluble praise, and the usual words of greeting had been exchanged, Miss Branner turned to him seriously.

"You remember I promised two years ago, James Rowley, that if ever I was in need of help I would come to you? Well, I've come. Maybe it isn't help I need, maybe it's only advice, but I thought you would be the one to come to and find out. You see I'm staying with a little family, a mother and two daughters, one a young woman the other a mere child of five. They've just moved into the old Garner house, the red brick, you know, that's been vacant so long. They don't know anybody around, and haven't even got a telephone in yet, though I mean to see to that tomorrow. The daughter works down the river at a defense plant and is away all day. The mother was there alone with the five year old girl, and fell in a faint while she was clearing off the breakfast table. The little girl, all alone and very much frightened, ran across the river on the ice and called for help at Mrs. Winthrop's, who telephoned for Dr. Ransom. He sent his office boy for me. That's how I came to be there. Mrs. Winthrop called in Valiant Willoughby and sent him home with the child, and later sent him down to tell the older daughter. That's the story, and there's nothing the matter with that part, for I happened to be just off a case, and am glad to help these people. They are dear people, and really need me for the present anyway. But last night something happened that worried me. In fact after I had thought about it a little it sort of linked itself up with something that had happened the first night I was there, and I thought I ought to tell somebody about it. I didn't want to tell the family, for they have just about as much to worry about as they can weather. I thought of the doctor, and of Mrs. Winthrop, but I sort of knew the doctor would merely laugh at me and tell me it was nothing and perhaps I ought to take a rest pretty soon. And I didn't like to worry Mrs. Winthrop. So I suddenly remembered you, and I knew you would be the one to come to. I knew if there was anything to it you would investigate it for me, or sort of protect the house for awhile or something. And if there wasn't anything to it I knew I could believe you. So, that's why I've come. But, there, your wife is calling you to your breakfast, and I want you to have those fish cakes while they're hot the way you like them. Go sit down and eat and I can tell you afterwards."

The big policeman grinned.

"Yes, I like 'em hot, but I like my stories hot too. Sit right down and have a cup of coffee with me, and go on telling. I might get called off, you know, and I wouldn't want to go without knowing what's on your mind."

So Nurse Branner sat down at the table and told the story of the man who had knocked at the back door a little before midnight.

Officer Rowley filled his mouth with one of his wife's delicious fish balls, and while he was chewing he watched the nurse's face as she told her story, his canny eyes twinkling now and again knowingly.

"You say he was short and thick set—stoutish?" he asked keenly as he laid down his fork and picked up his coffee cup to take a deep swig of the hot liquid.

Nurse Branner nodded.

"Have anybody with him?"

"Well, I wasn't sure. He went down the steps to the river and walked out on the ice and I thought I saw a shadow steal out from the bushes and join him. I guess it was a man. Taller than the first one. In fact it wasn't the first time I had seen a couple of men, a tall one and a short one, go by on the ice and look at our house. I didn't think anything of it that first night I was there. And then I happened to look out another night and saw those two going by again—in fact they were going *down* the river that time, and on the other side, so that I didn't realize it was the same two, until I saw them turn and veer over to our side of the river, and then I watched them go by. They were looking up at the house, even stopping an instant to point to the corner of the house. Then I saw they were the same two men. And so last night when that man knocked I realized that I had seen him before, at least I'd seen his funny chunky outline. But it didn't mean a thing to me even then until I got to thinking it over in the night. And then I saw that while I might be just fancying all this, there *might really* be something to it somehow, and somebody who would know how to handle it ought to hear about it. So, Mr. Rowley, what do you think? Of course it's none of my business at all. I'm just the nurse. But I simply couldn't tell those poor children nor their sick mother about it, nor even warn them not to open the door to a knock in the middle of the night if they should happen to be alone. So I've come to somebody I thought would understand and advise me right. What do you think?"

"I think you did just right, Nurse Branner. And I'll be glad to take over in your place and search this thing down to rock bottom. I'll let you know if I find there's anything to it. But to tell you the truth, your description of the man that knocked at your back door sort of tallies with a man we've been looking for off and on for several weeks back. Where did you say they parked their car?" and the burly officer took out a pencil and notebook and put down some incomprehensible marks.

"Now," he said, looking up with his pencil poised, "what time did you say he knocked at the back door? And approximately what time of night was it on the other two occasions you were sure you saw the two men?"

It did not take long to tell all she knew, and then the officer went on with his breakfast and smiled at the nurse.

"Don't you worry another little bit about this," he said. "I'll be glad to look after it. And in doing so I may uncover something valuable we have been trying to work out for some time. Just keep your attention out the window now and then and let me know any developments. You know there are a lot of Fifth Columnists going around these days. I don't say this is one, but don't let any strange men into your house, and tell your people not to. And if you happen to see me around anywhere don't worry. Though I shall probably not come myself. We'll kind of lay low on uniformed men to give these men a chance to show their hands. But don't worry, above all things. You folks will be thoroughly protected as long as there is the slightest doubt or danger."

Nurse Branner went out at last with a parting kiss for the baby, and a shower of blessings on her for the visit. She took her taxi quickly over to the place where she had roomed and got a small overnight bag filled with fresh garments. So she hurried back to the bridge, from which she placidly walked down to the little brick house, the light of the pleasant day shining in her face. She had done the best she could with the matter of the midnight visitor and now she meant to send Frannie out for a walk or some kind of a restful interval. If it only were not such a lonely neighborhood just now with all those vacant new houses, some of them not yet finished, she would insist that Frannie go to church. But perhaps it was just as well for her not to go far yet until she had established contact with a church, and could get acquainted with a few young people who might furnish an escort. But certainly not until Officer Rowley had finished his investigation, and reported, she did not want to be the one to urge Frannie to go out alone in an unknown district. Of course it wouldn't be right to count on seeing any more of young Willoughby. He had an important job, everybody understood, and then too he must have his own intimate crowd who would be expecting him. He was a popular young man, and it was wonderful that he had given a strange little girl as much time as he had given Frannie, even sparing time to help put up curtains. People naturally went with their own class, the ones they had been brought up with, and that was right. Only it went sorely against the grain for Nurse Branner to think of Valiant Willoughby as being paired off with Marietta Hollister. She never had liked that girl and felt pretty sure she never would.

If she could have known that Val had spent Saturday evening with Marietta at a concert she certainly would have been disappointed in him. For she wouldn't have known that the young man in question was thinking of his efforts of the night before with distaste, and wondering what would have been Frannie's reaction to the same lesson in orchestral music he had given, if he had tried it out on her instead of Marietta. Perhaps sometime he would. That was something interesting to look forward to. Provided always that the war had not swept over the land to such an extent that nobody had any time for symphony concerts.

Meantime, why couldn't he take Frannie to church somewhere? He had an idea she was a church girl, and would enjoy going, perhaps to some great rally with a fine speaker. There were often such meetings in the city. He went in search of the Saturday paper and turning to the religious page discovered a number of announcements that sounded interesting. Sometime that afternoon or early evening he would go over and ask after her mother and find out if she had any plans for the evening. Or, if the nurse was going out, perhaps he could sit there awhile and talk, just in a friendly way. Since Marietta's account of her call he wanted to look at Frannie with that in mind. Perhaps she would say something about her caller. He could almost visualize the twinkle in her brown eyes when she laughed at Marietta. He had a passing wish that he might have been present and heard the interview.

Then Val Willoughby chided himself. Was he idealizing that little Fernley girl because he had felt sorry for her, and because she seemed sweet and appealing? He mustn't be that kind of a fool. And of course there was something in what Marietta had said, much as he hated to acknowledge it. One shouldn't go too far out of one's own environment to form intimacies.

Yet Frannie had seemed so well brought up, so altogether refined. He remembered there had been the few pieces of fine old furniture, and some really good pictures, the daintiness of the white curtains, the thin old china on the table. No, surely, those Fernley's had not common tastes. And Frannie conversed well. She used well chosen words naturally, without awkward sentences. Surely Marietta had been utterly wrong. He felt in his heart that Frannie was worth cultivating as a friend. In fact he felt strangely determined to do it, and let the town gossips say what they would.

So Val did some serious reading that he had been saving for an hour of leisure, hung around until the usual five o'clock tea time that his aunt always made much of on Sunday afternoon, and then strolled out, up the hill to the bridge, and over the bridge to the little brick house with its cheerful friendly light shining down on the icy way.

As he walked he looked down the river, especially as he crossed the bridge, and thought of the lovely things that Lady Winthrop had said about it. Her "street of the city" she had called it. Her fancied way to the Heavenly City. With the silver moonbeams now upon its gleaming breast he could understand her similes. What a lovely lady she was, and how sweetly she was growing old. Taking her hardships and loneliness as if they had been blessings, giving her sons to the war, and taking what pleasure she could from the pictures the river formed for her. Thinking of her Heavenly Home as if she were looking forward to it with pleasure. He wondered if he would feel that way about the end of his life when he got there? That of course was a right way to feel. To meet it joyously, as an end in itself, and not a cessation of all that had been good.

He must not forget that Monday evening gathering she had told him about. He would go at least once and see what it was like. Perhaps knowing a great deal about the Bible and understanding what it meant had been what had kept Lady Winthrop's soul so sweet and young, so full of faith, and ready to look forward through growing old to the time when age should drop away, and life should become new and young and eternal.

So he pondered, as he walked across the river to see the little girl who lived on the wrong side of the bridge, and never knew that Marietta had seen him go by from her window, and attired herself hopefully, for his possible return.

Chapter 12

FRANNIE WAS HELPING the nurse to put away the supper dishes when Willoughby arrived, and the two were a bit startled to hear the knock at the door. The nurse thought at once of the man who had knocked last night and gave a quick glance in Frannie's direction. Perhaps she ought to have told the girl about it after all, but the policeman had seemed to think it wasn't necessary just yet.

"I'll go," said the nurse wiping her hands quickly on the roller towel and hurrying toward the front door. If it was that man again she would get rid of him in short order, and try to do it in a low tone so Frannie wouldn't have to know about it.

But Frannie was all too willing to let her answer the knock, for she was thinking of that obnoxious girl, and wondering if she had come again. If she had she did not want to see her, and she knew Nurse Branner would see that she did not have to.

But it was Val's voice she heard instead of Marietta's and her heart gave a happy little skip. That was pleasant. Nice of him to come over to see how her mother was, that was what she heard him say as he stepped inside the living room. And Frannie hurried to dry her hands and go in.

Valiant's smile was warm and hearty, like a very old friend's, and Frannie felt happy to think he was not going to try to be a stranger as she had feared. He had come back of his own accord, not just to be polite, but to be friendly, also. That was what his smile said. He might be an intimate of that hateful patronizing girl. He might even be the one she said was practically engaged to her, or some of her kind, but he wasn't going to look down on other people because of that, and he wasn't minding that she was living on the wrong bank of the river either.

So she came in without self-consciousness, just a bit of heightened color perhaps, and a shine in her eyes that had not been there before he came. He put out his hand and grasped hers wholeheartedly, making her feel that he was her real friend in spite of that other girl.

He was looking down at her as he stood, her hand still in his, and thinking how pretty she looked, with her hair in little rings of curls around her face, and no make-up at all, her pansy-blue eyes raised to his. Yes, she was lovely. He hadn't noticed it especially before. She had been almost too pale that first time he saw her, when she was so frightened about her mother. But she was beautiful, with those long dark lashes curling back from her wide sweet eyes. He had never been one to stare at a girl, or to analyze her features and think about beauty. He had often acknowledged that Marietta was beautiful, but it hadn't meant a thing to him because he didn't admire her character, and if a girl's heart wasn't lovely what did it matter how her outward features were formed? To be truly beautiful there must be no flaws of soul. The face must match the heart and that, it suddenly struck him, was the case with this girl. This face was no camouflage, it was a true delineation of the life within.

So he stood and smiled down into her sweet eyes, and spoke in an intimate tone:

"I just came over to find out how your mother is tonight, and then I thought if she was able to spare you for a little while, perhaps you would like to go somewhere to church with me."

Frannie's cheeks grew bright and her eyes lighted up.

"Oh, that would be lovely," she said breathlessly, "but I don't know but Miss Branner would like to go out somewhere. I was just going to ask her."

"No indeed," said Nurse Branner decidedly. "I went out this morning, you know, and really I'm a bit tired from it. I thought I'd read a little while to your mother, and when she gets to sleep, I have something I want to read myself. Go ahead, Frannie. I'd love to have you. Perhaps you can find a church you will enjoy."

And so with lovely happiness in her eyes Frannie hurried upstairs to get ready.

She seemed very sweet as she came downstairs in her slim green coat and her little green turban, her soft brown curls framing her face.

"I hope it's not a very grand church you're taking me to," she said shyly. "I haven't any fine clothes."

"Haven't you?" smiled Val. "They look plenty fine enough to me. But then I'm not much of a judge of clothes. I'm sure they look as if they suited you, and that's altogether satisfactory, so don't let's worry. Have you any choice of churches?"

"Oh no," said the girl. "I don't know the churches around here. I had it in mind to hunt up a pleasant place that would be near enough for my mother to walk to, but that would probably take time, and I'd rather go with you to whatever church you choose."

"Well, I haven't been living around here much until the last three or four weeks, and I haven't settled down yet. I've been going with my aunt to her church the last two weeks since I've been here because it pleased her to have me, but frankly I wasn't very well satisfied. The minister didn't seem to me to believe all he was saying, and I thought I'd like to go where there was a real message. There's one man down in the city who has the reputation of speaking pretty directly from the shoulder, and just now he is talking about what this war means and all the things that are happening in the world today, in relation to the message of God in the Bible. I thought I'd like to hear what he has to say. How about you? Would you enjoy that?"

"Oh yes," said Frannie earnestly. "I've wondered so much how the war can possibly fit in with God's loving the world and wanting to save them."

"All right then, we'll go and see if we get any light on the subject. And about that church for your mother, I'll be inquiring around to find out possibilities. Then, maybe next Sunday we can shop around a little and find a church nearby where your mother and Bonnie can walk. But tonight we'll go to the Fourth-Avenue Church and see what we can hear. Would you rather walk or ride? My aunt is not going to use her car to-night and she said I might take it. Pretty soon I shall have to have one of my own, but just now I like my skates as well as any form of locomotion. Although it wouldn't be just the thing to skate to church. I suppose the ice will decide to leave us some day and then we'll have to find some other method anyway. But tonight there is no reason why we can't ride if you'd like."

"Oh, I think I'd rather walk if you don't mind. Is it far?"

"No. Not over a mile or a mile and a quarter."

"Well, then let's walk. I haven't been anywhere around here and I think we'd get better acquainted with it walking, don't you?"

"Perhaps," said Val smiling. "I never thought of it that way. But it is a lovely night and I shall enjoy walk-ing down some of the pretty streets that are on the way to church and showing them to you. Then if you are tired we can take a taxi home."

"Oh, I shall not be tired," said Frannie with a little ripple of a laugh. "I don't get tired walking, and you know I have to sit almost all the days at the office. But you—you have to be on the go a great deal. Would you rather ride? Because I could enjoy that a lot too. I haven't had many opportunities to ride of late."

"No, I'd love to walk. I have always enjoyed it. Come, let's go. It is still light enough to see, and we'll go right by Lady Winthrop's home. You've seen it from the river, but I want you to see it from the street. It really is a lovely old mansion, with many delightful facings."

So they went out together, and Nurse Branner smiled and was glad at the way one day had worked out.

So that was how it came about that Marietta saw Val Willoughby and her hated little rival walking by her house together.

Marietta had not turned on the light. She was moon-ing by the window, thinking to open the door for him herself when he came back and stopped to call.

At first she could not believe it was the same girl, the girl from the wrong side of the river. The cut of her green coat was smart, and the little turban was jaunty and becoming. Of course it was beginning to be dusk and the sidewalk was some distance from the house, but Marietta's eyes were sharp, her intuitions were keen, and she knew who it was. She watched for a moment with growing fury in her heart. Had Val Willoughby done this just to tantalize her? Wouldn't he be sure she would see them? He was just trying to annoy her. To show her that he would defy her wish. Her blue eyes snapped like blue flames. She would have to do something extra specially annoying to him to pay him for this.

Perhaps he was even contemplating bringing her in to call. That would be unspeakable! That girl! If he dared she certainly would have things to say to the contemptible creature that would humiliate her forever.

But no, perhaps the best way would be to be out. To seem not to have been at home at all to see him pass. She would go at once, and run no risks of having such a dreadful thing happen. So she rushed up to her room to prepare for an evening with some friends, and watched her opportunity to escape across the lawn to get her car when there was no sign of them on the street.

But meanwhile all unaware of the tumult they were exciting in Marietta's angry breast, the two were walking briskly down Hilltop Road, and taking in all the beautiful homes along the way.

As they passed the Haversett home and Val told her it was where his aunt lived, Frannie gave a little gasp as she eyed the great stone mansion with its massive bay windows and stone arches, and evidences of wealth on every side.

"Oh!" she said softly. "To think that you live there in that lovely home, and yet you are taking time to be kind and go to church with me! *Me,* a little nobody, with shabby clothes, who lives on the wrong side of the river."

He gave her a quick look, and then he laughed.

"You sound like Marietta Hollister," he said and laughed again.

She gave him a quick look in turn now.

"You know her then?"

"Oh yes, of course, I know her. I've known her since she was a spoiled baby younger than your Bonnie. She never had half the sense Bonnie has now. But don't let anything she says or thinks worry you. I understand she's been to call on you."

Frannie lifted wondering eyes.

"How did you know?"

"Why, she told me herself, and my anger rose momently as she enlarged upon her visit. But I beg of you not to worry about it. She isn't worth it. She has money and an expensive education, but she has no soul; she's like a lovely showy flower without perfume. She is essentially selfish, and sometimes cruel in the extreme, if it suits her purposes. I don't like to talk about my acquaintances this way, especially to one who is a comparative stranger to them, but I feel that it is right that you should understand the situation. I hope you won't think me unkind in my summary of her character. You see she is so very beautiful on the outside that it is hard to realize she can be actually cruel. There! Now, have I said enough and can we put the subject aside and forget it?"

He looked down at her earnestly, and drew her arm within his own to emphasize his confidential attitude.

Frannie was looking down, her brow troubled, thoughtful.

"Why, yes, I guess so," she said slowly. "It wasn't exactly pleasant to bear, that call, and I practically knew it didn't matter, because I never would be likely to have my lot cast within even a near approach of hers, but of course I didn't enjoy thinking that a lot of tongues had been caused to wag about you as well as myself, just because you had been kind enough to bring a message to me about my sick mother, and then later to help me out in a free-for-all fight with those two fresh fellows. But I guess if we're not seen skating together any more the talk will soon die out. You see that girl and I really do live in different worlds, typified to her mind by which side of the river we live on, and we're not likely to cross each other's paths often, so I guess there isn't much damage done."

"Damage? Well, no, I should say not! But if you think I'm going to let that little gossiping baby-doll cheat me out of a new friend I hope I've found in you, you're sadly mistaken. Even if I didn't like you for yourself, and have pleasure in skating with you, which I very much do, I wouldn't let Marietta Hollister beat me out of doing what I want to do. So if you please, keep right on skating down to your work whenever you want to, and if you don't mind I shall join you when I can. I told that snooping little gossip as much myself. So you see you've got to help me keep my word. I told her you were a good friend of mine. And now can't we get to work and find some mutual friends, so we can prove that we didn't 'pick each other up' on the ice, as they are pleased to say we did?"

Frannie laughed.

"Why yes," she said gaily, "I guess we can. Did you have a friend named Ford Harrison when you were in college?"

Willoughby looked at her in surprise.

"Why yes, I did," he said. "How did you know?"

"Well, you see his sister Allison was my roommate in college. I've been trying ever since I heard your name to remember where I had heard it before, and at last it came to me that Allie used to speak of one by that name as her brother's best friend."

"Great!" said Willoughby. "That would surprise Marietta. She didn't know you had been to college."

Frannie grinned.

"She would think a girl who lived on the wrong side of the river couldn't possibly have gone to college," she said amusedly, looking up at him with a comical twinkle.

"No, please, I never said I agreed with that nonsense about the other side of the river. That's a lot of hooey the smart set got up. I never felt that way."

"No, I knew you wouldn't," said Frannie. "I knew you were bigger than that."

"But seriously, Frannie, tell me about your college life. I want to understand why I didn't hear more about you, because I was quite intimate in the Harrison home during my college days."

"Well, you see, that fall I roomed with Allison was the end of my college life. Father got sick, and we had to go west, and I never went back to college. There wasn't money enough after father's health and business both failed, and somehow those were pretty hard days. I had no time for just pleasant correspondence. It's been a pretty busy world for me ever since."

"I see," said Willoughby. "I do remember something about Allison Harrison losing her roommate that she liked so much. But I'm glad to know about it now. We are not just strangers to one another. We have a background of mutual friends through several years. We can start with that, and the next time we have a chance to talk about it very likely we'll find a few others, just for anyone who accuses us of picking one another up on the ice. But—this is the church, and the organ is playing. I guess we are just about on time. Shall we go in?"

Chapter 13

IT WAS A very solemn sermon to which the two listened, after the beautiful singing which preceded it was over. It took up the Bible outline of the national frontiers at the time of the end of the present age, as they are referred to in the seventh of Daniel and elsewhere. It showed how the nations would realign themselves so that two opposing groups would be separated by the line of the Rhine and the Danube, the boundary of the ancient Roman Empire. The speaker quoted famous war commentators' speculations which showed that it would be possible for the realignment to take place quickly, even within only a few weeks' time."

"Why, I never knew that the Bible told things like this," said Frannie. "Did you? I didn't know that it definitely told what was going to happen on the earth in these days that are so long after the Bible was written. I knew of course that there were prophecies of general things, but I never knew it went into detail. I never even tried to read any of the prophecies. I thought people weren't meant to understand them. Did you know all this?"

"Well, I knew in a general way that there were prophecies that had to do with the latter days of this age. I knew there were prophecies of wars, and one battle in particular, the last one, called Armageddon. Everybody was wondering in the last world war whether Armageddon was soon due. But I gather that not many of the church people have paid much attention to such things, only accepting them as a vague description of matters that would occur in the far distant future, like the Day of Judgment. People who had any Christian background at all have sort of taken these things for granted. It is only within recent years that any large number of Christians have seriously set themselves to study and discover what it is all about. I've been hearing a couple of young Christian students talk, and they mentioned a few of the things we heard tonight. That prophecy about the Prince of Rosh—it interested me a lot, so I thought I would like to hear some more. That's why I suggested coming here tonight. It's rather startling, isn't it? Did you enjoy the talk?"

"I thought it was wonderful," said Frannie. "I'd like to hear more. I suppose there are books or papers perhaps that would tell more about those things."

"I think there are," said Willoughby. "I know those fellows used to have a lot of books and magazines around their rooms, and now and then I would pick up one and read a bit. I'll find out their names and try to get hold of some of them. By the way, Lady Winthrop asked me to come to her house tomorrow night to a class they have, studying the Bible. Would you like to go? I'll ask her if I may bring you."

"Oh, I'd love it, but I wouldn't like you to ask her about me. You know I'm the girl from the wrong side of the river."

"Now look here! That's not fair. Lady Winthrop isn't like that at all! She seemed anxious to get all the people she could, and she wouldn't even know that your side of the river is not the aristocratic side. She's the most democratic Christian lady I've ever seen. If you'd like to go I'll see that she asks you. I know it will be all right, and I'll be calling for you a little before eight o'clock. I think from what she said that they are studying something along these lines of prophecy."

"Well, I certainly would enjoy hearing more about what we listened to tonight," said Frannie with a sigh. "I wish mother was where she could hear that man sometimes. I don't think mother has ever heard anything like that. Do you suppose that was all true, or is some of it just fanciful, just some imagination added to a few vague facts?"

"No, definitely not," said Willoughby. "This man we heard tonight ranks as one of the foremost Christian scholars in the city, and indeed I understand, in the country. He sifts his facts before he presents them to the world, and he is not only a scholar, but very spiritual, they say. Shall we go and hear him again sometime?"

"I would love to," said Frannie wistfully. "It is all so new to me. It makes the Bible seem real, and brings the prophecies right down to where we live, not as if they were away off and rather uncertain."

"Yes, it does," said Willoughby. "That's what struck me when I talked with those friends of mine. I thought at first they were just fanatical on that subject, but they certainly managed to make me wonder if there was something in it. And then I began to think what if it were true that Christ may appear any day. If it is it makes living in these days seem almost grand. Did you think of that when he was talking tonight about the silver trumpet sounding, and all those signs which precede the return of Christ to the earth later? Those were very interesting. I always supposed those signs in the sun and moon and so on meant the end of the world and the Judgment Day."

"So did I," admitted Frannie, "and I believe most people do who have read the Bible as carelessly as I have."

"Well, I guess that is true, but it's thrilling to realize that the times of those things may be almost upon us. And of course there were ancient prophecies fulfilled when Christ came to earth the first time. I remember studying that around Christmas time when I was a little kid in Sunday School. But nobody talked to me then about any coming *back* again. I always thought things were just going on and on this way till sometime there would come a day of judgment and then there would be Heaven."

"Yes, I guess I thought so too," said Frannie. "Of course they didn't study about anything like that in college, not even in the Bible course. It was mostly like a history course with some poetry mixed in."

"Yes, that's about the size of it. But I didn't take Bible in my course. In our university it was known as one of those easy make-shifts taken to escape really hard work. Of course engineering was my major, and I just took what went with it. But I see my mistake now. Of course if the Bible really is the Word of God, as my mother taught me, it should be the most important!"

"Yes," said Frannie, "I suppose it should. I never thought of that. And I have never counted it very important at all, although of course I've believed it."

"Well, you're one ahead of me," said the young man gravely. "I'm not sure I have, not always. Though of late, with this war, I've been thinking I was wrong to let doubts in. Doubts don't help the situation much in times like these. Not for men, anyway."

"No, nor for women either," said Frannie seriously. "It doesn't look very happy ahead in life for anybody, does it? Unless there is something to expect like what we heard tonight."

"That's right," said Willoughby.

They walked on till they came to the bridge, and looking down the crystal way they saw the moon shining, making the path of the river into beaten gold. They stood there for some minutes quietly looking.

"It is a glorious sight, isn't it?" said the young man. "I keep thinking what Lady Winthrop said about it. She had some Bible verses about the street of the city being pure gold, as it were transparent glass. I can see what she meant now, can't you? Look down toward the city and see those tall buildings. It isn't hard to imagine the unearthly beauty of a Heavenly City in this light, with the soft mist of the evening about it. That Lady Winthrop is a remarkable woman, and it doesn't seem as if she was old in the least. She has the naive childlikeness of a very young person, or she never would have thought of such similes, even with that Bible verse to start on."

"Yes, she seemed so to me," said Frannie, "though of course I saw her only a few minutes. But I do want to know her better. I thought she was lovely, and I know mother would love her. I hope we can be friends."

"I'm sure you will be," said Willoughby with conviction.

Then suddenly Frannie swung around and looked upstream.

"Look!" she said. "It's wonderful up this way too. Those are 'the eternal hills.' And see that tower of stone among the evergreens, and the river just below like a sheet of silver. It might be a part of the Heavenly City."

"Yes, it's wonderful!" said Willoughby. And then he turned and looked down at her with a great gentleness in his face.

"You're a bit of a poet yourself, aren't you?" he said with a tender smile in his eyes for the sweet girl.

After a minute or two longer he drew her hand within his arm, and they started on again.

"I'd like to linger here till the moon sets," he said half wistfully, "but you and I are both working people. We have to get to work early in the morning. I mustn't keep you up too late. Of course it isn't to be compared with the hour you would go home from one of Marietta's dances that she tried to tempt you with, but we aren't in her class, so we won't worry about that. Besides, I suppose you have to think about not worrying your sick mother by staying too late."

"Yes," said Frannie. "You're very thoughtful, and most kind. My mother will appreciate it I know. As I do also. But it has been very lovely tonight, and I've learned a lot. I shall never forget that sermon. It made me feel that the Bible is as real today as when it was written, and that it is for me as much as ever it was for the people in the New Testament days."

For answer Val Willoughby laid his hand over Frannie's with a quick warm pressure.

"I'm glad!" he said, and then added: "I'm glad we went. I think that sermon made me see a lot of things also that I've been missing for a long time. Somehow I think that you have helped, too. There's something in having a friend along who understands."

"Oh, thank you!" said Frannie. "Yes, I think I do understand. Because it's something I've never had myself, and always felt uneasy about it. Only I couldn't bring it out in the open, because I had to be strong for my mother's sake."

They were still for a long time as they walked slowly down the paved way from the bridge, and the bright silver street stretched away to where the softly-lit towers and turrets of Lady Winthrop's imaginary city stood shadowy against a star-pricked dome of blue.

As they turned to go up to the little old white picket gate of the brick house, Willoughby said in a tone that was almost like a sacrament:

"I'm glad I have found you. It is good to have you for a friend. In the uncertain days that are ahead of us both perhaps we can study this thing out together."

"Oh!" said Frannie softly, and her voice was so soft it was scarcely audible.

And while all this was going on two men had been waiting silently, back in the shadow of great alder bushes, up several paces from the inland side of the house, one a tall man, and the other burly, with a shovel held in his hard hand, the spoon part of the implement stuck sharply in the ground where the outer frozen crust had been removed for a foot or so. The man was leaning back against the stout handle of the shovel in an interval of his cautious labor. At his feet, well concealed by a pile of snow, lay a worn ōld tool box with a sturdy pickax beside it, both its pointed ends caked with frozen mud and ice.

"We oughtn't to have come so early," said the big man. "You don't have very good sense in your calculations, Mike. I didn't want any of the family around while we do this."

"Well, they didn't any of them go out *last* Sunday. They went to bed early. Every light out at eight-thirty. I figured they'd do the same this week. But anyhow, don't you worry. The young dame will be all absorbed in her boy-friend. She won't notice anything out of the way, and anyway nobody can see us from the house."

"Okay," said the other. "But it seems to me you've bungled this all the way through. What exactly did that agent say about the owner? Tell me again. Tell me every word."

"Well, he said he hadn't heard from him yet. He said the old chap was sick and had gone to a sanitarium, and he couldn't get in touch with him."

"But what did he say about a contract?"

"Said there wasn't any. Said they just rented the house and paid one month's rent down. Their month is up the seventh. He said if we paid a lump sum down we could take over, and he'd send a notice to the folks that the place was sold."

"The seventh! But that's too late! We've got to bring our stuff here now and get going. I've got big obligations."

"Yep. I tol' him that, and he said there wasn't no reason in the world if we wanted to, that we couldn't bring lumber here and park it on the back of the lot.

The tenants never asked how large the lot was. They just wanted the house anyhow. So I told Nick to bring on yer lumber tonight. That okay with you?"

"What? Do you mean he's bringing it here, tonight, *now*, in a few minutes? Why, the folks will hear. You can't get away with that."

"Oh *sure* we can. Not just in a few minutes I don't mean, for I figured it would take us a couple of hours to get these yere wires uncovered and pulled out the way you want. So I told him to begin to load up around ten and come in by the back road. You couldn't get a sledge down the river without making a whole lotta noise, and being an unusual sound it might be noticed, wake somebody up, you know. But coming in by the back road, if we have them boards *carried* in, one at a time, and lay 'em down careful-like there won't be a sound to give us away. And by morning they'll only be a pile of old boards. You know all of 'em are weathered stuff. And if they see 'em they'll just think they never noticed 'em before."

"Well, maybe so," said the big man uncomfortably. "But this ain't the way I intended to work it. I figured on playing safe every step of the way, and we *would*, too, if you had carried out *your* part of the bargain. If anything goes wrong on this deal I'll just lay it to your fault and pay you accordingly, understand that?"

"Say, look here now, you signed a paper saying how much you were willing to give."

"Sure I did, but there were things you were to do, and you haven't done one of 'em on time yet."

"Well, I couldn't help it, could I, if the old guy got sick and went to some sanitarium? I done my best to make things come out anyway though, and I think you'll find everything okay. The only thing I can't figure out is how you're going to get that there mike outta that there cellar. Why, they might discover it was there most any day now, especially when they go to clean the cellar. You know dames like that are apt to be pretty frisky about getting spic and span by spring."

"It's not the mike I'm worrying about," said Gran-

niss. "We could easy get another, but there are incriminating papers, maps, floor plans of defense plants,
and other stuff there that we've *got to have!* An' we've
got to have 'em before the seventh!"

"I see. But how are you gonta get 'em out without
wakin' up the folks?" asked Mike perplexedly.

"You just leave that to me," said the older man.
"I'm figuring to wait till some dark night when there's
a lotta wind, mebbe even rain, and do a swift job of
digging when we start, just tunnel under to that little
closet in the cellar and tap the wall. Take out the stuff
and the microphone and the recording machine and all
and install it in the new shed we're putting up back
here. Doing that we can go on using the same transmitter that we had before, and nobody the wiser. An' if
the folks in the house discover us working, well, they're
just women, and there are ways of handling them. I
don't intend to stop at anything."

"You don't say!" said Mike, looking speculatively
across the starlight to the other man, secretly planning
to leave any "rough stuff" to his partner in crime. "But
how come they didn't discover your arrangements when
these folks took over the house?"

"Oh, we had that all camouflaged inside. Even if the
cops had come into the cellar they couldn't have found
it. It was an extra bricked-in addition we built off the
far end of the cellar behind the furnace, and it was so
finished you couldn't have found the opening unless
you knew how. One loose brick that looked solid as
Gibraltar, and came out, and then behind a panel there
was the key hole. But even that you wouldn't have recognized. It was just a sort of slit, and the key was thin
as a knife blade. Oh, we had it all fixed up. It was great.
And of course when nobody lived in this house we
could come here any time and use it nearly all night
without any danger of discovery."

"So! That was the way it was!" said Mike thoughtfully to himself, laying up this knowledge for a time
when it would be more lucrative to remember certain
things than it now was to keep silence about them.

"Now, Mike, stop right about there where you are

and reach down with your fingers. See if you can strike any wires with your hand yet. I think you ought to have almost got it uncovered."

Mike got down on his knees and worked away beside his prone shovel, running his hand down farther and farther, bringing up handfuls of ashes and small stones.

"Yep," he said, puffing softly with his exertions, "I think I got her. Two wires, ain't there? *Say? Am I* liable to get a shock doin' this?"

"No, no shock, not to amount to anything. Got the two wires you say? Okay. Then we're safe. Now while we wait for the lumber suppose you do a little quiet digging. Go slow, not too continuous you know, else it might attract some dame's attention. Get as far as you can while we wait and have some bushes and weeds ready to put it all under cover in case somebody should come by. Hark! What's that sound? That isn't a cop's car, is it? Over there in the next street?"

"Naw, that there's the ten o'clock bus. She stops at that corner for three minutes and then goes on. I got this neighborhood pretty well memorized. You know I don't go into nothing like this without making sure I won't get caught. But what I don't understand is what you said the first day. You spoke about a powder plant, and I can't just figure how these two things work together."

"Oh, don't you? Well, you're not so foresighted as I thought you were. Don't you see the easiest way would have been to put up a rough building, call it a powder plant, make a small output of the stuff, enough to throw anyone off the track, and have only workmen who are wise to keep their mouths shut. Then we can use our radio all we please without exciting suspicion. That's why I wanted to buy the place. That would have been the easiest way, besides giving us the look of being deep in defense work. And that's what we will eventually do as soon as we can get entire possession. But in the meantime this lumber can be brought in very slowly, a little at a time, until we have enough here to begin to build. Then we can bring our own men here, put up a rough shell in a hurry, and not attract attention. You see it's wisest to keep attention away from here as much as possible. After we get the shell of a building up we can build a sound proof compartment out of sight. Of course if we could buy the house and put the people out of it at once, offer them a bonus or something, we could use the old arrangement, but if we can't get them out right away, we'll have to fix up something to do till we get possession. But there are always ways to get people out if you offer money enough. I figure this ain't any exception. Hey! What's that? Steps."

"That's the young guy bringin' his gal home. Just lie low. He don't stay long after he comes. He works early somewheres. Guess I'll sort of let up till he leaves."

The big man settled down on the tool chest behind the group of bushes, and the two remained motionless for several minutes, while they watched the lights in the little brick house. Someone came into the kitchen and got a pitcher of water and a tray. They could hear the tinkle of glasses and the clink of pieces of ice. Then the kitchen light went out and there was another interval. But they did not have to wait long until they heard the front door open; voices, footsteps, and then they could hear the young man going down the walk.

"Okay!" said Mike at last in a cautious voice. "The young guy has gone. Now we can work again. It won't be many minutes before all the lights go out, and the house will be asleep."

"Well, don't take any chances!" warned the big man. "What time did you say that lumber would arrive?"

"He didn't say what time exactly. He said he'd be along plenty late so we didn't needta worry. What's that?"

Footsteps! Footsteps! Quiet, steady, measured. A low word now and then stopping a moment, then passing slowly by.

"Sounds like cops!" murmured Mike.

"No brass buttons!" murmured Granniss.

The footsteps passed on, and the sound died away indefinably.

After a little Mike peered into the darkness after them.

"Where do you 'spose them two went? There ain't none of them new houses occupied yet, is there?"

"How should I know? That's your job. That's what I hired you for."

"Well, I guess I'm just getting jittery. I didn't like the way they stopped walking, but there ain't any place down that way where they could rightly go."

He got up and straightened his stiff back, took a step or two out toward the street.

"Hi! there, come on back and get to work," growled Granniss. "They went off toward the bridge. I'm most sure I heard them cross the bridge. Don't be a fool. You'll have that lumber on top of your work before you know it, and we don't want to stay here all night, you know."

"Keep your shirt on, man! You don't have to do a thing but sit still and see your orders carried out. And mind this, fella, I'm just as anxious to earn my money as you are to pay it, so pipe down and keep calm. And——*there*, I hear those footsteps going on now. They were most likely stoppin' to talk a little before separatin'. One has gone on across the bridge, and the other has likely taken the dirt road where his footsteps wouldn't sound. Now, let's get back on the job. You want I should foller them wires now, back to the leanto on the kitchen? Is that right?"

"Yes. Make it as deep as you can and then cover it over somehow. Little sticks across near together, covered with branches. Snow flung across it. Nobody walks across this place anyway. We've checked up on that in the past when we used the empty house."

"Okay!"

Later there were steps in the distance, but the two men were intent on the trench they were constructing, and paid little heed.

The night grew deeper, and the darkness more intense, with only the far dim stars above in the blackness of midnight blue.

And then at last came noiseless wheels and a muffled

engine, rolling down the incline of the back street almost imperceptibly, and Mike striding silently across the ruts of the field to stand in the road and wave and point out the stopping place.

Two dark figures slipped from the driver's seat and approached the load, rubber shod, lifting a single board and following Mike into the field behind the brick house. Mike went like a cat across to the place he had just cleared and indicated just where this first board should be placed. It was all done without talk, the directions given by motions, the men all acting as if they had been trained in a school of silence. Just once a board slipped and went down with a thud, and the crew looked fearfully about and crouched near the ground out of sight. Then after an interval the work went swiftly on till all the boards were neatly piled, low lying, and a few branches scattered over with some snow atop. It was a well camouflaged pile of lumber, and to all casual appearances had been there perhaps all winter. Only one very familiar with the scene would have noticed that the landscape was at all changed. Then the truck that brought them went away like a shadow into the darkness, and after a few minutes the two men slipped as silently away, Mike carrying the old tool chest on his brawny shoulder.

A few minutes later a canny little upstart of a moon peered brightly out from behind a cloud and went on with its journey across the sky, flinging down a flash of silver to the ice-locked river to sail like a bright twin up its length to the west and disappear with it behind the mountains.

And then two silent figures detached themselves from two of the little new empty houses up across the street, and went silently over to the late scene of activities behind the brick house, and carefully examined every inch of the way, bringing small pencils of light to bear in a flash or two upon the broken snow and branches covering the excavation, and the pile of lumber. They nodded at one another, and then together stole away.

And in the little brick house the family slept secure, and the moon rose higher, and smiled down on that street of the city that two young people had been talking about that evening as they looked down the silver way, till in her dreams Frannie almost thought she saw the tower and pinnacles of the Holy City, and she smiled in her sleep. Rest and peace and comfort and unawareness of the danger and the sinister plans that were working all about her, danger for the whole beautiful world of peace into which Frannie had been born.

Chapter 14

FRANNIE'S PIANO ARRIVED by way of the Bluebell Neighborly Truck Express, about the middle of the morning on Monday, and under Nurse Branner's direction was duly installed in the living room, giving the place a cosy air of homelikeness. With it had come two fine old oil paintings of a quaint grandmother with a white organdy cap and kerchief, and a grim grandfather in old time attire.

"I reckon she wants them pictures hung on the wall, don't she? I brung the hooks they was hung on, and I told her I'd hang 'em for her," said the old man who had brought them.

So the nurse went up to Mrs. Fernley for instructions, and when Frannie came home that afternoon there was her beloved piano in the place that had been left vacant for it, and there hung the old pictures in the same relation to the piano that they had occupied in Bluebell.

"Oh, this is nice, isn't it?" she said with a happy smile as she looked around the room. "It begins to look like home now. When do you think mother will be able to come downstairs, Miss Branner?"

"Well, she's going to sit up awhile today, and if her pulse says so, perhaps the doctor will let her come down tomorrow. He's coming again in the morning, and

I'll ask him. So perhaps we'll have another surprise for you tomorrow night when you come home. But don't get your hopes up too high. He may think she ought to stay upstairs another day or two before she attempts to come down."

Frannie ran up the stairs lightheartedly to see her mother, and her feet seemed to have the old spring, her voice the old ring as she entered her mother's room.

"My dear!" greeted her mother. "You sound more like your old self than you have since we came here. What has happened?"

"Oh, mother, I'm so glad to have my dear piano back again, and it looks good to see the pictures on the wall. Now it seems as if the family had the right setting."

Her mother smiled.

"Poor silly child!" she said smilingly. "I'm afraid you've got a bit of the old family aristocracy in you yet in spite of adversity. Don't encourage it. It always brings discontent."

Frannie laughed gaily.

"Don't worry, mother dear, I could live just as happily without the old family portraits and even the piano, though I *am* glad to have it, and it does make it seem more like home here."

"Yes, I know, dear. I was only teasing you. But now, sit down and tell me about your day, and about last night. I did so want to hear about the church, only the nurse was quite tyrannical. She insisted that I go to sleep before you came back. And most of all I want to know about that young man. Frannie, you've got to be awfully careful. Are you quite sure he's all right?"

Frannie laughed gaily.

"Well, you can feel quite comfortable about him, mother. I am sure you would like him. He seems to have been brought up with very much the same ideals you have tried to inculcate in me, and he's interested in real things. Books and music, and even the Bible. He's interested in knowing what Bible students think of this war in relation to the prophecies. That ought to take with you, mother. I'm sure he would please you."

"Well, yes, he is certainly good-looking, and pleasing in his manners. I saw that in just the few minutes when he carried me up to my bed the day I was taken sick. But——" Mrs. Fernley still looked worried.

"Oh, yes, I knew you'd say 'but' again, mother. But I'm sure you would like the way he talks about churches, and the way he looks at life. He seems what you call 'real.' And he was so interested in the sermon last night. We talked about it all the way home."

"Oh yes, how was that sermon? Is the man a good preacher?"

"Indeed he is, mother. He's your kind. He was most interesting. He knows the Bible so well, and he talks about it so clearly that he makes it most fascinating. Mother, he thinks that the return of Christ to the earth may not be far away! And if that's true, then what they call 'the Rapture' is even nearer. That's the time when He comes to the air to take up out of the earth the people who really believe in Him."

"My dear! That is very interesting. It makes everything seem so very near—as if we were going on a journey in just a few days and might begin to pack and get ready to leave. Of course we don't have to pack for that, for somehow God is going to make us ready, but it makes it seem so very much more real. And of course, it may not be as near as we hope, then again it may."

"But, mother! I didn't know you believed that Christ was coming back again."

"Yes, I have believed it a long time, but in a very vague way. I've read some books about it, in the days when I had time to read. I even joined a Bible class once where they were studying something about that. But then when your father died I felt so down-hearted and there was so much to do, and so much to be planned for, and it seemed so impossible to take hold of life again and go on without your father, that I didn't think much more about it. It almost faded from my mind, and began to seem like a dream, just a mirage. Your father was interested in it too, and after he was gone I couldn't bear to keep on thinking about what he had talked of so much. It seemed that a door was shut into what had been a bright vision."

"Oh, mother, I wish you had told me this before. I didn't think you knew about this hope that those people tonight seemed to have so clearly."

"Darling! I'm sorry I have been so remiss. Well, we'll have to get hold of things together now. But Frannie, this young man who took you to church tonight, was he really interested in all this, or was it just an excuse to have a good time with a pleasant sweet little girl?"

"No, mother, you mustn't think that about him. He isn't a bit flirtatious. He was really interested. He said he had heard about this preacher and his sermons on prophecy and he wanted to listen to him and see if he could get any light on the subject. I think he is really interested. We talked about it all the way home."

"Well, dear, that sounds pleasant and good. I am glad, of course, for you to have a friend who is interested in religious things. But there is one phase of it that I was thinking about all the evening as I lay here and thought about you. He may be very attractive, and have a wonderful Christian character, and yet he may not be especially interested in you. You'll have to remember that constantly. I hate to spoil your pleasure in the evening right at the start, but I'm sure you ought to be warned. It isn't just like going with the boys at home whom you have known all your life, all your growing-up days. You're a stranger here. You're lonely. And under those circumstances a bit of kindness, an invitation to go to church, means a lot more to you than it would if the boys you have known for years had asked you. What I am afraid of is that you will let your heart get set on this young man, when he really is only being kind and pleasant."

"Oh, no, mother!" said Frannie quickly, her cheeks flushing uneasily. "You mustn't think that. I know he is only being kind. Surely it's all right to talk about hereafter and that sort of thing with someone who believes as I do."

"Of course, dear. And I know I can count on my

girl to set a guard on her thoughts. Remember, you don't know anything of his circumstances. He may be engaged to someone else who is not here just now. Or at least interested in someone else. Miss Branner tells me this young man—Willoughby, isn't that his name?—she tells me he belongs to a wealthy family. She didn't know whether he was wealthy in his own right or not, but his aunt is very wealthy, a woman of society. And he is living with her at present."

"Yes, I know," said Frannie lifting thoughtful eyes to her mother, "we passed his aunt's house this evening. It is very beautiful, and costly looking. But he doesn't act as if he felt that he was rich. However, mother, it wouldn't make any difference. I'm not going to be silly and get a broken heart. I've thought all those things out, and I decided God sent him to help me over these new hard days when I was put in a strange new place, so I could be pleasant and cheerful all the time. But I'll keep sensible. One doesn't have to fall in love, mother, with every attractive man who is kind for a few days. But, listen! He wants me to go with him over to Lady Winthrop's house tomorrow night to a Bible class along these same lines. He says she wants to get new members for her class, and he had promised to go once anyway. He didn't know whether he could spare the time to go again or not, but he said he knew she would like me to come, and if it was all right with me he would call for me tomorrow night. He said she told him it would probably be over before ten o'clock. Do you think I shouldn't have agreed to go?"

"Oh, I don't see any harm in that, dear. He is just helping you to get adjusted to your new life. Going to a Bible study class doesn't mean anything significant. Yes, go, and get better acquainted with that dear lady who did so much for me when I was taken sick. Now don't worry. I just wanted you to be warned, and then I can trust you to be my wise true girl, and walk your sweet natural way, the way you always did at home."

"Thank you, mother dear. I'll remember what you say. And anyway I'm not out looking for somebody to fall in love with. I have a job, and whatever else comes my way I'll enjoy while I can, but I won't lose my head over it. Good night, mother dear!"

And Frannie kissed her mother and slipped away to her own room, thinking pleasantly of the nice time she was to have the next evening. And resolutely whenever the memory of a friendly smile or a pleasant look came to her mind she put away the thought of it, with a mere recognition that he had been very kind. And then she would go off in memory to the things they had talked over together.

So it was with a very happy heart that she hurried home that afternoon. Val Willoughby was not with her. He had told her in the morning that he had some extra work that would keep him late at the plant so she did not look for him as she sailed out into the crisp air. She had a recurrence of thanksgiving that the weather was still clear and fine and the skating still perfect.

On her way she got to thinking of the two fellows who had so annoyed her before, and wondered why she had not seen anything more of them. Could it be that they were really disabled? Or were they afraid to come back lest the knowledge of what they had done had crept back to the heads of their departments? Well, she was not missing them anyway, and was relieved that they no longer crossed her path. Still, she would be sorry if she had seriously hurt either of them. Of course skates were rather dangerous weapons. But they were all she had, and she felt sure that if she hadn't had them and if Val Willoughby hadn't come along just in time she would have had a serious time.

She ran gaily up the steps from the ice, swinging her skate shoes by their straps, and into the house.

"Ummmmm-m! How good that dinner smells!" she said. "How am I ever going to get along without you when you go to your next case?"

The nurse grinned. She was pressing something soft and blue, and as Frannie closed the door behind her she put down her iron, slipped the garment off the ironing board and handed it over.

"There!" she said triumphantly. "I guess that's all right for you to wear tonight. Your mother said this was what you would be likely to choose."

"Oh, but this isn't a party!" said Frannie with wide pleased eyes. "It's only a Bible class. I don't suppose they'll take off their coats and hats."

"Oh, yes, they will," said the nurse decidedly. "I went to one of those classes myself once, and some people just ran in wearing their bright dinner dresses, coats just thrown around them. A few came from a distance and wore coats and hats, but most of them were quite dressed up. You want a pretty dress on, especially since you are going with a young man. You don't want him to be ashamed of you, you know."

"Oh!" said Frannie with a bit of newly acquired dignity. "This isn't a social engagement, you know. Mr. Willoughby merely thought I would enjoy the study because of something in the sermon we heard last night. I don't think he would need to worry about how I was dressed. He is merely escorting me over there. Nobody will know, probably, that I came with him."

The nurse gave the girl a quick look with a queer little pucker to her lips.

"Oh! You don't say so!" said Nurse Branner. "Well, even so, you might as well look your best. I think Lady Winthrop would like that. Besides, she took the trouble to send word this morning and make sure you were coming with Valiant Willoughby. She said she was counting on your presence."

"Oh, how lovely!" said Frannie. "And you are sure that blue won't be too dressy for just a Bible class?"

"Yes, I'm sure. And what's more your mother was sure too. She told me where to find it in the big chest of drawers."

"Oh, all right. If mother thinks it is the right thing then I'll wear it, but I wouldn't like to feel overdressed."

"You won't!" said the nurse contentedly. "Take it from me. I've lived in this town long enough to know the customs."

So Frannie took the blue dress, thanked Nurse Branner with a warm hug and kiss and ran upstairs to kiss her mother.

"Mother dear, I feel very selfish going out two nights in succession," she said after the usual greetings had been exchanged. "Wouldn't you rather I would just explain when Mr. Willoughby comes that I feel tired and think I had better stay home tonight."

"No!" said Mrs. Fernley. "No! Not on any account. I certainly am glad to have you attend a Bible class, and especially when it is at that dear woman's house. And don't be a fool, Frannie! Just take this thing as you would have taken going to prayer meeting at home, or going to a church social with your Cousin Harry."

Frannie gave her mother a relieved smile.

"All right, mother. I'll do my best."

"And don't you think another thing about what we talked of last night. I didn't want to make you self-conscious. Just take it for granted that this young man is a friendly neighbor and let it go at that. Don't go to analyzing your feelings and his. I'm sorry I said a thing."

"There, mother, you needn't be. I'll do as you say. But do you really think I should dress up so much?"

"Yes. You can trust that nurse. She knows. Now run down and get your supper and then come up and get dressed so I can look you over before you go. Besides, I'd like to hear you play a minute or two on your piano if there is time. A touch of the Moonlight Sonata would give me a melody for the evening."

So Frannie ran down to her supper. They had a gay happy time laughing and talking, and Bonnie looked at her sister enviously.

"I wish I could go with you tonight, Frannie," she said wistfully. "I like meetings. I haven't been to a church in a long time."

"I know, dear," said the sister. "But you shall pretty soon. When mother gets well and we can all go together we will have nice times going to church and Sunday School every Sunday. And I am sorry to have to leave you behind so much, little dear, but you see I'm getting acquainted with places for us to go to. And tonight

Lady Winthrop has invited me to a Bible class at her pretty house where you were, and so I shall see it. You know you wanted me to see it."

"Yes, I wanted you to see it, Frannie dear," sighed the little girl. "Yes, I'm glad to stay with mother and Miss Branner so you can see my nice pretty lady. And sometime we'll go there together, won't we, Frannie? And go across the bridge?"

"Yes, sometime. Perhaps pretty soon. I'm sure there'll be a way."

So the little girl gave her sister a sunny smile.

"You have a nice time, Frannie," she said politely, like an older person.

Then Nurse Branner sent Frannie to get ready for the evening and got the dishes out of the way herself.

"You go on. You can't be sure just what time Mr. Willoughby will come for you, and your mother will want to see if you look all right before you go," she said.

So it was still early when Frannie went into her mother's room to be looked over. Presently the nurse and Bonnie came up to help with the inspection and they all pronounced that she looked all right.

"Just pretty perfect, Frannie," said little Bonnie quaintly.

"And now," said the mother, "I want to hear the old piano. Go down and play the Moonlight Sonata, and the Spinning Song, and then if you have time before you go give me one of the dear old hymns I love. But don't hold up your going if your escort comes before you are done. I'll carry the tune over in my heart till tomorrow night when you can finish for me."

So Frannie, in her pretty blue frock, with her coat on her arm, went downstairs and began to play. Softly, sweetly, and then gradually louder till the whole little house was filled with the glorious sound, and it stole out across the frozen river into the stillness of early moonlight, and filled the air about. Two men who were walking over on the other side of the river bank, reconnoitering, heard it.

"Say, if they'd keep that up we could get a lot of

work done tonight without any chance of being caught," said the big man.

"No chance this early," said the other shaking his head. "They're going out somewheres or else there's company coming. We better make it late tonight. They'll be good and tired and sleep sound."

"I guess you're right," said the other, and strode along silently, half annoyed by the tenderness of the lovely music that stole across to them.

But the Moonlight Sonata was only about two-thirds finished when there came a peremptory knock on the door that startled the nurse who had been waiting at the top of the stairs to go down and open the door when the young man should come. Somehow the knock didn't sound quite like his quiet summons the other times he had called.

But Frannie had not heard the knock, so sure she was that her escort would not come yet, and so intent she was upon the music. She knew her mother's critical ear would detect any lapses in her memorizing. So she played on and did not notice the nurse as she slipped down the stairs and went quietly to the door, did not realize that someone was coming in, as she swept on through several difficult passages to the end. And then suddenly it came upon her that there were others in the room.

With a bewildered look in her eyes she whirled about on the piano stool and looked at her guests, expecting to see Val Willoughby. But it was not Val Willoughby. Instead there were three people standing astonished just inside the room, as the nurse, also astonished, closed the door behind them to keep out the cold and looked from one to the other of the three young people who stood there staring at Frannie. It did not take her long to realize that one was Marietta Hollister. The two young men who accompanied her she could not figure out. She seemed never to have seen them before.

But Frannie knew. Suddenly and appallingly it was brought to her startled consciousness that these were three enemies standing before her, and she was so taken aback that for an instant she could not believe her senses. Then suddenly she lifted her delicate patrician chin and surveyed them, one at a time, coolly, haughtily, with a look that put them in the class of intruders.

She came at once to her feet.

"Yes?" she said in a clear cold voice. "Did you want something?" She addressed her question to Marietta who stood in the forefront, with the two abashed young hoodlums in her wake.

"Why yes," drawled Marietta in her most dominating tone. "I came to find you. I brought a couple of young friends to introduce to you. You remember I promised I would. And we thought we would take you over to our opening night and let you see what we are doing. I'm sure you will want to join us when you see what a gorgeous time we are going to show you to-night."

Frannie swept the faces of the two young men with a freezing glance. She had instantly recognized her two assailants, Kit Creeber and Spike Emberly.

"Thank you," she said turning back to Marietta, "it will not be necessary for you to introduce your friends to me. I have already met them under most unpleasant circumstances, and I do not care to have any further acquaintance with them."

"Oh, now that is rather rude of you, isn't it? They have come to do you a favor. They have come to ask the pleasure of being your escorts to the dance I told you about. If you have had some quarrel in the past just forget it and come along with us. We'll show you a perfectly good time, and you will forget your differences. Come on. Is this your coat? Mr. Emberly, put it on her and show her what a good sort you are."

"No!" said Frannie sharply. "I do not wish his assistance, and I do not wish to go out with any of you. Besides I am going out myself, and I shall have to ask you to excuse me for I must get ready at once." Frannie turned and would have hurried up the stairs, but Marietta angrily placed herself in the way of the stairs.

"Oh!" she said disagreeably. "Do you play in some night club? I wasn't aware you played. We might be able to offer you a small salary for playing for our dancing if you are interested. You really play rather well."

The very drawl of her voice was an insult, and suddenly Frannie felt tears and laughter coming upon her. But she must not go into hysterics before these, her enemies, sent to try her spirit perhaps. She was enabled to turn an amused smile upon her strange guests.

"I'm not interested," she said, "and I do not play in a night club." Frannie's voice was very quiet and courteous, as if the questions she had been asked had been perfectly genuine.

But suddenly there came another voice, clear, assured, dominating. Val Willoughby, standing in the kitchen doorway:

"Are you ready, Fran? I think it is time we were starting." Then his eyes swept the room, bringing his keen glance to bear straight into the eyes of the two frightened, furtive young men who tried to shuffle unobtrusively toward the door behind them.

"I guess we better be going then," murmured Kit Creeber nervously, edging nearer to the door.

"Yes, I guess you had," said Willoughby fervently, and stepping quickly forward swung the front door wide to let them pass. Then he turned, as they slunk by him, and looked at the startled Marietta who was too astonished even to be angry yet.

"So!" he said scornfully. "Is this the kind of company you keep, Marietta? Is it possible you know what kind of rascals those two fellows are? Or did I arrive just in time to give you protection?"

"Protection!" sneered Marietta furiously, suddenly aroused to the situation. "Just who do you think you are anyway? You're no one to preach? What kind of company do *you* keep? Are you doing slum work too?" Then she turned with head held high and angry eyes flashing and sailed out after her two commandeered escorts, slamming the door of the house behind her and stamping down the walk on her high expensive heels.

Chapter 15

WHEN MARIETTA REACHED her car which had been parked across the street from the brick house, there was no sign of her two escorts.

In vain she looked into the back seat, and turned on her lights to search for her erstwhile attendants, but they were nowhere to be seen. In quite a dignified lofty tone she called their names: "Mr. Emberly! Mr. Creeber! Where are you?" But repeated calls, varying from annoyance to actual anger, and then even fury, brought no response.

Once she thought she heard a cracking sound from over behind the kitchen of the cottage, and a floundering stir in the darkness, but when she took her flashlight from the pocket of her car and started over that way to investigate, she found nothing but a mass of disordered stones and bricks powdered with dirty snow, with sticks and branches in confusion. No sign of the two young men in their shiny dinner coats and rather shabby overcoats anywhere. And finally in disdain she picked her way over the roughness back toward her car. Stepping uncertainly, suddenly she felt one foot go down through the mass of branches into a deep place, so that she fell full length. She was about to cry out for help, till suddenly she remembered the merry eyes of that other girl. She couldn't stand Frannie's scorn. This seemed to be some kind of trough. What could it mean? In the back yard right behind the house! Why did anybody have a right to have a place like that in their back yard?

She called out again, guardedly. If those two horrid boys had any sense of honor they would come back and help her out. But of course what could one expect from boys who lived on the wrong side of the river and worked down the river at a factory!

Then she heard the front door open, voices, that ripple of a laugh, the memory of which had become so hateful to her! Mercy! She must get out of here. If she called out now Val would come and help her up, but he would read her a lecture, and the memory of his sneer about her erstwhile companions restrained her. Not for worlds would she let him know that her two knights had deserted her.

So she lay still with her hands plunged into the cold dirty snow that Mike had cast over the hole he had dug the night before.

She heard Val and Frannie come out the door and go down the street. She could hear the gay sound of their subdued voices as they walked toward the bridge. And when she heard them turn onto the bridge she tried again to struggle up, but only succeeded in plunging one foot down deeper and entangling it in some wires. Strange! Wires buried in a back yard. What did that mean?

She gave a quick violent jerk to her foot, and succeeded in losing her slipper down in that queer dark hole! What was she going to do now? Oh, she ought to have called Val Willoughby. He was always a gentleman. He would have helped her out, of course, and she would be on her way now. Even if he had tried to read her a lecture she could have given back as good as she got. He, lecturing her, when he was openly attending a girl like that who lived in a little insignificant house and worked down the river! He to presume to lecture her! Perhaps she had better go to Auntie Haversett and tell her what Val was doing, and get this ridiculous business stopped before it got too bad. She probably should have done that in the first place. Well, she'd got to get out of this hole, whatever she did!

So she wallowed about some more, and at last got a firm hold of the edge of this peculiar ditch into which she had fallen, and with edging and struggling was finally free. Out on firm ground again, she shivered; one stockinged foot was clinging to the brink. How was she going to get that slipper? Could she possibly hop over the rough ground to her car without it? No, that was out of the question. She had to find it. Then she remembered her flashlight and got it out of her pocket, turning it downward into the hole. Yes, there was the toe of her slipper, pointing upward, almost beyond reach. If she got down on the ground again, flat, she might reach it. How horrid, with an evening dress on. She wouldn't be fit to go to the dance afterward. It was all the fault of—well who was it the fault of? That girl, of course. If it hadn't been for that girl she would never have taken up this idea of helping downtrodden humanity to rise by means of dances. And she would never have asked the son of their gardener to bring those two fellows to help her in her scheme of providing escorts for the poor girls whom she was to help into a refined kind of social life in their own social class. But they were such good-looking fellows, really handsome in a way, quite challenging. How could she know they would turn out to be deserters? Cowards! Evidently Val and that girl had scared them stiff. Well, she had to get that slipper.

So down she got, carefully, and reaching as far as she could, just barely escaped touching the tip of the slipper's toe with the tip of her fingers. Well, she would evidently have to bend down a little farther!

Over she bent, stretched her arm to its fullest extent and found that the slipper had somehow entrenched itself in that mess of wire she had got into herself. So she struggled some more and finally lost her balance, and fell with her face in the frozen earth, cutting a gash in her chin on a sharp stone. For an instant she lay there struggling with angry tears that came unbidden to her eyes. She, Marietta Hollister, to be left deserted, lying in a ditch in an alien back yard on the wrong side of the river! And even the slum boys she had coaxed to come with her on this expedition had deserted her. What could possibly have made them do that? Young toughs they were. Why should they be afraid of Val Willoughby?

But at last Marietta by aid of her flashlight, and a strenuous effort, brought up her slipper triumphantly, and slid her foot into it, and then essayed to hobble over to her car, only to discover that the slipper was minus a heel!

Now what was she going to do? They were new slippers, too, and had cost plenty. Of course that didn't matter much, only to add to the annoyance. But she couldn't go to that dance without a heel on her slipper. She would have to go home, unless she could recover the heel. Even then, how would she make it stay on?

She turned back to the dark hole, and aimed her light down to its depths, but she could not find that imp of a heel. It was gone, away down to the bottom of Mike's excavations. And some day would he, or some other disloyal American, find that heel and wonder, and be afraid?

But Marietta had no idea of that now. She had to get to that dance, for nobody else could run things without her. And now that she had failed to bring the two young men she had promised, she would certainly have to hunt up two more somewhere.

At last she hobbled back to her car and got started on her way, growing momently more and more angry at Val Willoughby. For after all if he hadn't made a fool of himself with that strange working girl from the other side of the river she would never have got into all this.

So Marietta, blaming others for her own misdeeds, gradually in this way soothed her troubled spirits.

Frannie and Val went on their quiet way across the bridge, and when they had put sufficient distance between the brick house and themselves so that they were sure they could not be overheard by any recent enemies, Val said in a low confidential tone:

"Were you having a pretty tough time again, Frannie? I came in while you were talking. The nurse heard me outside and opened the door a crack, motioning me inside, so I got a fair idea of what was going on, but I didn't hear everything. Did I butt in too soon?"

"Oh no," said Frannie with a quick little breath of

a sigh. "I was so glad to see you, and to hear you. Your voice sounded like a refreshing shower on a thirsty day. It was grand of you! But—I hated for you to have to call down—your friend."

"My *friend!* Where did you get that?"

"Oh, isn't she? She implied the first time she came over here that you were something very special in the way of a friend."

"I know," said the young man, "she's been trying to imply that for a good many years, but it happens to be all on her side, not mine, thank you! But don't you worry about her. She's just a very determined girl who is trying to make everything go her way, and to run everything and everybody else. You see I've known her since we were youngsters and she was just that way when she was three. I was rather proud of your quiet voice and your smile in the face of her actual insults."

"Oh, well," laughed Frannie, "it was just funny. But how do you suppose a girl like that, a wealthy cultured girl, came to know those two unspeakable fellows that tried to get fresh with me?"

"Well, I think Marietta has taken up this war work the way she always does everything else, with a great deal of energy and no common sense. I used sometimes to wonder if she *hadn't* any sense. I guess she has, but she doesn't use it. I don't know where she ever picked up those two kids. She probably saw them somewhere and thought they were good-looking, or else some fool told her about them, and she thought they were plenty good enough for the kind of girls she was planning to help into what she calls 'social life.' However it was, they were good and scared when they saw me come in. Did you notice? I never in my life saw anything slink away as fast as those two did. I fancy they were afraid we would complain to the authorities. Have they been seen at your plant since your encounter with them?"

"No, I haven't seen them anywhere. I was almost afraid I might have hurt one of them with that skate. That really wasn't a very pleasant weapon to use on a face."

"Well you used it most effectively. I think I noted a scar on the chin of that one they call Spike. I trust it taught him a good lesson."

"Oh, but I didn't mean to do anything like that!"

"No, of course not, but remember how much worse they might have done for you if I hadn't come along and taken a hand. Well, let's forget them."

"Yes, let's. But why do you suppose that girl wanted to come here again? I'm afraid I was pretty rude to her the first time."

"Don't worry about that," said Val. "I'm quite sure she gave you plenty of reason to be."

"But I don't want to hate her," said Frannie with a troubled voice.

Val smiled down upon her in the moonlight.

"My mother used to tell me that I couldn't always like the things that people did, but I could love them because God did, or something like that. Did you ever hear that?"

"Yes, my mother taught me that, too. She said that we were to love everybody that Christ loved, but we didn't have to love what they did, and that made it possible for us to love them even when they were doing some very unpleasant things to us."

"Well, it's not always easy to get that point of view, is it? But it seems to me you have come mighty near to it. And now let's forget her too, and get ready to enjoy what's before us."

They turned in at the big white gateway and walked slowly toward the house, and then they saw more people coming from every direction.

"Why, they are turning in here," said Frannie. "There must be a lot of them."

"Yes, there are about fifty or sixty in the class, Lady Winthrop said," said Val.

"So many? Isn't that wonderful? I'm so glad you invited me!"

"Even though you had to miss the dance?"

They arrived at the door in a burst of giggles, which perhaps more than anything that had so far happened to them, made them feel better acquainted. And then

they entered the wide beautiful hall and were welcomed
by the sweet old lady in a soft gray gown with her
pretty white hair in lovely waves to frame her face, and
a look of joy in her eyes. And right away she introduced
them to this one and that one:

"These are two dear young friends of mine. I want
you to know them. I hope they are going to enjoy our
study so much that they will want to be with us every
week." Frannie's heart gave a pleasant little thrill of
pleasure. It was so nice to be taken into the inner circle
as it were by this sweet old lady.

"Our Bibles! We didn't bring our Bibles!" whispered
Frannie as she looked around at the rustling leaves of
the many Bibles.

But almost instantly the need was supplied, for Lady
Winthrop touched Val's arm and motioned toward a
pile of Bibles on a table by the door, and he quickly
brought some, for them and for a few others who had
come Bibleless. And then the meeting started with a
song—somebody at the piano, Frannie couldn't see
who—and everybody taking part. It seemed somehow
different from ordinary singing. It was so heart-felt. She
stole a shy look at her escort and noted his fine clear
voice. His singing bore other voices along.

And then a young man to whom they had been
introduced, and who was sitting near the piano arose
and began to pray, exactly as if he were seeking personal help for each one for the evening's study.

And so the lesson began.

Frannie found she knew her way about her Bible
pretty well, although she was greatly amazed at the
startling truths that developed through this well-versed
teacher. It had never occurred to her before that the
Bible was so linked up together, every word definitely
proved by some other word elsewhere spoken.

And as they went on through the lesson Frannie
grew more and more absorbed in the thought of how
the Bible itself claimed to be the Word of God, not in
just a casual way, but in a clear indisputable way, up-
holding its claims with unanswerable truths that she

had never thought of before. As an undercurrent she
sensed its demand to be accepted and put to the test.

It had never occurred to Frannie before, nor perhaps
to Val either, that the Holy Spirit was a real Teacher,
who was ready to make clear the meaning of the
Bible to any soul willing to accept and believe it even
before it was proved. But now they were amazed to find
that all these people looked on the Holy Spirit as a definite Person. They heard that the moment a soul ac-
cepts Christ as his Saviour then the Holy Spirit comes
into that soul to abide, never to leave it. That was all
new to them. The Holy Spirit had been a part of their
traditional belief, inherited from their families, but there
had been no knowledge that He was a real Person. If
they had heard the words before they had not taken
them in. And now suddenly it was as if the Holy Spirit
had come into the room, and been introduced to them
personally, so that hereafter there could be no Christian life or even thought, without this consciousness of
another Person within them who had power and
rights and likes and dislikes.

Lady Winthrop sat across from these two new disciples, and watched their speaking faces, saw how new
and wonderful it seemed to them, this teaching that was
practical. She began praying in her heart for them. For
she suddenly knew she loved these two whom she had
watched going down her "street of the city" on their
flashing skates, and whom she had been praying for.
She had so wanted them to come to this class, yet she
had been afraid they wouldn't. They were so young and
bright and gay looking, and they were of the age when
young people want the pleasures of this world rather
than study about another world that can only be seen
by faith. Yet here were these two poring over the pages,
and finding the references as eagerly as the regular
members of the class, their faces bright with interest,
their eyes shining with each new nugget of truth they
took in. And Lady Winthrop's prayers took on the
semblance of thanksgiving.

They lingered a little while in the neighborhood of

the teacher. Asking an intelligent question of him now and then, as did others, and when the gathering finally broke up they went thoughtfully away.

"I begin to see," said Willoughby as they turned onto the bridge, "that there are questions ahead of me that I've got to face and settle before I'll be fit to go on. It seems to me that they must even take precedence of my war work or I won't be fit to do it rightly."

Frannie looked up thoughtfully.

"Questions?" she said half wonderingly. "What questions?"

"Whether I'm saved or not," said the young man. "I never considered that at all. I thought I was living a pretty decent sort of life and that would be all that was expected of me. But I see now that I must know whether I've really accepted what Christ has done for me, whether I have my papers all made out, my 'application' as it were. It's just like getting in the army, or enlisting in defense work, only vastly more important of course, and strangely I never gave it a thought before. I thought that people who kept talking about being saved were cranks who wasted a lot of time and didn't amount to a row of pins. But now I see it's the basic principle upon which this whole thing rests. Christ made it so important that He was willing to die to accomplish it and I have just passed it by and tried to get into the procession without filling out my papers. Any day now my work might get more strenuous, even more dangerous, and I don't feel that I want to go on with it any farther until I have this matter settled beyond a doubt, so that whatever comes I've a rock foundation under my feet and some One to trust in. How about you, Frannie? Have you settled this question?"

"I think I did when I was a little girl, just before I united with the church, but I haven't been doing much about it since except going to church regularly when I could. Doing a little church work now and then, like playing for prayer meeting, or waiting on table at a church supper, or even teaching a class in the primary room. But I know those things don't amount to anything. I see now that what God wants is for us to let

His Spirit have His way in our hearts, and it's up to Him then to direct us to do 'church work' or 'home work', the way they said tonight. I never really let Him do anything in my life. I think I'll have a talk with God tonight, and tell Him I want things to be different after this."

Willoughby's hand slid around Frannie's little gloved hand that rested on his arm.

"We'll do it together tonight," he said quietly. "It seems wonderful that we can really talk such things over with the great God, doesn't it?"

"Yes," said Frannie softly. And then just before they left the bridge she pointed down the river to where the lights of the city twinkled and brightened the sky and shone golden in the river.

"Look! Look! See, there's the Heavenly City shining out that way again. It almost seems as if it really were a picture of the City we are to see some day."

"Yes," said the young man gravely. " 'And the street of the city was pure gold.' I looked that verse up today. Lady Winthrop told me where to find it. It struck me as something to look forward to."

Chapter 16

AN HOUR AFTER the little family in the brick house were asleep with every window dark, there came two stealthy figures stealing over the fields and approaching the back of the cottage where the covered trench was located. They halted, and looked about.

"It was right here I fell. Turn on your flash, Spike, and give us a glimpse around. It ought to be easy to find. It was a white card, and there were some other papers with it. Give us a flash. What's the matter? Can't you find it?"

"No, Kit, I don't seem to have it. Guess I must have

forgot to take it out of the pocket of my overcoat when I changed to this sweater. Here's some matches. They'll do."

"Well, go easy! A match scratching might wake anybody, and I don't want to run any risks, not with guys like those two. I don't want us to get pinched. Not at this stage of the game."

A crisp sound and then a flickering light, quavering over the pile of dirty snow and earth, and dying out with a fizzle.

"Heck! Don't you know how to keep a match going? Give it to me!"

Another light struggled out from the damp matches, floated mistily over the heap of rubble, disclosing little, and died away again.

Match after match illuminated the ground for a brief space and faded away, until they were all gone, but not a card was disclosed.

"Well, I guess it ain't here!" said Kit in a discouraged whisper. "But I know this is where I fell, right over that big lump of snow. I cut a big slit in the knee of my pants. What's that you're picking up? Is that a card?"

"Naw, it's only a rag. It's a fancy nose rag. Some dame dropped it here. Got perfume on it. Smell that!" and Spike held out a delicate bit of finery.

Kit sniffed, and then reached for the handkerchief and smelled again.

"Say!" he exclaimed. "That's the same perfume our dame wore when she brought us to this house this evening. It's hers!"

"You poor fool you, how would it get here? Look how far this is from the gate where we came in. And there's no wind."

They stared at each other in the dim night. Then Kit looked around him, turned his head toward the house, and then toward the gate where they had entered earlier in the evening.

"That dame must have chased after us, and likely fell down the way I did!"

"I told you we oughtta have gone across the road and stayed behind that car till she come out and then told her we found we'd forgot an engagement ur something."

"Not on yer life, I wouldn't have risked meetin' that guy again. Ef he'd slung you across the ice on the river the way he did me you wouldn't either. But say, we've gotta hunt up that dame and get my pass. I'll lose my job ef I don't have it. What did she say her name was?"

"She's that old Hollister guy's kid. They live acrost the river in that house with all them towers and pinnacles."

"They do? Well, we gotta go over there and ask for her."

"Not me!" said Spike. "It ain't my pass that's lost. Go yerself ef yer fool enough to try it, but you'll go by yerself. I don't crash into no swell's house like that!"

"Okay! I'll go by myself then. I ain't gonta lose my pass and lose my job. You know I'll lose my job if I can't find my pass in the morning. Mebbe if I'd go over to that dance we was planning she'd be there yet."

"That won't do any good," said Spike. "Don't you remember she said these dances she wanted us for were over by midnight because all the girls were working girls, and couldn't keep their jobs ef they stayed out too late? So that's out. It's way past midnight now."

"Then I'm in real trouble. That dame won't be up early enough in the morning for me to get my pass."

"What makes you think she's got it?"

"Oh, she likely picked it up ef she fell down. See all these footprints. She fell all righty, and I sure am in real trouble now."

And then a heavy hand fell on his shoulder.

"Yes, you sure are in real trouble, unless you can explain pretty good and quick what you're doing at this time of night, lighting matches around the back of this house."

Spike made a quick movement to leave, but the other shadow that had come quietly up with the first man, put out a strong hand and grasped Spike with a firm hold, and though he struggled his best he was unable to get away.

"I ain't in this," gasped Spike in a scared voice. "I just came along with him because he asked me."

"I wasn't doin' nothin'," growled Kit shakily. "I was just tryin' ta find my pass I thought I might a dropped here awhile ago when I went across lots in a hurry. I gotta have that pass ur I lose my job."

"Yes? Well, you better look out you don't lose something else on the way. What were you doing with matches here? Trying to make a fire this time of night?"

"No sir: I wasn't tryin' to make no fire here. I was just tryin' to find my pass card. It oughtta be around here somewhere."

One of the two men swept his flashlight around the place, but no card showed up.

"You see," he said scathingly. "You just come along with me to the station house and we'll see if we can't get to the bottom of this business."

"No, sir, I can't go to the station house. I haven't done nothin'. I've gotta go see that girl and see if she picked it up and was goin' ta return it ta me."

"What girl?" said the officer sharply.

"Why, she's some rich girl that was takin' us to a social club she started. And she brought us here to get another girl from this house."

The officers exchanged a quick look.

"Did she go? The girl from this house?"

"No, sir. She said she had another engagement, so we beat it. We figured we'd had enough."

"I see. So you came across the back of the lot. But what became of the girl who brought you?"

"We don't know," said Spike gruffly. "We didn't wait ta see."

"Then why did you think she might have your pass?"

"Well, we didn't hear her car right away so we figured she mighta chased around tryin' ta find us, and mebbe picked it up," said Kit eagerly, persuasively. "I've just gotta go ta her house an' see if she's got it. I need it in the morning."

"Who is this girl who brought you. What is her name?"

"Marietta Hollister. She lives across there on the ridge in that big house with a cupola on the top. Her father's some big guy."

"And you expect me to believe a story like that? That a daughter of Foster Hollister was taking a couple of young hoodlums like you to a dance? You must think I'm crazy. Come along with me. We'll see about this."

"Why, you see, it was a dance for young workin' girls an' she hired us to go along and be pardners fer the workin' girls, see? She was payin' us five bucks apiece fer goin' an' havin' a swell time besides, good eats and some fun."

"Oh, she was paying you for going, was she? And yet you two ran away without your pay! Another likely story."

Then suddenly an interruption occurred. A window at the back of the house was cautiously raised, and a moment later a clear voice said:

"Who is out there? What are you doing there?"

The officer who was holding Kit looked up calmly.

"It's all right, Miss Branner. This is Officer Rowley. Nothing the matter. Just a couple of kids hunting something they thought they lost here when they went through the lot awhile back. Don't worry."

"Oh! All right! Thank you!" and the window went softly down with none of the rest of the sleeping household the wiser.

So Spike and Kit went off in the custody of Officer Rowley and the little brick house beside the frozen river slept on quietly.

About two hours later two more stealthy figures arrived among the bushes, and took up a stand alertly.

"Well, I guess we've got the coast clear tonight," said Granniss. "I began to think we'd got every light against us, last night. But it's much better to come at this hour. Practically nobody would be around now. Better go down and look at our digging and see if it's been tampered with at all, hadn't you? Make sure before the lumber truck arrives, and then what nobody doesn't see won't do any harm. Go easy on that flash though. You know even a sound sleeper is waked up by a light moving around the wall."

"I ain't puttin' any light on anybody's wall," growled Mike. "Whaddaya think I am?"

"Well, now don't get touchy, Mike. This is no time to develop a temper, just when things are going our way."

"Okay!" said Mike glumly, and strode out to the trench he had dug the night before. He stood for a moment turning his light this way and that, studying the ground carefully. Once or twice he stooped and put out a hand, feeling of the roughness of the earth, brought his flash to bear on something on the ground, and finally picked it up, a button that Spike had burst off when he struggled to get away from the second officer as they made their way to the hidden car by which the two officers traveled. Then Mike went back to the covert where Granniss was watching him.

"Well, how did you find it?" questioned Granniss sharply.

"There's been somebody there," said Mike. "In fact several."

"What do you mean?" asked Granniss, anxiety in his tone at once. "How could you tell?"

"I mean there's been some people there," said Mike calmly. After all it wasn't his funeral, he told himself. "I know by the footprints. There's been quite several. And the ground has been considerable tore up."

"What kind of footprints? Men? Or boys."

"Men," said Mike. "It looked like at least three, mebbe four. And there was one girl with spike heels."

"A girl!" said Granniss. "Do you suppose it's the girl that's living here in this house?"

"I couldn't say," said Mike dryly.

"What would a girl want with coming out there?"

"Mebbe heard us the other night. Mebbe got scared, and came to see what was going on."

"Mebbe hired by the government to spy on us," said Granniss bitterly. "Might be, you know."

"Aw, yer dreamin'!" said Mike disdainfully.

"Well, did you make any attempt to find out if our wires had been tampered with? Do you think they could have dug beyond where we went?"

"Could be," said Mike speculatively. "Do you want I should tear it all up and find out?"

"Well, I don't know as we'd have time before those lumbermen get here. Perhaps we better wait till they've gone."

"Not me!" said Mike decidedly. "I gotta get some sleep. I got a job to carry on tamorrow."

"You got a job to carry on tonight, man, have you forgotten? If you do it right it's worth a heap more than any job you have tomorrow. Remember that!"

"Okay!" said Mike getting up with a sigh from the place he had flung himself down. He yawned. "If this has gotta be found out tonight here goes. I ain't waiting on no lumber. I'll have plenty branches to fling in if we hear 'em comin'."

So Mike went to work, carefully laying aside the stones and dirt and branches, where they could be put back in a trice, and now and then bringing a powerful flashlight to bear on the hole. He was working fast. He didn't care to have to do this over again after the men left.

And across the street on the side porch of one of the little new unfinished houses the two officers who had returned from the police station parked themselves comfortably and invisibly where they could easily keep tab on what went on. Somehow they knew that this job about the old brick house was not half finished yet.

But Mike was working away for dear life. He had sighted strange turmoil in the dirt he had thrown in around the wires, and something dark and foreign was tangled firmly, as if a hidden foot were sticking up. Had somebody dug this whole trench up since last night? There was one place where it seemed the fingers of a small hand had been drawn along, burrowing in. Breathlessly he worked and at last was able to dislodge Marietta's slipper heel from the wires where it was as firmly caught as if the fastening had been intentional. He brought it up and stood bent over, the flashlight turned full on it, and studied it.

"Great jumping goslings!" he ejaculated. "Now how could that get into my nice clean ditch?"

Granniss came near.

"What is it, Mike, have you found something? Have they disturbed our wires?"

"Wal, I ain't just sure yet," said Mike loftily. "It's something mighty queer. It's the heel of some dame's shoe. Down in by them wires, all tangled up in 'em, as if somebody had stepped into 'em, or else was trying to pull 'em out. Some swell dame too, 'cause they don't make heels like that on cheap shoes."

"Where is it? Let me see it," said Granniss in alarm.

He took the absurd high heel and held it in his hand, sensing the soft leather with which it was covered, the art of its lines. Then he held it under his coat and turned his flashlight on it, studying every part of it carefully.

"It's been wrenched off," he announced in a guarded whisper. "Somebody tried to step over there and the ground gave way. She went in unintentionally. Nothing to fear from her, I guess."

"I think you're wrong," said Mike abruptly. "There's marks of hands down there. The whole place has been mauled over, mebbe by more than one pair of hands. I tell you I seen it, I know the signs."

"Well, if that's so there's nothing for it but to get at the wires and see if they've been tampered with. Get a hustle on and be quick about it before the truck gets here."

"But what's so important about them wires? We could replace 'em, couldn't we, ef they've disturbed 'em?"

"Oh, it's not the wires. They are only the beginning of the aerial that goes up a tree. It's what they lead to. Man, there's papers in with that transmitter in there that would put us all where we don't want to be, and no mistake about it. Besides if they've tampered with those wires we've got to destroy all evidence and then beat it with no time to lose. What I want you to do is find out if those wires are still uncut between this ditch and the wall of that kitchen. Find out if anybody has traced 'em to their source this evening. And do it mighty quick, too."

"Okay," said Mike in no hearty voice. "But I ain't partial to workin' in double quick time. Not after I've worked all day in the plant."

The whispering ceased. Mike climbed down in the hole again and went to work, wishing he'd never taken over this job, no matter how big the pay promised. But at last he reached the place where he had ended his digging the night before and found the wires still undisturbed as they came out of the solid ground about a foot from the brick wall of the kitchen. So he laboriously climbed out and went back to the big man who was seated on the tool chest.

"Well, they're all okay. Just look as if they'd been pulled a bit, kind of taut, that's all. I guess they didn't think it was worth while going no further. Ur mebbe they got tired and decided to come back another night."

"Well, that looks bad," said Granniss. "I guess we better arrange somehow to make a grab right away and get out of this for good. If those wires are still there as you say then that's a perfect guide to the place where we expect to break through the bricks, and since someone has tried to get down there tonight they must have discovered the wires. Lost a heel doing it. That would be enough to make a thoughtful person suspicious. Say, Mike, you don't think you could go on and break through tonight? It can't be much farther, and in case we can locate the loose brick we might be able to do the whole job tonight and get away. I don't like this outlook. It means somebody is suspicious, and once get somebody suspicious, it's first come first win. Mike, we gotta get that stuff tonight!"

Mike dropped down on the hard ground wearily and shook his head.

"Nothin' doin'," he said shakily. "Whaddaya think I am? A machine? You'd better get some other man if you want the world moved in a night."

"What's the matter with you, Mike? Getting cold feet

with the goal just in sight? I didn't think you'd play out right at the end and lose all that dough."

"Lose it?" said Mike excitedly, raising his voice above the stipulated whisper. "Who said I'd lose it? If that's the kind of a guy you are, I can quit right now, and make more money snitchin' on you than I can diggin' solid ice caves an' breakin' into honest people's houses while they're sleepin'!"

"Look here, Mike! If you're a stinking yellow sucker like that I could put you in the jug in no time for digging this trench into honest people's houses, and taking part in an act of treason to your country, and how much of a chance do you suppose you would stand, your word against mine? I'm a respectable business man, well dressed and educated, and you're a poor laboring man. So get down off that high horse and get to work. See what you can accomplish before those lumber fellows get here. Remember, you don't know what evidence I could bring against you when I get my hands on those papers."

"You wouldn't dare!" muttered Mike in a low undertone, but he went slowly back to the trench and lowered himself out of the other man's sight. He was getting angry clear through, and thinking out a plot whereby he could get Granniss into real trouble with the government.

Then suddenly they heard the lumber truck coming, and Granniss arose in a panic and began to kick branches and stones into the trench.

"We better take a couple of those shortest boards," he said, "and lower them into the hole, and then cover them up. We can't have our men falling in there, and getting tangled up in this jam. Get outta there, Mike, and help me move a couple of boards, quick, and shovel some of that snow back over them."

Mike was glad enough to get out of the hole. He had reached the place where nothing short of a good strong blow or two with the pickax would get to the brick wall, and he was scared to try it on a calm clear night like this. He had in mind the voice of the quiet elderly woman who had opened the door and looked him down the night he first came here. He had a feeling that

she was capable of doing almost anything, certainly
calling for the police. He was sure there wasn't any
telephone in here yet, but there was no telling how soon
one would be put in with a woman like that nurse on
the job.

Halfheartedly he helped lift two boards and sprinkle
some rubble over them, piled a couple of branches and
some snow atop, and went out to the road to meet the
truck.

The truck men knew their job. They carried their
lumber swiftly and silently and put it in place, received
their pay and went their way, as the moon slipped over
the rim of the horizon and left the world in darkness.

The two men stood for a moment discouraged, looking at one another, and then by common consent
stepped over to the trench.

"You made a pretty good job of camouflage if you
did do it in a hurry. Suppose you just fling a few more
shovels full of stuff across the top, and we'll let her go
for tonight. I guess we'll be safe. One more night
ought to get us through the wall. If the weather would
only favor us. A good warm rain, or even a melting
snow would melt that ice, and cause it to crack, and
then if a wind would come up we'd have plenty of noise
to hide our movements. There! Put some of that snow
on the top. Now come on, let's go! Tomorrow night
we'll break through that wall and get our stuff, and
then we can take our time getting the rough building
put up. I been figuring it out while I sat here, and it's
going to seem just like another operation of the same
carpenters that built those houses over there. I think
we'll get by. You're a good fellow all right, Mike, and
here's an extra ten bucks for a little velvet for you, so
be here on time tomorrow night."

They went away toward the parked car which had
been left in a new place that night. And as soon as the
sound of the car's going died away two figures separated
themselves from their hiding place and slowly made
their way over to the scene of the night's action.

Their rubber shod feet made no stir of sound in the
silence of the place. They picked their way over to the

trench, and with their flashlights bored into the carelessly placed covering to the enlarged trench. Quietly with heavily gloved hands they removed enough of it to discover the boards. These they studied for some minutes, conversed with sketchy gestures, now and then a whisper, finally removed more rubble until they could move the end of one board enough to get a narrow view of the concealed wires sticking out of the brick wall. After carefully examining the layout, which included reaching in and tapping the wall gently, the two men softly returned the rubble into place, and stepped over to the newly arrived lumber, which they looked over carefully. Then they retired to a distance and turned their glances up to the tree tops.

"Say, Tom, if that's a radio there's an aerial around here somewhere. Which tree do you think had it?"

Tom looked up speculatively at the tree tops, and finally pointed to the tallest one.

"I think that there one, Rowley."

"Yes, I shouldn't wonder. Think you could climb that tree and find out? We gotta get this thing all figured out before we clamp down on them. We gotta know just what to expect."

"Sure thing!" said Tom. "Yep, I'll take a try at her, but it ain't necessary to go all the way up ta find out. Them wires will be going up the tree trunks somewheres around here, ef it is an aerial."

"Okay! Look around and cipher it out. I'm figuring they'll have to show their hands pretty soon. Maybe tomorrow night, maybe the next. We better have a posse ready when the time comes. You can't tell just what those babies have got up their sleeves, or what they're figuring to do. We've gotta be ready. You know it might just be they're planning to put dynamite under that brick wall."

"What fur would they do that?"

"Well, fer some reason they wantta get possession of that house. Look's like they've had an illegitimate radio hid there somewhere, and mebbe some incriminating stuff. You know there's been a lotta messages leakin' through to the enemy. There's bound to be several places where they send off messages."

"Okay, Boss," said Tom, and was off.

It was sometime before he returned.

"I found the aerial all right," he said. "Far side of that tallest tree, behind them evergreens."

"I thought so," said Rowley. "They must have a radio transmitter hidden away. They may have had it going there for some time. It's good and lonely here. Nobody would suspect. You had to look hard to find that aerial. Nobody would notice it, going by, and nobody even went by here for several years."

"But if it's a mike, they could easy get another."

"Yep. It's something more than just a mike. Something incriminating or I miss my guess."

"Watcha goin' ta do about it, Rowley?"

"Ain't sure yet. Gotta think it over. Come on, let's go!" and the two men slowly faded out of the picture.

But up in the third little bedroom where Nurse Branner had been sleeping since Mrs. Fernley was better, she was lying awake listening. She hadn't heard anything definite, but she was almost sure someone had been whispering. Yet when she slid over to the window she couldn't see anyone, for it was very dark. The little moon was tired of its walking across the sky and had dropped down behind the hills to rest until another night. Yet Nurse Branner was much comforted by the thought of Officer Rowley, and his reassuring voice, and also by the promise that the telephone would be installed tomorrow morning. At last she too dropped off to sleep again.

About that time Marietta Hollister, driving home from an evening of revelry, passed just across the river from the little brick house, and cast a baleful glance in that direction. To think that Val Willoughby had dared to come into that house while she was there and openly taken that girl out somewhere! Where had they been going? And why had he mentioned Lady Winthrop? She had scarcely had time to consider that point since it happened, so excited she had been about falling into that hole at the back of the house, and about the two missing escorts. Besides, one of them had called up that morning to know if she had found a pass into the shipyard where he worked. And then he asked her when they were going to get their "dough." Imagine it—when they had simply checked out and left her alone!

Chapter 17

WILLOUGHBY HAD TOLD Frannie on the way home from the Bible class that he was probably going to be called to Washington for a conference, and it might be several days before his return. He had arranged for someone to look after his job while he was gone, but he was worried about her.

"If I were you I wouldn't go down on skates for a couple of days. The weather reports say there is going to be milder weather and a likelihood of the ice melting. Also storms in the offing. It won't be too safe on skates. Ice is treacherous, you know, when it begins to melt. I wish you would promise me to stay off the ice for a few days."

"But surely I could tell if the ice wasn't safe," said Frannie. "I've been used to skating since I was a very little girl."

"Well, it isn't always easy to predict what weather will do to a frozen river. Besides, there are undercurrents to be reckoned with. And besides number two there are those two fellows. If Marietta has them under her wings there is no telling what the three of them might not plan. Just go quietly downtown on the bus that passes the next street over behind your house. It goes down and crosses the river at the lower bridge, and comes around by your office. You will get there a little ahead of your opening time. Will you do that? If you don't I shall be uneasy all the time I am gone, and remember I haven't settled my score entirely with those two hoodlums, and if they find out I'm gone they may take advantage of you. They are cowards, I know, but I think they are fairly scared of me, and would delight to get the better of you in my absence. Besides Marietta hasn't helped matters for us any by what she did tonight. So, stay off the ice while I'm gone, will you?"

"Why, yes, I can if that will help you any, but really I don't see why you should worry about me. I'm not in the least afraid."

"Then all the more I'm worried. You see I feel as if you had in a way been put in my hands to look out for until you get thoroughly acquainted with the place. And anyhow I want you to, please."

So Frannie smiled and promised, and told her tumultuous young heart not to make anything out of that. He was just courteous, and felt that a gentleman ought to protect a lady. Any lady. He wasn't singling her out because he had any particular interest in her. And then their talk drifted back to the subject of the Bible class, and how pleasant it was to have opportunity to get this study.

"It's going to be a great privilege to go to that class," she said. "And when mother gets well she'll want to go. Bonnie can go too. She always behaves beautifully in church."

"That's a fine idea, only won't she get pretty sleepy?"

"No, she's been used to going to church evenings all last summer, and she can sleep it out the next morning if she will."

So Frannie did not expect to meet Willoughby the next morning, and got up a little earlier to be ready for the bus. She cast a wistful eye toward the ice, as she started out to the bus corner, but after all it was milder, and there were gray clouds with a sullen look off toward the east. As she got out of the bus she felt a drop of rain. Rain? So soon? Perhaps the weather man had been right about it, as the young man had suggested. Probably he usually was. Frannie never read the weather man. She usually took weather as it came with a smile, whether dark or bright. Well, she was glad that she had come by bus. It certainly would not be good to have to skate home in a torrential rain, but as for safety, she smiled. Surely a little rain couldn't break up that thick ice that she had traveled so happily on for so many days. But it made her feel sad to see the rain come pelting down now. She hurried into the office and as she hung her hat and coat away she looked out the back window and saw the rain come down in a regular torrent, as if it had come to stay. It made her sad to see it pelting down so hard that it fairly leaped up again, it had such a determined destructive look, and she almost felt a pity for the clear ice that had carried her so safely. Would it come again that winter? Would there yet be cold fierce enough to make a solid street of it again? Probably not until another year. As she went to her desk there was a heavy sadness upon her. This threat to the ice meant more than just losing the skating. It probably meant an end to her acquaintance with the young man whose friendship had made such a bright spot in her drab life. Probably that was a good thing, for it could not naturally go on to a lifelong friendship. That Marietta had made quite plain, even if she herself had not had sense enough to know that he belonged among a different class of people. Even if he was sensible and democratic and all that, he had a family, hadn't he? An aunt at least, who lived in that beautiful house, and companied with people on the other side of the river where she, Frannie, did not belong. Yes, it was probably a good thing that this storm and separation had come before it was too late for her to realize that she was getting far too much interested in this young man who had been so very kind.

So Frannie went hard to work, and accomplished a great deal on that long gloomy day, and did not allow herself a moment to turn aside to think. She must be true to the right and the life that God had marked out for her. And she tried to think, every breathing space that came, how grand it was going to be to have mother come downstairs again.

The rain continued according to schedule, all that day, growing harder and harder, steadily through the night. The two figures that crept through the darkness at the back of the old brick house on the wrong side of the river, came in an old car of ancient make, and parked it this time up the back street, hidden behind bushes. Also they wore rubber coats and rubber hats, and they waited until the nightly load of lumber was landed safely before they began operations. But when the lumber truck was gone they went at it in earnest.

"You get that trench cleared right up close to the brick wall, Mike," directed Granniss, who was togged out in old clothes and looked like a laborer himself. "Get a pile of stuff each side of the trench and then we'll lay those two boards across to cover us while we work. Maybe a couple more. We gotta work fast, and this is just the kind of a night we wanted. Listen at that ice cracking. Sounds like a gun. A little pounding won't be heard. This is great. The river'll be breaking up pretty soon. Come, let's get to work. I'll get the car ready to receive the stuff when we get it out. I brought some boxes along so we won't get the papers wet. Got some important maps and plans in there."

So Mike went down on his rubber shod knees with pick and shovel, and soon had the upper end of the trench cleared, placing the rubble in a pile either side, and laying the boards across.

The wind arose and howled about the place, and shook the bare branches of the trees until now and again one fell with a crash, but there were so many crashes that it would not be noticed. And in a short time the bare brick wall lay close ahead, with the wires sticking out. Mike found himself quite excited to think he was at last so near to the goal, and actually working now out of sight under cover, where he could guardedly use his flashlight.

Of course Mike could not know that there watched two across the street, who were well aware of strange activities going on, and that the guarded little flashlight whose sharp brightness danced and gleamed through the rain like diamonds, was entirely within their sight. Mike did not know that when he had accomplished the feat of chiseling a brick or two loose, so

that he could put his hand inside and feel around
for things he had been told to locate, one of the two
across the street in hiding, had quietly slipped from
his covert to his secreted bicycle, and noiselessly
pedaled away to a telephone station not too far off,
where he had arranged to call the Police Station and
give instructions. Then he went back to Rowley who
was carefully watching developments, listening to every
movement.

And about that time Frannie, who had not been
able to get to sleep with her usual promptness, thought
she heard a sound like a blow on the back wall of the
house. She listened for a moment to see if it could be a
tree fallen with the wind which rose now and then
with sudden vigor, and then died down again. There!
There was that sound of a blow again, as of a sledge
hammer, on the back wall, down low, as if it were
striking the foundation. The wall seemed to tremble.
Could that be a slight earthquake? Did earthquakes
ever come to that part of the country? Or was this
purely imagination?

Then suddenly she remembered the new telephone
which had been put in that morning. It was located
down in the living room so that it should not annoy
the sick mother, and it seemed a long way downstairs
in the middle of the night. But again she heard that
dull thud that seemed to shake the little house. Strange
Nurse Branner hadn't heard it, but she was sleeping in
mother's room tonight because she was afraid the wind
and noise outside would make the invalid restless.
Frannie's room was partly over the back of the house,
and that was where the sound seemed to come from.
There it was again! She must do something about it.
What was a telephone for if not to use in emergency?

But she mustn't let the nurse get awake, for that
would likely waken mother, and she mustn't turn on a
light for if there was really somebody outside trying to
get in they might have a gun and see her through the
window and shoot her. Oh, but this was fantastic. It
probably was nothing at all but the wind rattling some-

thing, a loose shingle perhaps. But even if it wasn't any safer to go down in the dark than the light, she felt much more comfortable going in the dark. So softly she stole up, careful not to waken Bonnie, threw her bathrobe about her, stepped into her soft slippers, and stole slowly, cautiously to the head of the stairs. Maybe she was a fool! Maybe she ought to go back and try to go to sleep again, but at least she could go downstairs and see if the same sound was clearer down there. Perhaps she could find out what it was, and calm her mind and then she could go back upstairs and go to sleep like a sensible girl. She needed her sleep if she were going to be alert and worth her wages tomorrow. She was a working girl. She had no right to stay awake humoring herself with fancies and fears. She was brave!

So she went on step by step, avoiding carefully the stair that squeaked. She had had plenty of practice at that while her mother was so very sick at first.

And in due time she arrived at the foot of the stairs, went across to the little alcove between the bottom step and the coat closet where the telephone had so newly come to reside, and then tried to think what to do next.

Of course. She must call the police. But she didn't know their number, and she mustn't make a light to look it up. But surely the operator would know! So with shaking hand she took down the receiver, half hesitated, and then in a trembling voice spoke, very softly:

"Will you please give me the local police, quick!"

"What is your number, please?"

Her heart was beating so wildly now she could scarcely answer, and then almost at once she heard a man's voice, cool, deep, dependable, like one who was used to constant emergencies, and it gave her reassurance.

"Is this the police station?"

"Yes, what's wrong?"

"Oh, I don't quite know, but it sounds as if somebody was trying to break into the back of our house. It's number ten, Rosemary Lane, the little old brick house that has been vacant so long, they tell me. Would you please tell some officer who is near here to go behind our house and look? It sounds as if somebody was pounding on the bricks and it sometimes shakes the whole house. There it is again. Oh please, quick, could you send someone?"

"Number ten, Rosemary Lane. Why sure, we'll take care of it, sister. Don't you worry. Is the house lit up?"

"No, I was afraid to turn on the light."

"Well, that's right. Keep it dark till we get there. Then if everything is all right we'll knock on the door and tell you."

"Thank you. But please don't knock loud. My mother is sick and I don't want to frighten her."

"Okay, lady. Just keep the house dark till we come. We'll take care of you."

So Frannie dropped down in the big chair by the front window and tried to stop trembling. Somehow calling the police had made her more sure than ever that there was something dreadful the matter, as if she had created the interloper herself out of her imagination.

It seemed to be very still here in the dark living room, and then she began to think it had all been a mistake. There wasn't anybody pounding on the back wall. There wasn't a sound anywhere except the snapping of great branches, their thud as they fell to the ground. And how like a fool she was going to feel when the police came, and found nothing was the matter. Her face grew red in the darkness at the thought. Everybody would hear of it. Maybe it would get in the papers, and people would laugh. Only there was nobody around here to laugh whom she would care about, except Valiant Willoughby, and he was away. Maybe he would never hear of it. But if he did he would think she was a little blunderer and a 'fraid cat, always getting into trouble and needing to be taken care of, and she simply couldn't have him feel that he had to go around feeling sorry for her, and taking care of her all the time. And then have that girl, that horrid girl, maybe come and laugh at her in her own house and tell her that was what it meant to live on the wrong side of the river, with no servants around to guard the place.

Then suddenly into the deep quiet there came an extraordinary blow, as if given by a heavy sledge hammer, pounding over heavy folds of canvas or some heavy cloth, and the whole kitchen floor shook, so that the dishpan which Bonnie had left in the sink rattled.

Frannie jumped and caught her breath. "Oh!" she said, and put her hand over her heart. She struggled to her feet and stood staring around her, wondering what to do next, and yet mindful of the officer's warning that she was not to turn on the light.

The rain was still pelting down and rattling on the improvised roof over the trench where the two men worked. And now the big man was by the side of the stout man, sliding into the trench beside him as the rattle of bricks in a shower could be heard mingling with the rending sound of breaking ice. Then all was suddenly still. Frannie, creeping trembling to the kitchen window to look out, saw two dark figures step across the street swiftly and come up close to the house, and two more follow behind, and then two more. Had the police come so soon? It didn't seem possible since she called. She knew the station house was at some distance from their home. But now she could hear voices.

One voice, Miss Branner, who had been wakened by the last rumble of the wall, recognized as belonging to Officer Rowley. He was speaking with clear authority, that could be heard in the little house even above the roar of the storm.

"That will be about all," he said, putting a mighty grip on the flabby shoulder of the big man. "Just what do you men think you are doing breaking into another man's house at night while the people sleep?"

"Oh," said the big man clearing his throat importantly. "This isn't another man's house. I've just bought it, didn't you know that? And I'm going to make some changes in the place. I wanted to see the architect tomorrow and have the plan drawn up so I thought I better come over and do some measuring up tonight."

"Yes?" said Rowley. "Well you can just walk out of here and down to the police station with me and do your measuring up there. I fancy somebody else will need to measure you before you go any farther. Come on, step out of there. Brewer, snap those bracelets on him and look out for him."

"Now, man, who are you?"

"Oh, I don't know anything about this business," said Mike airily. "I'm just a laborer he hired to do some digging for him. Getting extra wages because of the storm, you know. Comes in handy when you have a big family, see?"

"Yes," said Rowley, "I see. Well, come on over to the police station and see if you can make them see. Come on. Hustle out of here. We haven't any more time to waste."

And then into the noise and storm of the night came the clear siren of the police car in front of the house, and Frannie stole to the front door and opened it, to find two policemen standing there, and a red car with bright lights standing at the gate.

"Well, ma'am," said one of the policemen, "I guess it's all over. They've just arrested your two men, and I think there's men here enough to take care of the house tonight."

"Oh, thank you," said Frannie, with a sound of tears in her voice. "I was afraid you were going to scold me for being scared at nothing. I've been hearing sounds several times, other nights, but I thought I was silly."

"No, ma'am, you weren't silly. You did the right thing callin' us. But you see our men were onto the fellows. They'd been watchin' several nights, only they wanted them to give themselves away completely before they pinched 'em."

"Oh!" said Frannie. "But what would they want to get into our house for? We're not rich people. We haven't anything much to steal. The few solid silver things we had mother put in the bank for safe-keeping. She was sort of afraid to live in such a secluded place so near to a big city, and yet not in it."

"Well, that's what the men wanted. The seclusion.

They're what is called Fifth Columnists, I guess. Anyhow they've been operating a broadcastin' station illegally, givin' away our American secrets to the enemy, and this was a nice quiet place where they could send messages. At least that's what we figured was the matter. I haven't been in charge of this case, but there's others like it nowadays, and I guess they musta had some of their stuff hid in the cellar. You folks come unexpected and moved right in and they had to get it out before it was discovered. But you don't need to worry any more. Our men will take charge of the premises, and nobody can't bother you any more. Them fellers are gone to the police station, and there they'll stay tonight, and there ain't any chance of anybody else gettin' into your house. There's too many police around."

"Oh, thank you," said Frannie, relieved.

"You're welcome, miss. Call us any time you need us!"

And then Nurse Branner stepped up.

"Officer, is Mr. Rowley anywhere about here tonight?" Her voice was crisp and self-possessed, and Frannie looked up penitently.

"Oh, did I wake you up?" she asked. "I'm so sorry. I tried to be quiet."

"No, you didn't wake me up," said the nurse, smiling. "It was the pounding on the wall woke me. Did you say Mr. Rowley is around here, officer?"

"I think he is," said the policeman politely. "Would you like to see him?"

"Yes, I would very much," said the nurse. And in a moment more Officer Rowley appeared dressed in a rubber uniform, dripping from every point and fold of his coat and boots.

"What was the matter, Mr. Rowley? Did you find anything down there?"

The big policeman grinned.

"We sure did, Miss Branner. Just a little matter of a radio transmitter used for spy purposes. You see they've been using this as a hideout till you folks moved in, and they had to vamoose in too much of a hurry.

So they just sealed everything up, and planned to come back and get it later. I haven't looked everything over, but I guess there's some pretty important papers for the government to see. Anyhow we're taking possession of them and will keep them safe till the government expert gets here. Sorry we couldn't have pulled this off sooner and saved you any further worry, but we had to keep them under espionage till we could find out just what they were at, so we could catch them red-handed. But we watched them carefully, and you weren't in any danger, we made sure of that. So now you can get your family back to sleep and you won't be bothered any more tonight. I'm leaving a force here to guard the house, and I'm having the break sealed up. If you'd just let us go down cellar a minute or two, then we'll be in a position to take care of everything."

Quietly the men went down the narrow cellar stairs, investigated everything including the movable brick and the slit of a keyhole, and then as quietly returned and went out into the rain, bidding Frannie and the nurse get a good rest. And so as the stormy morning grew toward dawn, sleep gradually came to the excited little household in the brick house.

While down the beaten silver way the rain continued to fall, unlocking the icy fetters, and making it into a river again.

Chapter 18

THEY WENT TO sleep after a little, just as the dawn was creeping into the sky, but they did not sleep long. Their nerves were too tense, excitement stirred in their blood, and they were up early, tiptoeing around, careful not to waken the mother who mercifully had slept through the night. Lulled by the storm which she believed to be harmless, she had not heard the excitement.

They slipped out into the bright morning that had come to succeed the rain and wind, and went cautiously around to the back of the house where a couple of grim policemen still patrolled the yard. They looked curiously at the trench, now lying exposed, cluttered with bricks and mortar and other debris. They stood back and looked into the gaping hole, now large enough for a man to enter, but they saw only a large caselike frame against the side of the wall and an old wooden chair. Everything else had been taken out by the officers. They did not know yet what significance there had been to this night raid. They wondered about the men who had been found battering into the wall, trying to obtain entrance. They looked and went away in awe.

"Well, I'm glad your mother isn't able to walk around yet," said the nurse. "She would have had to know all about this thing, and I'm afraid she never would have felt comfortable in her home again. She would want to move right away."

"Yes, I'm glad she can't know about it yet," said Frannie, "but my mother is very sensible. She would not be frightened if she had to know. She might take some extra precautions against any further possibilities, but she would never run away from here. And after all, Miss Branner, those men, even if they were still at large, wouldn't be likely to do the same thing in the same place again, now that they have been found out."

"Well, perhaps not," said the nurse. "Still I think the memory of what happened in the night might be hard to forget."

"I don't feel that way," said Frannie thoughtfully. "I think there is great comfort in the knowledge that the police could get here so quickly in any time of need. And then—Miss Branner, don't you think God may have had something to do with taking care of us?"

"I surely do," said the nurse in a fervent tone. "And I guess He always takes care of His own that way, whether there are any police around or not. Only sometimes. He does use the police."

"Of course," said Frannie.

Then they suddenly looked at the clock and found they had to hurry to get Frannie off on time.

So, with two policemen wandering about the back yard, and a big hole in their back cellar wall, Frannie had to get on the bus at the corner above the house and go quietly to her work in the city. As she settled herself in the bus she cast an anxious glance back, and a quick trustful prayer upward for a guard over her dear ones. Another hard day to go through and she needed keeping power herself that she might be calm, and keep her mind on her work.

Two or three times she wondered what Willoughby would think if he knew what had been going on, but she quickly chided herself for that thought. With his innate courtesy, of course, he would have wanted to do something about it right away for her reassurance and her comfort. But she mustn't let that longing for his presence well up in her heart. It was a good thing he was not at home, and could not possibly find out about last night, for it would just have been another excuse for his protection, and she knew very well she had no right to expect protection from him, nor to think of him as in any way her property. She was a working girl and as such was beginning to experience some of the annoyances and anxieties that other working girls in the days of war probably had to experience. She must just take things day by day as they came, and try to remember some of the wonderful things that had been said in that Bible class Monday night.

"Nothing can possibly come to one who is God's own child, that God does not permit. And even though it may be hard to bear, and seem to be a calamity, whatever it is it will work out for good and to the purpose of God. For that purpose is to make His redeemed ones into the image of His Son Jesus Christ."

So when there was a moment of time she cheered her heart with these thoughts.

Willoughby hadn't told her just how long he was to be gone. Perhaps he didn't know himself. There were a great many secrets and mysteries in these days about the movements of any man connected with war work.

He would come back when he came, and maybe—her heart shrank from the thought—maybe he would not come back at all. It was perfectly thinkable that he might be transferred to another place or country hastily, with no time even to come back and say farewell to anyone, even his closest friends. Well, here was something that was possible and she must be quite prepared for it. Why should it matter to her? He was only a casual acquaintance who had been kind to her.

For three days this went on, and then the fourth night when she got home, there was her mother sitting up in the big chair in the living room!

"Mother *dear!*" she exclaimed, rushing swiftly over to the chair to kiss her. "Oh, this is good, *so good!*" and there were actually tears of joy on her face.

A little later there was a knock at the door and there stood the young man from the agency where they had rented the brick house. Frannie opened the door and let him in, glad that her mother was back in a sheltered corner behind the piano, and wouldn't feel the draft from the door.

"I just stopped by," said the young man, "to tell you the deal's all off for the sale of the house. The fella that wanted it has gone to jail for a good long term, enemy alien, and the deal's off. You can go on staying here as long as you want. The owner telegraphed this morning he didn't wantta sell, anyway. So you don't need to worry."

Frannie gave the young man a bewildered look.

"But of course we understood the house was not to be sold," she said with dignity.

"Yes, but I stopped by last week and told the lady somebody was buying the house, and you'd havta get out. But now that's all off. You can stay!"

Then Nurse Branner stepped forward.

"Yes. I am the lady you saw when you called last week. I understand. And now, did you bring that contract? I don't think we'd care to stay here any longer without it. Not after the way you've acted. Did you bring the contract?"

Frannie turned a frightened look at the nurse, and Mrs. Fernley arose from her chair and stood watching the young man alertly.

"Why, no, ma'am. I didn't bring any contract, but the owner said you could stay."

"Very well, then you can bring a contract. Make it out for a year. Don't you think so, Frannie?"

"Why, of course," said Frannie, catching the idea quickly. "We certainly wouldn't want to have any uncertainty about it. There are other houses we can get. I saw one today."

"Why, yes, ma'am. You can have a contract. I'll bring it around tomorrow night. I'll have it all fixed up for you to sign."

"All right," said the nurse firmly, "you may bring it, and in the meantime we'll talk it over and decide whether we want the house for another year. You know there are a lot of things about it that need fixing, repairs on the roof and so on. We'll talk it over. You bring the contract and we'll see. The quicker the better."

"Why, I could go back to the office tonight and get a contract," suggested the alarmed clerk. He knew he had overstepped himself in trying to break the lease with these people in the first place, and didn't want them to move away and leave him to bear the blame.

After the young man had gone, the Fernleys turned in bewilderment to Miss Branner.

"What is it all about, nurse?" asked Mrs. Fernley.

"Well, Mrs. Fernley, you just sit down in your comfortable chair and I'll tell you all about it. That's it. Now pull that afghan over your knees again and don't look so frightened. Nothing has really happened, and nothing is going to. I may have overstepped my rights perhaps in talking up to that washed-out youth, but when he came here last week and tried to tell me that you had to move by the seventh I felt it was up to me to keep you from finding out anything about it until I had a chance to inquire into things and find out what your rights were. I meant to tell you last night about it, Frannie, but I forgot entirely with all the things we were doing. I did try to call up a lawyer I know to ask him, but he was out, down in Washington on business, and I thought it wouldn't matter if we waited a few days till you were able to think about things, Mrs. Fernley. But now it seems to have settled itself, and of course in case you want to stay here I suppose you can almost make your own terms. Demand a few repairs, you know, or something like that. If you ask me I think that youth is plenty scared at what he did, telling you to move when he had no orders from the owner, and I guess he'll be as reasonable as you want him to be."

"Why, that's all right, of course, nurse. You always know the right thing to do I'm sure, and we're very much obliged to you for taking the initiative in our interest, aren't we, Frannie?"

"Yes, indeed, mother. Miss Branner has been simply wonderful. I don't know what we would have done without her."

So the matter was smoothed over, and they talked a little of the different houses that were to be had, deciding from what they knew of rents that the brick house was really the only one they could afford. And then suddenly in the midst of their talk the young agent arrived back breathless with a crisp new contract. After reading it carefully over they finally signed it, and Frannie drew a breath of relief as he rode away on his bicycle.

"Well, the house, such as it is, is ours for a year," she said as she locked the door.

"Yes, and that clause that allows you to sublet in case you find something more suited to your purpose will help too," said the nurse.

"Yes, I'm glad you suggested that, Miss Branner," said Mrs. Fernley. "I've thought of that possibility several times."

And so quite contented they all went to bed and to sleep.

The weather was mild for several days, and the thick ice broke up, and floated away down the river to the sea. The beauty of the great silver street was gone, the skating was gone. Would it come again before another year, Frannie wondered, as she rode daily to her work, and sighed a little? She loved to skate.

Lady Wintrhop took advantage of the mild weather to drive over and call on the Fernleys, and it happened that Mrs. Fernley was downstairs, doing a little mending, carefully watched over by the nurse who wouldn't let her work long at a time.

Bonnie, always wanting to do whatever her mother or sister were doing, sat near on a little stool painstakingly sewing two patches together which she asserted were for a quilt for her doll.

Lady Winthrop had brought a roasting chicken all stuffed and ready for cooking, a basket of apples from her farm, some sweet potatoes and two jars of fruit for the invalid. She settled down like an old friend and talked. The two ladies had a delightful hour together, and told each other bits of their life history, until when the car came back for Lady Winthrop they felt very well acquainted, and Frannie's mother had promised to bring Bonnie and come over with Frannie to the next Bible class, if she was allowed to go out so soon.

"I'll send the car over for you," called back the dear Lady Winthrop happily, as if she were talking to an old friend.

"Oh, but I shall soon be able to walk," said the other woman, with a pleasant ring to her voice and a light in her eyes. "That isn't far."

So when Frannie came home that night there was good cheer in the brick house, the smell of roasting chicken, and a dish of big red apples on the table in the living room. It seemed almost cheerful as she entered, and she was able to put aside her sad thoughts about how lonely she was every day with no young people around with whom she felt like being friendly. Well, perhaps she would find some congenial companions at the plant pretty soon, that is, when things at home were going well, and mother was up and around all the time to make home a place where she could bring some girls now and then. That would be nice.

So she entered into the gala spirit, enjoying the

chicken and sweet potatoes and fruit with the rest. It was almost as pleasant as it had been when they first arrived in the house and felt that they were anchored for a while and were going to be happy, as happy as they could be without the husband and father who had been so much to them all.

Frannie was congratulating herself that she had scarcely thought all day of the young Mr. Willoughby who had been such a delightful companion before he went away. He hadn't said he was not returning, just said he didn't know how long he had to stay. So perhaps he knew there was a possibility that he would not be sent back. Perhaps Washington had some bigger, more important job for him, and she was glad if that were so, for his sake, but she sighed a little that perhaps she would never see him again. And to cover up that sigh she smiled.

"It's so good to have you down at the table again, mother dear!" she said happily.

And the mother smiled.

"Yes, it's nice to be down," said the mother.

"Are you warm enough?" asked the nurse. "Wouldn't you like Bonnie to run up and get your little shoulder shawl?"

"Well, perhaps I would feel more comfortable with it," said the invalid. "Isn't it getting colder again?"

"Why yes," said Frannie, looking up from her unconscious absorption. "I noticed it on the way home. I had to turn up the collar of my coat. My, wouldn't it be nice if it would get cold again and the river would freeze over? I promised Bonnie I'd try to find my old skates and teach her to skate."

"Oh, well, it will be time enough for that next year," said the mother. "I don't believe it will freeze solidly again, after melting off entirely this way. That wouldn't be likely to happen."

"It might," said the nurse. "It does sometimes. I can remember one winter in my girlhood when it did that three times before spring, but of course that was unusual. Still it isn't late in the winter yet, and I read somewhere that this was going to be an unusually cold winter. That would be nice for you, Frannie. You really need the exercise you get skating back and forth to work. And, of course, you can't walk all that way."

Frannie looked up, smiled, and was about to burst into eagerness, but then she suddenly remembered. She had promised Val Willoughby she would not skate down to her work while he was gone. Surely that promise would not be binding indefinitely. He had spoken as if he were returning soon when he bade her good-by, but suppose he never came back? Surely she would not have to refrain from skating the rest of her days. How silly! If he never came back he would have nothing more to do with her, and of course she had a right to do as she pleased.

But from that moment the hope that the ice might return lost its thrill. Certainly she didn't want to go skating without him so soon after her promise, even if he did not come back this winter.

So she plunged into the ceremony of dishwashing with a vim, making a game out of it with Bonnie for helper, and tried to forget the ice and all the nice evenings and mornings she had spent on it, for somehow they seemed to be running away from her with a sort of a hopelessness that she could not conquer.

Later that evening there came a timid knock at the door. When Frannie opened it thinking it was the little girl who sold magazines she found Kit Creeber standing there with averted face.

"Oh," she said as he stepped inside the room. "It's you again. What is it now, another dance?" and she smiled at him amusedly.

He twirled his cap embarrassedly, and grew red in the face.

"Aw naw! Say, we didn't get that dance stuff up. It was that fool girl with the yellow hair. She offered us five bucks apiece to take some girls to a dance, and of course we were out for the dough. But we didn't mean any harm. We meant to carry it through, honest we did, till we saw who you were, and then we beat it. And say, I wantta apologize for the way I treated you that first day at the plant. We didn't mean anything but just kidding. But when you took it that way Spike got mad. But afterwards we saw you were a real lady, and I'm sorry. I hope you'll forget it."

Frannie looked at the embarrassed boy in astonishment.

"Why, of course," she said coldly. "I guess I didn't quite understand. But you didn't need to come and apologize."

"Well, you see I lost something that time I came here for the dance, and I thought I'd come and ask you, did you find it? It means a lot to me. It's a pass I had, and I'm expected to show it at the gate where I work. I can't find it anywhere. The gate man is getting awful hot about it, and I thought I'd take a chance asking you if you found it. It was in an envelope in my coat pocket, and when I got home it wasn't there."

"I'm sorry," said Frannie, "we didn't find anything. I'd be glad to give it back to you if I had. But if you go to Mr. Chalmers the head of the second floor department and explain it to him, he'll maybe fix it up for you. He's very kind and fair."

"Well, but I don't work there any longer. I'm over at the powder plant."

"Oh, I see," said Frannie. "Well, I'm sorry, I don't know what to suggest then. But usually if you are frank about a thing and tell the truth they will meet you half way."

"Thanks awfully," said Kit, and took himself away with haste.

Frannie sat down weakly in her chair and stared at the wall.

"Well, did I ever!" she exclaimed softly to herself. To think that boy would come and apologize! What did he do it for? Was he afraid that somehow he would get connected with the men who were running that queer radio? Or did he maybe have something to do with it? Well, probably not, but at least she needn't be afraid of him any more. It was good that he no longer worked in the same plant with herself. He might try to get fresh with her again sometime if he was still there. She was glad the nurse and Bonnie were still upstairs and wouldn't ask questions about him. She didn't want to tell about that trouble with those two boys. Her mother must never hear of it.

She didn't think long about it because she found that such thoughts inevitably brought Val Willoughby into her mind, and that was what she was strenuously trying to avoid.

When she went to bed that night and looked out of her window there she saw the river spread wide and dark, with a sheen of silver beginning to gather from the rising moon which was growing nightly larger. It gave her a twinge of sadness. Why did the moon have such power to take one back over past days, or nights, and spread sorrow over one's heart? But there! She must hurry and get her garments ready for the morrow, and then get to bed. She had no time to sentimentalize. It would be hard enough to get up early in the morning without that! Then when she opened her window the fresh breeze swept stingingly in. Yes, the air was decidedly colder. It wouldn't take long at a temperature like this to freeze that river again. But what good would that do her when she had promised not to skate while Willoughby was away?

Chapter 19

THE COLD CAME steadily down that night, freezing everything it touched. It laid an icy clutch on the river and began slowly turning it to glass. The moon lingering late showed a solid stillness where there had been a dark limpid heave and quiver at sunset hour. The river had definitely succumbed to the cold again, and if there were any little fishes in it anywhere they must have hurried shivering to their homes to put on their seal overcoats. And sharply and smoothly down the glassy surface shone the pale silver of moonlight.

Frannie looked out before she crept into her warm bed, and said sadly: "The skating will be coming back soon," and sighed as she laid her dark head down on her pillow. Sighed and shivered, and fell asleep from sheer weariness of trying not to think.

"No, I will not be silly," she said over and over to herself. "I shall never give in to disappointment nor have a broken heart. Everything works together for good to those that love the Lord. It will all work out right. I must just trust and wait till He helps me to see how right it is, and then I shall be glad and not feel badly any more."

Lady Winthrop looked out of her window in the early morning and saw the ruby light of the first flash of sunrise stealing in a wide crimson sweep over her river, like a flaming carpet. She could see it from her bed, as she lay softly there in the great old-fashioned four-poster, with its fine linen draperies. It was a sight she loved to waken early just to see.

"The street of my city has come back!" she said softly to herself. "It has come back to stay awhile longer. And I shall again see those dear young people go down to the city on their flashing skates. They will go down together this time and I shall watch them, many times perhaps before the springtime comes and takes away my street of silver."

She lay looking at it for sometime, as the sun rose higher and flashed over tall buildings and towers and pinnacles, studying out her vision of the fair city that hovered in her imagination. And then she went on softly to herself again:

"And some day, some great day, *I* shall walk down that street that is 'made of gold, as it were transparent glass,' and I shall step up the crystal way to the bank of the city. I shall go on into the city and see the face of my King, my Saviour, my Lord Jesus who died for me. I shall look on Him, and be like Him, incredibly like Him. With all my mistakes and sins; it is so wonderful that He can make me like Himself some day. And I shall not be afraid nor ashamed."

Silence again as the sun climbed higher, and the way

where the darkness of the river had been grew broad
and rosy.

Then the soft voice went on:

"And I shall live there among those Heavenly mansions, far more spacious and beautiful than my dear
earthly house, and I shall walk those golden streets. I
shall stand on the crystal banks and see the fire mingled with glass that will sometimes come in that great
street of the city, my city, my Heavenly Home. Please
God, make me ready for it when the time comes,
dressed in the white linen garment of Thine own righteousness, because try as I could all my life I can get
no righteousness of my own. And I shall dwell by my
street of the city, all the days, that shall never end! And
my dear ones whom I have lost awhile on the journey
here will be there! My City! My street of the city. Oh,
I'm glad it has come back again for awhile!"

Three days later when the supper dishes were done
and the Fernleys were just settling down to a few minutes' pleasant talk before the mother was remanded to
her room, Frannie stepped to the window and looked
out. The great hole in the back of the house had been
thoroughly bricked up and cemented and reinforced,
so that they felt secure from unexpected intrusion, and
there was a cosy cheer over the whole place. They all
felt it. And yet there was a sadness in Frannie's heart.
She couldn't but think of the days, though they had
been very few of course, when she and Willoughby had
had pleasant companionship. Was it possible that even
those few days had spoiled her sweet content, her joy
in life? Well, that was silly, and she had told her
mother that she didn't intend to be silly, she *would* not.
So she put on a cheerful tone.

"Oh, mother, you should come to the window and
look out! It is such a lovely sight. The ice is like a
piece of glass, and the moon is almost full. It is worth
while living here just for this sight even if for no other
reason. Come, mother, come and look. You can see
Lady Winthrop's 'street of the city' as she calls it."

For Frannie had long ago told her mother all the

lovely tales of the sweet old lady that Willoughby had told to her.

So Mrs. Fernley went over to the window and stood with her arm around her daughter looking out on the winter beauty.

"Yes, it is indeed a lovely sight," she said, "and a lovely idea. I am looking forward to the time when I can go over to that Bible class and get to know that sweet woman better."

But Frannie said nothing about skating to her work yet, and her mother, knowing little of how long it took to make ice safe for going, was glad. Somehow it always seemed a big risk for her little girl to go sailing off alone down a river of glass.

"And now," said Nurse Branner, "it's time you and Bonnie went to bed."

It was just then that there came a low tap at the front door, and then the knob turned and in walked Valiant Willoughby!

Frannie turned and looked at him, her eyes wide with a great joy, her face blooming out in smiles.

"Oh, you *did* come back!" she said, almost as a little girl would have said it.

And Val had eyes for no one else, his rare smile filling the room with good cheer.

"Why *sure!*" he said. "Didn't you know I was coming back? That's what I've been intending to do all along." He went and stood by Frannie and took both her hands in his, looking down at her as if she were the sweetest thing on earth.

And then, with her hands still in his he turned to the others. "Hello, Bonnie, and Nurse Branner. I'm glad to see you all looking so well. And now, Frannie, aren't you going to introduce me to your mother? You know I've never rightly met her, just picking her up off the floor and putting her to bed. That isn't an introduction."

And so he led her over to her mother, who had gone a few steps toward the stairs as he came in.

Frannie laughed.

"Mother, this is Mr. Willoughby. I know you'll want

to thank him now you've got well for all he did for you when you were taken sick."

"Oh, yes," said Mrs. Fernley, giving him a smile that made him think of her daughter, it was so sunny and kindly.

Val reached for one of her hands and folded it with Frannie's within his own clasp, a kind of symbol of the united friendship they all felt. "You know," he said gently, "I *like* mothers. My own is gone Home, and so I almost envy everyone who still has one left here on earth. I am very glad to know you."

Mrs. Fernley gave his hand a warm pressure and smiled again, trying to thank him for all his kindness to herself and her daughter, but he waved her thanks away.

"It was nothing," he said. "But I mustn't keep you standing. You are still an invalid, aren't you? May I help you upstairs? Is that where you were going? And may I ask a favor of you? Do you mind if Frannie and I put on our skates and go out on that ice for a few minutes, just to celebrate my getting back? They tell me the ice is solid as the Rock of Gibraltar, and I'm aching to try it. Do you mind?"

"Oh, is it safe? Why of course, go for a little while. Frannie has done nothing but work since you went away. She needs a bit of exercise."

"Well, that's all I've done too, so I think we can both enjoy it. The ice is perfect. You look out your window and you'll see us skimming along."

"I will," smiled the mother. "Go, Frannie dear, and have a good time."

"Oh, mother, and can *I* go sometime too?" pleaded Bonnie.

"Why, of course, you can, Bonnie," said Willoughby, "I'll come over sometime before it is bedtime and Frannie and I will take you out, one in each of your hands, holding you up, till you learn for yourself. I think I can find a pair of skates at my aunt's that will about fit you. My little cousins used to skate and I'm sure I've seen some small skates over there. Will that please you?"

"Oh, muvver! *Can* I?" asked Bonnie entranced.

"Why yes, dear, that will be wonderful!"

So Willoughby gathered up the little mother and carried her easily up the stairs, and they said good night. And then Frannie got her skates and they went out together into the clear cold night.

He helped her down the steps to the ice, and knelt before her to help her on with her skates. Then he looked up to her face and caught the starry look in her eyes.

"Oh, Frannie, Frannie *dear!*" he said suddenly, taking both her hands in his, "it is so good to get back to you! It seemed forever before I could get away and come back. Did you miss me at all, Frannie? Or is it too soon to expect that from you?"

Frannie lifted shy eyes.

"Yes, I missed you—very much," she confessed. "I thought I ought not to, but I did."

"You darling!" said the young man, stooping suddenly and laying his lips on hers. "Frannie, I love you! Oh, my *dear!*" Then he lifted her up, and put both arms about her, drawing her close in his arms, laying his firm cold cheek against her glowing one, his lips on hers again. Frannie thrilled to his kisses, her heart full of wonder and joy. He loved her! Think of that! And she had been trying to forget him, because she thought he didn't belong to her world, because she thought he did not care for her, was even perhaps engaged to some other girl. But he wasn't. He loved her! The thoughts tumbled themselves over and over in her brain until she was just in a tumult of joy.

Then suddenly Val remembered.

"Can they look out the upstairs window and see us?" he asked with a comical grin. "We might be a couple of gold-fish in a glass bowl for all we remember the world now. I don't care if you don't, of course, but we don't want the whole world in on our sweetest privacy, even on a moonlight night. Wait till I get my skates on and we'll go away by ourselves for a little."

He made her sit down on the step while he adjusted his own skates, and then together they glided away from the shore and out into the middle of the

stream, remembering to turn and wave to the three
shadowy figures in the upper window who stood watching them, and waving back, especially the smallest one
most vigorously.

On down into the silver pathway they flew, joyful in
the touch of shoulders, the clasp of hands, the look in
their eyes as their glances met.

"Oh, I *love* you, little girl," said Val. "Do you think
you can love me enough to want to marry me, so that
we can be together always?"

Such sweet converse they had that they scarcely saw
the gold in the silver way before them, as they glided on
and on, almost down to where the river joined the sea.

And when they turned and came back they went
more slowly and touched in their talk on the sweetness
of loving one another. Val began to tell her how she
looked to him when he first saw her, and how different
she seemed from the silly girls he had always been so
bored with. And little by little she told him how desolate her young heart had been after he went away.

"But it was only a few days," he said. "I told you I
would be back. I did not know before I went that they
would keep me so long, but sometimes it seemed to me
it would never end. I did not realize I would feel that
way for just a few days, when I left. But when I got
away where I could not see you any more I began to
realize what you were. I met a couple of girls I used
to go around with when I was in college but they only
made me long for you."

Frannie's hand lay warm in his as he told her this,
and she nestled closer as they glided on.

"What were you doing down there anyway?" she
asked suddenly.

"Oh, just the kind of work I was doing here. You
see, I was taking the place of another man who was
very sick and couldn't keep on. It was work that one
had to have special training for, the kind of training I
have had. That's all I can tell you now, because on
account of the war these things have to be kept secret.
So it was important there should be someone there
who understood. The man I was substituting for is

rather high in his profession, and he turned out to be sicker than they thought at first, but at last he got better and then they let me off. I got back early this morning, but I went straight to the plant. I haven't been home yet. I wanted to see you so much. But there was a lot to be done at the plant. I couldn't get away any sooner. You see the men I left in charge here were rather green at the job, and I found a lot of mistakes to be rectified. But oh, I'm glad to be back, and glad, *glad* to have you again."

He suddenly flung his arm about her and drew her closer, and so they glided on in the silver night, so close they were like one body, so much a part of one another that they seemed a single figure.

And in the dim distance the mountains girded round about the river, the towers and turrets of earth's mansions took on their unearthly semblance, and seemed like outlying parts of Heaven to which they were traveling.

And then they looked up at the beauty of it all.

"Look, look!" said Frannie. "How beautiful. Doesn't it seem like a picture of what Heaven might be?"

"Yes," said Val reverently, "our Heavenly Home. And to think that we can be *sure* that we are both going there. All our lives we can go on looking ahead to going there, to being with the Lord, *our* Lord, forever. Oh, I am so glad we are both saved. There doesn't have to be an uncertainty about it ever, because we accepted His word, and He has promised. I've been thinking a lot about these things while I was away. In fact that was one of the main reasons why I was so sure I loved you, because you were interested in these vital things. Because we thought alike. I can't imagine a happy married life without that. People have to think alike to enjoy life together, I guess."

"I guess you're right," said Frannie softly. "I couldn't feel the same toward one who didn't understand my deepest thoughts and feelings."

"Dear!" said Val pressing her little mittened fingers tenderly. "Of course. And now, Frannie, I think I ought to take you back. Mother will be watching for us to come even if she has retired, and besides we both have to be up early in the morning, remember. But tomorrow night I'm coming over early and have a little talk with your mother about all this, and *we'll* talk it out together, you and I. Make our plans, you know. I don't want to be away from you any longer than I can help."

"Oh!" said Frannie with sudden dismay in her voice. "Plans. Yes, of course. But listen. You know I have responsibilities. I couldn't leave my family high and dry—"

"Of course not!" said the young man heartily. "But your responsibilities will become my responsibilities now, you know. There'll be two of us now to take care of your mother and sister. And remember I haven't any mother or sister of my own, so I'm going to enjoy yours a lot, and shall delight to make life happy for them both. Shall we do it together, dearest?"

Frannie looked up at the eager face above hers and a great joy flashed into her eyes.

"Oh, you are wonderful!" she said in exultation. "I didn't know there were men like you. And to think the *only one* should be mine! I can't see why God could be so good to me!"

"And just for that we're going to stop till I kiss you again," said he, whirling her over to a wooded place in the bank, and holding her close in his arms to lay his face against hers for a moment. "You darling!"

Slowly at last they glided on back to the little brick house, and took off their skates.

"I heard at the plant today that you folks had had a little excitement up this way a couple of days ago. Is that true? I meant to ask when I first arrived, but I was so taken up looking at you that I forgot it. What happened? Or didn't you know about it?"

"Know about it?" said Frannie. "I should say I did! For a few minutes I thought I was the only one who knew about it. I heard a noise and slipped to the window. It was during that worst storm. The wind was shrieking, it was raining fiercely, and we heard a great pounding on the back cellar wall. At least I did, and

the nurse came too, pretty soon. But I had slipped
down to the telephone and called up the police and
asked them to see if someone was trying to break in."

"Brave girl! I wish I could have been here to help!
But what was it? Was someone trying to get in?"

"Yes, it seems they had a radio transmitter walled
up in our cellar. They had been using it to send messages, intelligence about war plants and such like to
the enemy, and when we suddenly moved in that
spoiled their plans. So they wanted to get their para-
phernalia out, and they didn't dare come and tell us
about it. It seems they had some incriminating papers
there, hidden behind the furnace in a walled-up place
they had built while the house was vacant several years.
They couldn't come and open the place from inside lest
they would be arrested, so they chose a stormy night
and tried to work in from outside. They dug a trench,
and when they got close in they began with pickax and
sledge hammers, and it was pretty awful for a few minutes in the middle of the night. But just think, mother
didn't hear it, at least if she did she thought it was just
branches breaking off the trees in the storm, and she
slept all through it. Wasn't that great?"

"Pretty great I should say. Oh, I'm sorry you folks
had to go through all that without me here to help. I
shall have to begin right away to take care of you all
very hard to make up for it. And by the way, you
won't need to work any more, you know. I mean you
shall have a beautiful and comfortable life from now
on."

"Oh, but I'm doing defense work now, you know,
and all the women of the land are asked to do that, so I
guess I should keep right on at my job for a while, as
long as I'm needed. I guess our work at the plant is
pretty important, and it isn't good for them to have to
change helpers when they have someone taught."

"That's true, I know, and of course if you put it on
that score I'll have to withdraw my objections. We've
all got to help win this war. But as much as I can I
mean to take care of you and make life easy. Of
course I'm talking rather 'biggity' for a man who hasn't

even asked permission of your mother to court her daughter. Do you think she will offer serious objections?"

"Oh no," giggled Frannie, "only she will tell you, I am afraid, that you are thinking of marrying a girl from the wrong side of the river, and that isn't being done, you know."

Valiant threw his head back and laughed loud and long, and the echo of that laughter, mingled with a ripple from Frannie, reached up through an open window in the Hollister mansion and caused a beautiful young lady to turn uneasily and sigh in her sleep.

Then Frannie spoke more soberly.

"Mother admires you very much. I'll tell you later all the nice things she said about you, and she was glad that you are a Christian. The only thing she is afraid of is that you may not care for me and will break my heart, and she warned me not to let my heart get entangled. She has heard that you belong to a wealthy family and live in a fine house, and she has no aspirations toward wealth. She doesn't trust it, perhaps. She had some wealthy relatives herself."

"Well, if that is all the objection she will offer I can easily quiet her mind. You can tell your dear mother that I am anything but rich. I have a few thousand invested that was left over after my father's estate was settled, and beyond that I have only my salary for the work I am doing. I have an aunt who is fairly well off, but that has nothing to do with me. She has children of her own who will inherit her money, so you see I'm not a poor little rich boy, and your dear mother needn't worry on that account. You can tell her too, if you like, that I have a fairly promising education which will probably make it possible, if all goes well, for me to support you in a modest way, so she needn't think I am a lazy-good-for-nothing, either. Just a plain young man with health and a job, who loves you more than anything in life. Now, do you think I will pass?"

"I'm sure you will," whispered Frannie with her face against his, her lips close to his ear.

"And oh, here's another thing," said Val, suddenly

holding her back and looking into her face. "How do I rate with Bonnie? Is she going to be terribly upset to have a big brother?"

"Oh, no," said Frannie, her face wreathed in smiles. "She simply adores you. She will be delighted. But truly, you know, none of my family have been presuming enough even to dream that you would ever want to marry me, a plain working girl from the wrong side of the river." And then her eyes twinkled merrily and her laugh rang out again with his hearty one.

"Well," said Val, recovering from his mirth, "hadn't we better call it a day and quit? I don't know how I'm going to tear myself away, but I guess it's got to be done if we want to keep our jobs till the end of the war."

As they reached the door and turned to go in, Val pointed to the river, bright in its silver sheen.

"Look," he said, "our river! *The street of the city* where we met. By which we may travel to the end and find the City Eternal waiting to welcome us some day."

"Yes," said Frannie softly. "I found a verse this morning in my Bible. It sort of fits now. 'Here we have no continuing city, but we seek one to come, a house not made with hands, eternal in the Heavens!' "

And so they said a tender good night, and Valiant Willoughby went on his way. And the next day was a new day!

Novels of Enduring Romance and Inspiration by

GRACE LIVINGSTON HILL

Bantam Book Catalog

It lists over a thousand money-saving best-sellers originally priced from $3.75 to $15.00 —bestsellers that are yours now for as little as 60¢ to $2.95!

The catalog gives you a great opportunity to build your own private library at huge savings!

So don't delay any longer—send us your name and address and 25¢ (to help defray postage and handling costs).